ARNOLD FALLS

CHARLIE SUISMAN

Dedicated to you

CHAPTER ONE

Time of the Signs

I t's a good forty minutes until sunrise and the roads of Arnold Falls are empty, except for one silver Rascal mobility scooter making its way toward the courthouse.

Stopping at the corner of the park, Dubsack Polatino hops off his ride, singing a pidgin Italian version of "O Mio Babbino Caro"—"*O mio brand-new caro, mi race car, è bello bello*"—as he walks over to the "Jenny Jagoda for Mayor!" lawn sign. After pulling it out of the ground, he returns to his scooter with the sign and stake, singing in full grand-tenor mode, "*Vo'andare with Portia de Rossi,*" narrowly missing the actual lyric.

He drives along the sidewalk until he arrives at the next sign. Same routine, again and again, until the Jagoda signs are gone and only 'Rufus for Mayor' signs remain. He surveys his domain, pleased with his work as well as his version of the aria, humming it again, traversing several of the surrounding streets performing the same operation.

It's starting to get light, so Dubsack Rascals to the back of the courthouse and tosses his haul into its large dumpster. He spots Hamster, the courthouse maintenance man, watching him from a second-floor window, and curtsies to him.

When he's finished, Dubsack jumps back onto his scooter and cruises to The Chicken Shack on Hester Biddle for breakfast, singing the climax of Carmina Eurana's "O Fortuna," letter-perfect, with hammering, war-cry fervor.

CHAPTER TWO

Wiccan Bongo Night

The hail comes down the size of crab apples just as I open my front door on this clear and mild September evening. Run-of-the-mill hail, of course, emerges from run-of-the-mill cumulonimbus clouds, but Arnold Falls doesn't bother with such niceties. We have Old Testament-style barrages of idiopathic hail several times a month, irrespective of cloud cover, temperature, or best-laid plans, something scientists have failed to explain beyond stating that Arnold Falls is a microclimate with "no known correspondence."

I ignore yet another shingle that the hail has dislodged from my roof and make my way to a campaign meeting at Argos, the town's favorite watering hole. My pal Jenny Jagoda, born and raised in Arnold Falls, has decided to mount a challenge against the incumbent mayor, her old schoolmate Rufus Meierhoffer.

Taking a slight detour toward Bonebox Point at the southern end of the steep bluff over the Hudson River, I opt for a bit of communing with nature as the sun sets.

As I pass a grove of frowzy evergreens, I notice a baby carriage that someone has dumped next to a tree, only to discover that it contains what looks, in my judgment, to be an actual baby, swaddled in a pink blanket. What fairy tale have I stumbled into?

A man calls out from within the trees, "She's fine. We'll be done soon. She's fine."

"Well, okay, if you say so," I reply.

A woman's voice: "Is that Jeebie?"

I say, "Yes, yes, it is. I don't recognize your voice and I think we should leave it that way. The baby's fine?"

"She's fine. Have a good night."

"Good night," I say.

I head down to the railing at the promenade and give myself over to the view. Looking downriver, it occurs to me that you don't have to be lost to find yourself in Arnold Falls, though it does seem to help. You just go a little further north than you planned—that's how most people turn up.

Geography as destiny—how could it have been otherwise? Defying logic and common sense have been Arnold Falls hallmarks ever since it was settled in 1803, after a sketchy ringleader named Hezekiah Hesper and his gaggle turned up unannounced in Poughkeepsie one fine spring morning. The denizens of that town took a quick look at this collection of misfits and miscreants and said, uh-uh, absolutely not, and chased them north with an invective-rich invitation not to return to Poughkeepsie. By the time they caught their breath, Hesper and Co. were on this very escarpment, where there were only two houses as far as the eye could see, built by intrepid Dutch families on a patch of land so barren and forlorn that the Native Americans would have nothing to do with it.

A motorboat enters the scene, cutting its engine. I try to concentrate on the crimson remnants of the sun but my view is being interrupted by a moon—two moons—the backsides of two drunk men in the rocking boat, laughing as if this were the most original sight gag ever. I am sorry to say that you have now met Arnold Falls' mayor, Rufus Meierhoffer, and his accomplice, Dubsack Polatino.

To make it worse, I had been hoping for the smoky smells of autumn to go with the sunset, but at the moment, all I'm getting is a strong whiff of sulfur, origin unknown. This suggests it's time to move along, reinforced by the bell from the tower of the Chapel of Our Lady of Lourdes ringing the hour in, as always, five minutes early.

Even though our campaign meetings rarely start on time, I hurry toward Argos anyway, reflecting that old Hezekiah Hesper hasn't exactly left a shining town on a hill for Jenny to inherit. Hesper was never anyone's idea of a role model—in 1853, AF celebrated the fiftieth anniversary of its founding with a bonfire burning all documents having to do with Hesper, so that you tells you something right there. And legend has it that his wife murdered him with a scythe. Or possibly he was disgorged into the Bonebox Point ravine by persons unknown. Alternatively, I've sat through more than one disquisition claiming Hesper died from spontaneous combustion, and the longer I live here, the more plausible it sounds. Scythe, cliff, or combustion, the guy was destined for a bad end and one way or another he got there.

The moment I step into Argos, Sofia, its longtime

bartender, shouts out a hello. She hands me a glass of Tempranillo as I reach the bar, saying, "Your crew isn't here yet, Jeebie."

I nod to Hamster, the maintenance man at the court house, who's sitting a few seats down, and wave to my postman and his wife, who are at the end of the bar.

"Let me ask you something," Sofia says.

"Anything," I say gamely.

Sofia rests her forearms on the bar and looks me in the eye. "Why the fuck does Jenny want to do this? I mean, *Arnold Falls*?! I grew up here, too, and I'd rather clean up the puke of drunk guys every night for the rest of my life than run for mayor."

I love that about Sofia: no mincing of the words. She's a great listener, too, which makes her an ideal barkeep— although she's doesn't exactly look the part, if you'd cast someone plump and lusty along the lines of Mistress Quickly. Sofia is tall, thin, and all sharp angles as inclined to brooding as she is to merrymaking.

"Rufus is too stupid to know better," she continues. "Jenny *should*. Arnold Falls is incapable of changing."

Sofia has a point. Incorrigibility is part of the Arnold Falls DNA. Some places make sense and some places don't. Arnold Falls doesn't and never has and you have to lay that at the feet of the aforementioned Hezekiah Hesper and his gang, who launched Arnold Falls on its confounding course by naming Arnold Falls in honor of Benedict Arnold, a tribute they made explicit by also naming the street into town Benedict Arnold Way and a park Benedict Arnold Park. Why all the infamous traitor love? No one knows; the founders took that to their graves in Benedict Arnold Cemetery.

And as for the "falls" part of Arnold Falls, we have no waterfall whatsoever, the nearest being twenty miles east as the crow flies. In an effort to address this geographical misfortune, someone had long ago, in the 1950s, I think, posted a sign next to an unused haul road near the railroad tracks that read *"Access to Falls Closed Due to Dangerous Conditions"* and, ever since, that's all the town has cared to say about it.

"Jenny thinks she can do some good. So do I. You know in that black heart of yours that she'll fix a lot of things that have been broken for a long time."

"God, I hope you're right, Jeebie."

Through the bar's picture window, I see a large party bus covered in neon swirls pull up, blaring Florence + the Machine's "Shake it Out."

"Sofia! What is *that*?"

The phone behind the bar rings and as Sofia goes to answer it, she points to a poster on the bulletin board. I turn to look at it while a group of women toting bongos, wearing black and too much eyeshadow, pile into the bar and head toward the back terrace. The flyer reads *"Wiccan Bongo Night at Argos! Celebrate the Coming of the Harvest Moon With Us."*

"Not sure how doctrinaire they are," Sofia says, hanging up the phone, shouting over "Shake it Out," which is rattling Argos' front window. "They used to do the harvest moon thing in Midden Park but apparently the coyotes hated the drumming sounds and finally sort of attacked them last year while they were singing 'New York, New York'."

Madora, the owner of Argos, comes out from the kitchen. "Oh, Christ, look at them lined up at the popcorn machine. Sofia, I think I made a big mistake here. Hi, Jeebie."

"I thought everybody is welcome at Argos, Madora."

"We may have our first asterisk," she says.

The ladies have indeed lined up to help themselves to the free popcorn dispensed from a vintage popcorn cart once used at the old Queechy County fairgrounds.

"I wonder if they vote," I say.

"Not many of these girls are local. More from around," Madora says as the first of the kernels gets thrown at a sister Wiccan.

Manny, Argos' waiter/busser, brings out a clean rack of glasses and passes it to Sofia, then goes off to take drink orders.

In comes Jenny with three of our campaign strategists, though "strategist" may be putting too fine a point on it. Jenny's a thirty-something, bespectacled, spiky-haired force of nature and for a moment I consider Sofia's question about why she would attempt taking on Rufus McDufus (as he is widely known). For one thing, the town can do a lot better than this astonishingly dim future old-boy. For another, a win for Jenny would cast off the icy grip of that old-boys network. And I think Jenny likes the idea of being Arnold Falls' first female mayor.

I say, "Sofia wants to know why you're running. She'd rather clean up puke every night than be mayor."

Jenny laughs her rumbly laugh. "I hear you, Sofia. But I like a challenge."

Sofia hands her a glass of Jim Beam neat, which Jenny dispatches promptly.

Hamster, who had been staring into his beer until now, looks over to us and says, "Tell you something. Can't win without signs."

"We have signs, Hamster," Jenny says,

"Not at the courthouse you don't," Hamster says.

"But we—"

He puts up his hand. "Not'ny more you don't."

"No!" Jenny says. "Rufus?"

"Dubsack. Yesterday morning. Tossed 'em in the dumpster behind the courthouse. Watched him do it. I got 'em back for you. Put 'em in the shed."

"Was he on his Rascal?" Though fully ambulatory at age thirty-seven, Dubsack uses a mobility scooter while running errands.

"Yup. Having a grand ole time. Singing opera."

I buy Hamster a round. "We're going to have to deal with this, Jen."

Manny returns with the Wiccans' drink order. "They want Harvey Wallbangers."

"How many?"

He hesitates. "Sixteen."

"Oh my fucking God."

"I'll make more popcorn," Manny says. "I think they have the munchies."

"Thanks, Manny. Now, where the flying fuck is the Galliano? Hey, who died?" she says to someone over my shoulder.

I turn around to see Duncan Elmore, my best friend since we were tykes, walking toward us, looking uncharacteristically glum.

He gives me a kiss on the cheek.

"What's the matter?" I ask.

"Le Perroquet is closing," Duncan says.

"No! They're one of your biggest customers."

"Our biggest. This is bad. No one is eating French food anymore."

"Here," Sofia says. "Glenfiddich. On the house."

"Thanks, Sofia," Duncan says.

Sofia adores Duncan—they're both part of the Evergreens, an environmental group that has fought many threats against Arnold Falls. And why wouldn't she adore him? He's smart, handsome, sporty. And kind. I should have said kind first. Duncan and I have known each other since first grade and okay, yes, I've always had a crush on him and we did make out once when we were fifteen, but by that point he had concluded that girls were pretty great. He's married to Marybeth, whom I also love, and they have a four-year-old, Sadie, my goddaughter. After visiting me up here so often, they bought Pluggy's Farm. It was once the largest farm in the area but parcels were sold off as time went by. Duncan and Marybeth use the remaining three acres to grow heritage vegetables and specialty items for chefs and restaurants in the Hudson Valley and NYC. The closing of Le Perroquet will be a big financial hit for Duncan.

The Wiccans launch into a bongoed version of "Day O."

"What's that?" Duncan asks, and I can see the beginnings of a smile around his mouth.

"Wiccans. Bongo night. Harvest moon."

A grin spreads over his face. Much better.

"Can you find new customers to make up for Perroquet?" I ask.

"Yeah," he says. "It may take a while. They bought half our Tom Thumb."

He's very proud, and justifiably so, of his Tom Thumb celeriac. After Duncan orders another scotch, I say, "Does Annie send you much business?"

"Some," he says.

Annie O'Dell is Annie O'Dell, the chef—I suppose in her early 60s—who has a following for her TV series *Annie's Farm*, shot at her place in Arnold Falls, which celebrates the table part of farm-to-table, but mostly just celebrates Annie O'Dell.

"I heard that Miles is opening a new restaurant," I say.

"I thought you two weren't speaking," Duncan says.

"We're not *not* speaking. We just haven't spoken in a long time."

"Years," Duncan said.

"Years," I agree. Miles and I were in a long relationship that didn't end well.

"I'll send him a note."

"Thanks, Jeebs, but you don't have to do that."

"It's just an email," I say. "And you need the business."

"'Daylight come and me wan' go home,'" Jenny sings into my ear. "Let's do some work."

"Gotta get this young hussy elected mayor," I say.

"Jenny's tab?" Sophia asks me, then nods when I arch one eyebrow at her.

Our little campaign crew settles in at the big table in the back corner and hashes out that which needs hashing. Over the next hour, the Wiccans provide our soundtrack, an unholy mixtape of howling at the moon, instrumental bongoing and singalongs to your favorite hits from the '70s, '80s and '90s. Jenny points out that golden oldies is exactly the nostalgia Rufus and his chief benefactor, Ivan Borger, will be peddling when the old boys did whatever they wanted with, and to, the town.

After we're finished working, we get up to order a nightcap but no one's behind the bar. Jenny and I head to the back patio where the thoroughly Wallbanged Wiccans are in high spirits, sending good vibrations to the coming

Harvest Moon. They've teed up "Mambo Number 5" and everyone's dancing and bouncing around the terrace.

And when I say everyone, I mean the full coven of Wiccans, plus Sofia, Manny, Madora, and Duncan. Jenny and I look at each other and when they get to "A little bit of Monica in my life," we join in.

CHAPTER THREE

The Corner of Nowhere and Nothing

"Assassins! Everywhere I look, assassins! This worm of a town is turning and it needs to stop," Ivan Borger rants.

Rufus Meierhoffer, current mayor of Arnold Falls, looks at the real estate developer and thinks Ivan's nickname, "Seventy-thirty"—short for "70% comb-over, 30% venom"—isn't quite right this late in the evening. More like "Fifty-fifty." Rufus grins at the thought.

"This is *funny* to you?!" Ivan shouts.

"No, Ivan. I was just thinking—"

"*Not your strong suit!*"

The Lodge members look over for a moment. Ivan is always insulting him like this, but Rufus knows he can't be *that* dumb: he's the *mayor*.

"You've got some grease there," Rufus says pointing to his own lip.

Ivan wipes off the grease from the Chicken Shack

drumstick he's been gnawing. "Are you gonna win this race or are you gonna let a girl beat you? Who the hell is Jenny Jagoda?"

Rufus glances at the Elks Lodge's Schlitz clock and sees it's almost eleven. His wife's going to kill him.

"Stay with me, Rufus. You know what 'Jagoda' means? It means 'blueberry' in Polish. That's what you're running against. A blueberry. Squish her." He taps his greasy index finger and thumb together to make the point.

Mange, the Lodge's craggy-faced Exalted Ruler with a gray, walrus mustache, comes over to Ivan and says, "Hey, Ivan, you're not supposed to bring in outside food. House rules."

"House rules? House *rules?* How many kitchen inspections have you failed, Mange?"

"All of them."

"Exactly. And yet somehow, they allow you to stay open. I wonder how that happens. I want to see you eat some of the curried ham salad right now."

Mange's pupils dilate. "That wouldn't be a good idea."

"What do *you* think, Rufus?" Ivan says.

Rufus says, "Mange, leave us alone."

Ivan turns back to Rufus. "What are you doing to win this campaign thing, *Mr. Mayor?*"

Let it go, Ivan. No one's going to vote for Jenny Jagoda. "We've been taking down her campaign signs . . ."

"What the *fuck* are you talking about? You listen to me. I've got a lot of money sunk into this godforsaken redneck hole at the corner of Nowhere and Nothing. I need you to win, Rufus, because if that blueberry wins, I'm going to hear 'environmental' this, and 'preservation' that, and Rufus," he says slowly and quietly, "I don't want to hear a word about preserving the Dutch House—that hut is coming down before it falls down and a rubber factory is going on the property, *my* property, and that's all there is to it. I've got major Japanese funding on the line. Lotta folks in Albany want to see this happen. But we need to move on it because of the Zoning Board."

"Zoning Board?"

"I have better conversations with my Dalmatian, not the brightest and dead eight years. How old are you, Rufus?"

"Thirty-five."

"My land is zoned light industrial—"

"Thirty-*six*. Hard to keep track. Lot on my plate."

Ivan looks at him and exhales loudly. "My land is zoned light industrial and I need *heavy* industrial. How many board members' terms are up this year? Four. How many are on the board? Rufus?"

"Ten?"

Shaking his head, Ivan says, "S*even*, Rufus. Do you see any relation between *four* and *seven*?"

"Four is less?"

"Four is a *majority*," Ivan says through clenched teeth. "And who appoints the board members?"

"I do?"

Ivan pauses, mid-bite on a drumstick.

"*I* do. I see where you're going with this. Gotcha, gotcha. But I don't know about the rubber thing, Ivan. People don't use rubber bands as much as they used to. Or do you mean condoms? People still use condoms. Don't worry, Ivan. Jenny can't win. That fried chicken smells delicious."

"GET OUT."

"But it's the Elks, Ivan. You can't . . . "

"OUT!"

Rufus chugs the rest of his beer and scurries out.

The Wiccans have honored the Harvest Moon until they could honor her no more. The place is finally empty and quiet which, Sofia thinks, is the building's preferred state.

As she dries tumblers behind the bar, a gust of wind slams the screen door shut. It was so mild out today, but now the weather's turning Novemberish. Sofia glances at the six clocks of the world on the wall: just after one a.m. in Arnold Falls, five o'clock in Sydney. *Tomorrow afternoon, not yesterday, right?* she wonders for the thousandth time. Manny has already mopped and split. She's counted the drawer, put the cash in the safe, swabbed the bar.

She pulls up a bottle of Clagger from under the counter and pours herself a jigger. "Burn, baby, burn," she says out loud as she swallows it. It really is wretched moonshine, but it's *Arnold Falls'* wretched moonshine. Although maybe not the hill she wanted to die on. And deviations over the years from the original recipe *had* proven quite fatal, Elbridge Bartlett's Farewell Wassail being the best-known example.

One of these days, she thinks, one of the thin, young things that now throng Argos on the weekends is going to make an "artisanal" Clagger and the shark will be well and truly jumped. She could think of a million things to depress her, but the idea of artisanal Clagger would be near the top of the list. Maybe if Jenny becomes mayor, she can help Arnold Falls hold on to the things that make it Arnold Falls.

Sofia sees the fire truck hurtling down High Street, sirens blaring. *Take care of your furnace, people!* Why do people not take care of their houses? She pauses for a moment to let the irony of her question sink in.

She goes to the front door, locks it, and turns off the outdoor lights, then the bar lights. A passing train blows its horn—long twice, once short, once long. Sofia grabs her bag and coat and heads out through the kitchen. Kitchen lights out, through the back door, same as a thousand other nights.

Across town, the light is on in Jenny's den next to the Raymond Loewy-designed BarcaLounger she inherited from her dad. Jenny's reclining in the chair, her head back, eyes closed. She's wearing gray sweatpants, a T-shirt with a picture of the Ramones on it that says "Hey ho let's go" and a Red Sox baseball cap. She may look like she's sleeping, but her mind is in its insistent hey-ho-let's-go mode, full of verbs in various future tenses. Jenny has spent the past couple of hours working through a spreadsheet, counting votes. It's 52 days to the election and even if there are more maybes at this point than she'd like, she can see a path to winning.

She's also trying, without success, to get "Mambo Number Five" out of her head. Jenny opens her eyes and glances at the clock: just after one. Unfurling herself from the chair, she grabs her flannel shirt from the floor and buttons it up as a fire truck rumbles by, sounding its Q-siren. Rufus wouldn't know the difference between a Q-siren and a Q-tip. She thinks back to a conversation she'd had with Jeebie, when he suggested she run for mayor. He had laid out the case for it, emphasizing the need to throw off the yoke of the old-boys-network. No argument there. But there was more to it than that.

"I might have an ulterior motive for running," she had said.

"Everyone has an ulterior motive," he'd said. "So what?"

She picks up a photograph from the side table by the

lounger and stares at it, walks it to her bedroom nightstand, and carefully places it there.

The fire truck turns off its siren, which means the call is nearby. She looks out the window, but can't see anything amiss.

"Mayor Jagoda," she says out loud.

At the sound of the siren flying past, Annie O'Dell sits up in bed and pulls off her eye mask. Her husband, Julius, is snoring. She stares at the clock. Just past one. Annie shakes his shoulder and he grunts, turning away from her. He used to be so good-looking.

"You could lose a few pounds yourself," he mumbles.

She must have misheard him. Can he read her mind while he's sleeping? Ridiculous. Or maybe not. After thirty-five years of marriage, he often knows exactly what she's thinking. And she *has* put on weight, but that's what chefs do. Especially since her TV show, *Annie's Farm*, is taped right in the kitchen downstairs. Her fridge has to be impeccably stocked at all times—her fans would expect no less.

A coyote howls in the woods behind her farm and there's a howl in response. They're creepy, those coyotes, the way they howl and especially the way they walk. She'd never get used to them. Growing up in Boston, the wildlife was refreshingly sparse. She'd hardly ever *been* on a farm when she and Julius had purchased this property that they stumbled on eight years ago after missing the turnoff to their friends' house. Annie had fallen immediately in love with it and Julius had waved the white flag after a two month war of attrition. Within a year of moving in, she had turned the whole thing into a spotless Potemkin farm, ideal for photoshoots, which, in addition to the TV show, were now its most frequent use.

But the ratings and the buzz had been trending downward this past season and she was hell-bent on reversing that. People need so much novelty these days. What to do, what to do?

"Sleep, just sleep," Julius says.

She puts her eye mask back on and stews, on low heat, for hours.

CHAPTER FOUR

Up the Ladder to the Roof

Something is beeping loudly. And, oh! The smell of smoke.

I jump out of bed, dressed only in my boxer shorts and a T-shirt, and think, okay, smoke alarm. Smoke. Smoke! Did I leave the oven on? Fire? Gotta go. What things? I grab my cell phone, keys, and, anything else? Yes, the small oil painting of my grandmother painted by my grandfather. Grab it. I run into the hallway—it's starting to get smoky—but the only option seems to be to keep going, so I do. Downstairs, I take the sweatshirt hanging on the coatrack and run out the front door, dialing 911.

This is a really a bad feeling, when you think your house is about to burn to the ground and there are no sirens yet, just silence. My feet are bare and the grass is cold. How did I forget shoes? I am still holding the small painting, which feels strange, so I go to my car and stash it in there. I realize I didn't take any of my mother's paintings and I feel a stab of guilt.

It is a long, a *very* long, three or four minutes more, but then I do hear sirens and I still don't see any flames, so I think things might turn out okay. The truck arrives with four firemen in full gear, adjusting their breathing masks, jumping out of the truck.

"Mr. Walker? Is there anyone inside?" one of the guys asks. "Any pets?"

"No," I reply. "I think it could be the furnace. If you go in the back door over here, the stairs down to the basement are on the left."

Smoke is pouring out of my basement windows but in they go. I shake my head at their courage. Thankfully, it isn't long before they are back out.

As I suspected, the furnace was the culprit. A clogged filter. The firefighters couldn't be nicer but they say I need to get the furnace serviced regularly, which I don't tell them I've let slide. After I promise to have an HVAC person come out, they are on their way. I'm shaken up, but at least my house is still standing. I retrieve Granny from the car, return inside, and open windows to let the smoke out.

Then I do what I always do in times of stress: make two pieces of cinnamon toast and wash them down with a glass of milk. I sit quietly at my kitchen table and let the cinnamon aroma settle my nerves.

The vintage farmhouse kitchen sink is doing the slow drip, as it has since I moved in and surely before that. Sometimes the sound is soothing but not right now. I make a note to add it to the rather long to-do list that the house demands.

Munching my toast I conclude this is a very bossy house. Imperious. "Fix my drip. Caulk me, Jeebie . . . A little WD40, please, for my old bones, Jeebie. . . Jeeeeebie! Do something! There are leaves clotting my gutter! HVAC on line one . . ." Honestly, I'd rather have an obstreperous, china-smashing ghost than a tottering house with a bucket list.

In my defense, the plan was that the two of us, Miles and I, would buy this tired Queen Anne and do the work together. Then that all went to hell, but I bought the place anyway. And now it's me who's tired.

I finish my milk. A kindly ghost would be fine, too. Lovely, even.

———

The next morning, it's still smoky downstairs, so I head out for breakfast at the Chicken Shack. And who's sitting there? Rufus himself, so easy to spot in his no-iron golfwear, aqua-color shirt and yellow ochre slacks, a thirtysomething going on seventy. I sidle over to a table near where he's sitting, but just out of eye range. Perfect.

"I'm not here," I say quietly to the waitress, Aunt Doozy, nodding my head toward the Rufus and Dubsack booth.

"Wouldn't have noticed if you were," she says, "'cept you smell smoky. Chicken and waffles?"

"Yes, please."

"Coffee's self-serve today."

I note that Doozy, now a wispy ninety-three, is wearing the World War II Bronze Star that was awarded to Chester Jordan, an Arnold Falls native who was in the 761st Tank Battalion and was killed in 1944. They would have been married after his tour of duty.

Doozy's been here as long as anyone can remember.

And so has the Chicken Shack. Since the day it opened in 1937, it's been Arnold Falls' favorite place to gossip, complain, scheme, and eat. In all that time, the Shack has never had a makeover of any kind. The tall, brown, wooden booths were there on the sweltering August day the eatery opened, though the matching brown tables are now covered with thousands of flirtations, insults, and lewd doodles.

There have been only two concessions to modernity: air conditioning was added in 1974 and in 2014, Wi-Fi. The Shack has never had any real decor, except for one framed image to the left of the French entrance doors: a picture of JFK, placed there in 1963.

Rufus hasn't spotted me, and neither does Dubsack when he enters, making a beeline for the mayor's booth.

"Morning, Rufus," says Dubsack, sliding in opposite Rufus.

"How did you do today?" Rufus asks.

"Musta got twenty," says Dubsack.

"From the courthouse?" Rufus asks.

"Did those yesterday."

I very much doubt we had twenty signs left.

"Jenny Jagoda—*not* gonna be mayor."

"That chick is going down," says Rufus.

"I hear that's her thing!" says Dubsack, slapping his knee, both men laughing loudly.

Doozy stops at their table. "Coffee, Dubsack?"

"Yes, Aunt Doozy."

"It's over there," she says.

"Her arm is bothering her," Rufus says in a stage whisper.

"I can hear that," says Aunt Doozy. "Old, not deaf, McDufus. You visit your grandmother lately, Rufus?"

"I will this week."

"Mm-hmm. Then do it. Sick people don't live forever. Breakfast, Dub?"

"Scrambled eggs and sausage."

"Naw," says Aunt Doozy. "You don't want the sausage today. Repeating on me something turrible."

"How come you let me order it?" asks Rufus.

I get up for coffee, careful to stay under cover. Doozy is no fan of Rufus, that's clear. And she is someone you want in your camp, being a walking piece of town history, the daughter of one of Arnold Falls' most successful madams, Miss Georgia, who presided for decades at the only black bordello in town. The sex trade had long been Arnold Falls' crucial plot development, its golden ticket, tracing back to the very first house, which belonged to John and Isabel Pumphrey. The Pumphreys ran a tavern on Hester Biddle Street, a couple of blocks down from here, and shrewdly decided one cold winter's night to put their upstairs storage room to a more profitable use than Clagger aging, since Clagger's distinction as moonshine is that it starts poorly and gets worse with time.

Did the Pumphreys appreciate the irony of plying their trade on Hester Biddle? I think they must have. Biddle was a Quaker who had lived in seventeenth-century Britain and published the short, censorious, and frankly tiresome *Woe to Thee, City of Oxford* and the hit companion piece, *Woe to Thee, City of Cambridge*, which decried urban life as smothered in filth. Poor, sad, virtuous Hester. What good in the end does woe-hurling do? Biddle's got her name on the main drag of our historic red-light district, the only place she's memorialized anywhere, as far as I know. For their part, the Pumphreys became local heroes, given all the sailors and merchants turning up looking for "Clagger and a bagger."

Doozy would have gone to work for Miss Georgia but a lifelong problem with flatulence had ruled out a career in her mother's line of work. Instead, Doozy got a job at the Chicken Shack in 1943 in spite of her condition and patrons learned to ignore it. She's never left the Shack's employ.

I'm perusing the headlines of the day when Doozy sets my breakfast on the table. As I tuck into chicken and waffles, I think about the Shack's history as a home away from home. It was a color-blind eatery long before laws were passed, welcoming everyone from presidents (Bill Clinton) to the hoiest of the polloi. Not to mention its amazing fried chicken, a reputation that was sealed by *The New York Times* in 1982, when its critic called it "the best fried chicken north of the Mason-Dixon Line."

Doozy makes her way toward the kitchen. Halfway to the goal, she sings out in a robust contralto, "Open them doors!" which everyone knows means the Shack requires additional and immediate ventilation.

Sal, the manager, flips the switch for the overhead fan and a man sitting next to the entrance reading a book opens the French doors without taking his eye off the page.

Conversation resumes.

When Rufus and Dubsack finally leave, I pick up my phone and call Jenny. She answers with a feeble morning voice.

"Are you still in bed?" I say with just the right amount of accusation.

"Yes," she says. "Did you hear the sirens last night? Probably some idiot's furnace."

"That idiot would be me."

"Jeebie, I told you to call Addie's!"

"Yes, well, priorities. I'm trying to get the lesser of two

reprobates elected mayor of this little town. And speaking of which, I'm at the Shack and Rufus and Dubsack just left. Dubsack is still stealing your signs. I suggest a countermeasure."

"Okay, General Walker, let's slay the Old Boys. What's the plan?"

"Haven't gotten that far," I say.

"Something with a woman. Or booze. He likes opera," Jenny says. After a moment she says, "Dubsack's a hypochondriac."

"Ah! That makes it easy. He's at Argos most nights early, right?"

Jenny says, "Yeah. What do you have in mind?"

"We call Sofia and have her give him a message he won't like."

"Like what?"

"'Dub, it was fun but I've got chlamydia. You should get tested,'" I suggest. "The caller doesn't leave her name."

"Yes! Perfect! When?"

"Tomorrow night. I'll bring my camcorder. But maybe you shouldn't be there. It would look bad if someone figured out you were involved."

"I wouldn't miss it for the world," she says.

We agree to meet near Argos tomorrow at seven-fifteen for Operation Dubsack Payback.

As I make my way from the Shack to High Street to run errands, I pass the long-abandoned Bartlett's detachable collars factory, which was thriving until Troy began producing collar stays in the 1920s, a bit of comfort one-upmanship besting the stiff and starchy detachable collars, from which Bartlett's never recovered. The building is a beautiful ruin that could be restored if only the money were there, the same cul de sac that plagues the town on so many issues.

Sofia's fair question about why Jenny would want to be mayor of Arnold Falls comes back to me. The town has always prided itself on its unruliness. Even after the New York State Police conducted a military-style raid in 1958 and shut down the bordellos in one fell swoop, AF retained its illicit cred with a sprinkling of gambling dens and profligate municipal corruption spanning many administrations. But shorn of its sex-trade economic engine, Arnold Falls finally fell victim to the urban decay of the sixties and seventies and that might have been that, but for the flight of one antique dealer from Manhattan to High Street, followed by another and then another.

It's now a shabby-chic Brigadoon that awakens as the weekend nears, a place where the High Street shopping is luxe, the sidewalks third world, and carefully restored houses are cheek by jowl with abandoned, crumbling wrecks. And while the pepperoni sandwich is one of the town's rare culinary achievements, you can spend thirty-seven dollars for a take-out roasted chicken. Don't do that.

Arnold Falls continues to thrive on those who went a little further north than they planned: the eccentrics, an old guard, a once-new guard, earnest hipsters, artists, art dealers, drug dealers, rat-race refugees, recluses, self-medicators, the brilliant and the dim, the delightful and those who should be avoided at all costs. In short, the falutin here can be high or low.

Entering High Street my peripheral vision detects Bridget Roberts with her Brussels Griffon in a small tableau of chaos: Bridget yanks Gussie's leash to stop him from peeing on the flowers in front of the flower shop as she blows her nose into a tissue and rebalances her sagging bag of farmer's market produce—one apple having escaped onto the sidewalk. Gussie yelps when his leash is pulled and lays on the sidewalk upside-down in protest.

If you live in a city, peripheral vision can save you from getting sideswiped by a speeding taxi. If you live in the countryside, it can alert you to a peckish bear sampling your compost pile. And if you live in a small town, it can give you a fighting chance to avoid the mystifying juju of Bridget Roberts.

Bridget goes to retrieve the apple and I see my chance for a detour to the left. But alas, now that I've hit my forties, my very early forties, my reflexes are not what they used to be, so Bridget, with impressive fleetness in spite of some nascent roly-poly, turns Gussie right-side-up, drops the apple back into her bag, stuffs her Kleenex into a recess of her tunic, and calls my name before I can flee. She clomps her way to me. That's when I notice the boot she has on one foot.

"Jeebie!"

"Oh, hello, Bridget."

She gives me a hug and I bend down to scratch Gussie under his chin.

"Isn't the weather glorious?" she asks.

It seems a harmless question, but with Bridget you never know.

"What's with the boot?" I ask.

"Plantar fasciitis," she says.

Her moppety salt-and-pepper hair, I note, has been henna-ed into the kind of orange feather duster you'd find in the hand of a French farce maid.

"And what's with the henna?" I ask.

"I have a date tomorrow. I might have laid it on a little thick."

"Very fetching," I say. "Who's the lucky gal?"

"Her name's Trudy. Private art dealer. Lives in Blue Birch Corners. We met online."

"How much does she know about you?" I ask.

"Quite enough," Bridget says. "I can be very well behaved."

"If you say so. Any scuttlebutt for me?"

She offers up several nuggets of dubious provenance, the last of which is an allegation involving Rufus who, according to Bridget, had been spotted yesterday afternoon in his city vehicle at the end of Urchin Lane with a woman who was not Mrs. Meierhoffer. This must have been before he knocked a few back and took his motorboat for a spin.

"What were they d—Hey! Bridget!"

"Yes, dear?"

I give her my sternest gimlet eye and put my hand out. She stares right back, raising her eyebrows, and then, after a pause, returns my wallet.

Before she became a successful theatrical agent, Bridget was an accomplished pickpocket—or "sleight-of-hand artist"—and it is a persistent pastime.

"Bridget Helen Roberts! Aren't you too old to be purloining people's wallets like some ancient Fagin in an Eileen Fisher tunic?"

"I like to keep my hand in," she coos.

She's used that line many times and I wasn't in the mood to have a beautiful autumn morning spoiled with her dark arts. Although, to be fair, she managed to pull off the heist while holding a leash and a bag of apples, which I think speaks to her skill.

I start to walk off and she calls out my name.

"Yes?"

She hands me back my cellphone. I tip an imaginary hat to her and make my way up High Street.

I pat my pockets to confirm that my wallet and phone are still on board. My routine on Saturday mornings is a stop, before the farmer's market, into Long Strange Trip (known by all as LST). It's a record store run by Ben Hubble (known by all as Bender), who is related to the astronomer Edwin Hubble—great grandnephew, or something like that —and he smokes a pipe like Edwin, just not tobacco. He's an old soul in a young body.

Most of ye olde shoppes in Arnold Falls have a bell that jingles when you open the door. Bender has it set up so that the beginning of "Wipe Out" by the Surfaris plays, a long falsetto laugh followed by "Wipe Out!" I'd have cooled on the idea after the first five hundred or so plays Bender, in his hipster-bearded, knit-capped, infinitely chill way, seems good with it.

Bender opened LST a decade ago when he was in his twenties and Arnold Falls was in backwater status. He's managed to make a go of it by selling a quirky selection of vinyl and CDs, and an equally thoughtful selection of weed strains. The weed is stored in the back, the accessories proudly displayed in a tall antique vitrine next to the reggae section.

His music and weed pairings are the stuff of legend. Indeed, in a town often riven by disagreements over matters great and small (mostly small), there was harmonic convergence about Bender's contribution to the general well-being of the community. His best-ever recommendation to me was Shirley Horn's album *You Won't Forget Me* and a bowl of Blue Dream after eleven p.m. The man is a genius. *And* he told me once that I have most comprehensive knowledge of seventies soul of anyone he's ever met, a compliment I am particularly proud of.

I wave to Bender. On the turntable is "Up the Ladder to the Roof" by the Supremes, their first single after the departure of Diana Ross. As I begin looking at the list of new arrivals, I notice a black woman in the corner flipping through albums, in her thirties, I would say, tallish, full-figured, attractive.

She says to Bender, "I always liked the Supremes after Diana Ross better than with her."

"Wh-wait," I sputter, interjecting myself into the conversation. "You cannot be serious!"

"I am."

"I have *never, ever* met anyone who preferred the later Supremes."

"You have now."

"Well, we haven't met," I try lamely.

"I'm Lanelle. Friends call me Nelle. You can call me Lanelle."

Her name was familiar to me—not surprising in a town of seven thousand—but I couldn't place it. As I begin to form a riposte, she continued.

"What's your name?"

"Friends call me Jeebie."

"G. B.?"

"Not G. B. Jeebie.

"What did I say?"

"You said, G. B."

Bender taps his hotel-style desk bell a few times. "How about we go back to Diana Ross versus Jean Terrell?"

"Very well then. You are telling me, Lanelle," I say with my best prosecutorial voice, albeit trembling with emotion, "that given the choice, you would *prefer* to listen to the Supremes *without* Diana Ross?!"

"Miss Ross? That skinny little bitch?"

Bender interrupts. "Dude, you know there's no swearing in here."

Emphasizing his point, Bender turns to his most prized eBay win: a biggie-sized 1970s NCR cash register with dozens of buttons on the left side and a big plastic rectangle on the right side that one bops with the side of a fist after entering the price of an item. Once bopped, the numbers make a satisfyingly crunchy, turning-of-gears sound before the amount charged rolls into formation at the top.

And so Bender bops, the crunchy sound follows, and twenty-five cents appears on the register.

Lanelle says, "Jean Terrell was fierce. She starts this song, 'Up the Ladder,' all purry, like that skinny little bitch—"

Bop, crunchy sound. Fifty cents.

" . . . All purry, just to show you she can do it. And then," she continues, "she blows it out at the end. And you can tell she had more power than she was using. She did *not* want to blend."

In addition to my "comprehensive knowledge of seventies soul," I do voice-over work for a living and I have a thing for Motown. You could say I am an aficionado and I wouldn't disagree. And I have never once considered the possibility that someone would prefer the Supremes without Diana Ross. Diana Ross was *the point*.

But making Lanelle's case at just that moment, Terrell got to the lyrics "As we go on, our love, it will grow/Much stronger, stronger" and gave the word *stronger* a gospel punch that I had to admit Miss Ross couldn't have done.

"Well, I'll be damned."

"That's twenty-five cents . . . G. B." Bender says.

"Put it on my tab," Nelle says.

I nod graciously to her. "I suppose, Lanelle, you're going to tell me The Temptations were better after David Ruffin left."

"No, I wouldn't do that. You couldn't handle it. Besides, I agree with you, David Ruffin was the man."

I take this small victory to cut short my record-browsing. "Well. See you later, Bender. Have to get to the market. Nice to meet you, Lanelle."

She responds with a dead-on impression of Diana Ross, singing in that reedy way, "'Cause you don't really love me / You just keep me hangin' on . . ."

Jean Terrell over Diana Ross! I take a few deep breaths as I enter the farmer's market. Approaching Eiderdown, everyone's favorite apple stand, I hear chef/evil spirit Annie O'Dell giving marching orders to Will Shaffer, the sweet-faced young beanpole who mans Eiderdown's table.

"I need," Annie is saying in that booming voice of hers, "your Cox's. All of them."

"I'm sorry?" Will says.

"Cox's. I need your Cox's."

"It's polite to buy us some beers first," Will says.

"What's the matter with you?" Annie asks. "Your Cox's Orange Pippins. All of them. I know you don't harvest many and I want them."

"Oh, well, I'll have to check with Ed and Louisa. The

Pippins haven't come in yet. And I think they were going to hold them back this year for family and, um, friends."

"You tell them that Annie O'Dell wants their Cox's. I need them for my Thanksgiving special. Tell them I'll pay double. I've left three messages for them—three!—and they don't call me back. You're the only one who has juicy Cox's and I can*not* make the apple pies without them. It's just not the same. And I want the rest to decorate the set."

"We have a lot of Cortlands," Will says.

Annie fixes him in her sights with a beady stare. "I am not going to dignify that with a response. Cox's. Orange. Pippins."

"Okay, sure, I'll tell them, Mrs. O."

And with that she trundles off to spread her cheer elsewhere. Will turns to me.

"Hey, Jeebie."

"Looking for Cox's and offered Cortlands. There's a parable in there," I say. "I'm lucky to be alive."

"That's a good outlook to have," Will says.

"No, I had a major fire last night. Escaped with my life!"

"*Really*? I'm sorry to hear that," he says, grinning in odd counterpoint to the subject at hand.

"Why are you smiling, Will?"

"I'm just glad you're all right. How much damage was there?"

"Minimal. To none."

"Good you escaped with your life. Hey, want to see one of this year's cards?"

"Cards?" I feel I haven't quite gotten the appropriate amount of sympathy from him for the fire.

"You know, the monkey cards for the holidays," he says.

"Oh, right."

Will makes seasonal greeting cards with monkey illustrations that come with a little story, and the money earned goes to Jane Goodall's foundation. I think he told me he sent three hundred dollars last year.

He's a bit of a camel, this gangly guy, designed by committee. When he's just standing there with his Aviators on, as he is now, and his side-slicked brown hair, waiting for you to pick out your apples, you'd say there's a touch of forties-movie-star glamour to him. A bit remote. But when he talks, and especially when he grins, he's rather disarming.

He pulls the card out of his backpack. "This year's theme," Will says, "is Hinky Monkeys."

I was afraid I might OD on whimsy but I'd forgotten that his watercolor and ink drawings were really good—crisp and funny. The portrait is of a chimp named Peaches, wearing a string of pearls around her neck, whose eyes are wide like she's been caught in the act and whose lips are stretched in an oh-crap-I-am-so-busted smile. The bio says "Peaches was indicted in April on racketeering charges, including embezzlement of union funds. The jury was deadlocked and a mistrial was declared. She likes tribal house music, termites and hanging with gibbons."

"The rest of them are up at my Etsy store," Will says.

"I'll have a look," I say, "but I can tell you I'm taken with Peaches. She's . . . quite a catch."

"I'll pass that along to her," Will says. "Any apples today?"

"No, I still have some from last week. I'm actually on the hunt for horseradish root."

"Try Dragon Hill," Will says.

"Good idea."

"Are you cooking tonight?" Will asks. He's put a long

green bean lengthwise in his mouth so that the ends are poking out of each side.

"Yes, mackerel with horseradish cream."

"Sounds delicious."

Was there an ellipsis at the end of that sentence?

"Why are you gumming a string bean?" I ask.

"Looks funny," he says, making the string bean wiggle.

"Well, enjoy. And don't play with matches."

I look up at him but he's already helping another customer. My face feels flushed.

The days are growing shorter. Looking out the kitchen window, the sun is setting and it's not even seven o'clock. The smell of smoke still lingers, reminding me to call the HVAC guys. Good job not self-immolating, my little half-hearted Queen Anne cottage. It's a solid house, all-in-all, but as I mentioned, a bit needy.

Removing the mackerel from its wrap, I nod approvingly, then give myself a generous pour of Sancerre from an open bottle in the fridge. I step out onto the back porch and stand for a moment, looking at the Japanese dogwood already tinged with red, which an arborist with whom I was briefly involved said was probably close to a hundred years old.

As I go back in, I think that some Ella would be nice, but before I push play, I change course with a Supremes album post-Diana Ross that I've hardly ever listened to. The first song, I'm amused to note, starts off with bongos, prompting an unexpectedly warm rush of feelings for our local Wiccans.

I grab the horseradish from the hail pail next to the sink.

A hail pail—otherwise known as a repurposed milk pail—is unique to Arnold Falls, as far as I know. Everyone says you should have one with you at all times within town limits, for protection of the old noggin against hailbursts. Most people in Arnold Falls don't actually heed their own advice—as it relates to hail pails or most anything, come to think of it.

My eyes water as I grate a couple of teaspoons worth of the horseradish into a ramekin. What was that woman's name at LST, anyway? Lanelle. Very sure of herself in her dismissal of Diana Ross. This song's not bad. Didn't Smokey Robinson produce it?

Such weighty thoughts occupy me as I prepare the fish and the horseradish cream to go with it. An easy recipe. I set the table for myself, plate the fish with leftover salad, and pour myself another glass of wine.

As I light a votive candle, I hear Will saying "don't play with matches" and recall him smiling when he said it. Seems a bit callous. I text Jenny, reminding her to drop the lawn signs off at Pluggy's tomorrow. As the album finishes, I pick at my salad, and I think how underrated peace and quiet are.

CHAPTER FIVE

Sidekicks

Jenny drives into Pluggy's Farm and stops near the fenced-in area at the side of house, where Marybeth Elmore is sitting on a tree stump, watching her four-year-old daughter, Sadie, who is twirling to make herself dizzy.

"Hello, Jellybean!" Jenny shouts.

"Hello, Jennybean!" Sadie shouts back, running unevenly toward the gate.

"Oh, Jenny, you didn't have to do that," Marybeth says. "I could have picked it up."

"We're a full-service campaign," Jenny says as she hands Marybeth the lawn sign. Then she kneels down and throws out her arms to Sadie, who runs into the embrace. "You are getting so big."

"I'm almost five," Sadie says.

Though it was Jeebie who had first suggested to Jenny that she run for Mayor, it was Marybeth who had finally persuaded her to do it. They had been having a late-night heart-to-heart, drinking Manhattans at Argos, when Marybeth said she wasn't sure she wanted Sadie to grow up in Arnold Falls.

"It's like Arnold Falls is in the middle of a Venn diagram," Marybeth had said, "where a thriving community and civic neglect overlap. The schools, the parks, they all need a whole lot of TLC. When you were young, the schools were pretty good here, right?"

"Right. Would you really move from Arnold Falls because of the schools?"

"I would, if I thought they weren't going to improve. You'll feel the same way, Jenny, when you have kids."

Slipping two gummy bears to Sadie, Jenny asks, "Where's Duncan?"

"He's inside, doing the bookkeeping. Guaranteed to make him grumpy." Marybeth says. "And our biggest customer, Le Perroquet, is closing."

"No! What are you going to do?" she asks just as Chaplin, one of three Narragansett turkeys the Elmores had inherited from the previous owners, comes out of the barn to greet Jenny, tucking his head down for petting.

"We'll get past it," Marybeth says. "But it's a drag. Have to be thankful for what we've got, and all that."

Now six, Chaplin is a handsome fellow, grading on the poultry curve, with his spray of black, tan and white feathers. Gentle and sweet, Chaplin is the most popular turkey in Queechy County, but also, unquestionably, the neediest. He will do anything for attention.

"Hi, Chaplin!" Jenny says, stroking him. "You have to take extra care of your family, buddy."

Chaplin gobbles.

When schoolchildren come to visit, he struts, snood and

wattles out, showing off his feathers, walking his bow-legged walk. If his audience's attention wanes, he'll flap his wings, gobbling for laughs, and work the crowd like the plaid-suited vaudevillian he is at heart.

"And I hope I can count on your vote."

Chaplin gobbles.

"If I were as popular as you, Chaplin, I'd win in a landslide," Jenny says.

His fellow Naggs, Venus and Serena, have long grown bored of his act, and have learned to sit in a corner until the show is over. Jenny looks into the barn and sees them sleeping. Duncan walks out the kitchen door carrying a mug of coffee.

"Hey, Jen. Want some coffee? Fresh pot."

"No, thanks. Totally caffeinated already."

"I just get a text from Annie O'Dell."

"Ooof, what does she want?" Marybeth asks.

"She didn't say. She asked if she could stop by."

It might be helpful to have Annie's endorsement, but Jenny knows she won't get it. Annie stays away from town business unless she needs something.

"She come by a lot?" Jenny asks.

"God, no," Marybeth says. "I can't even stand to watch her show. Oh, crippety, here she is."

Perfect, Jenny thinks, she's driving an Armada now. Annie gets out of the SUV smile first, accentuated by crimson lipstick, nodding her head as if acknowledging a warm ovation, her round face framed by the familiar bob cut of shellacked blond hair. She looks exactly the way she does on TV, except in person, the guile is unmistakable.

Annie stops outside the fenced area. "Hello, Elmore clan . . . Jenny. I didn't know you'd be here."

"Likewise," Jenny says. "I hope I can count on your support, Annie."

"Jenny. You are *so* brave," is all Annie says.

Only one way to deal with her. "I saw a video of your sister's TED talk last week. She's *so* insightful."

Annie's face curdles. "Yes," Annie says. "The Ambassador to Andorra is a fount of wisdom, isn't she? An endless, endless, endless fount."

"Can I get you coffee?" asks Duncan, coming to the rescue.

"Thank you, no. I can only stay a moment. Modulating her voice to emulate chumminess, Annie continues, "I wanted to talk to you about something. I'm planning my Thanksgiving special and it's very important to the network —and therefore to me—that the ratings are a substantial improvement over last year's. Not that they were bad, but even the best recipes can use a new twist."

Jenny catches Marybeth's eye.

"What I wanted to say was, since Chaplin has such an outgoing personality, I would like to buy him from you so he can be a . . . sidekick. Or a mascot, really."

Marybeth says, "Annie, I'm sorry. Chaplin isn't for sale."

As if on cue, Chaplin runs after Sadie, who screams with delight.

"I know that cash flow is always such a problem when you're running a farm," Annie says, wrinkling her forehead in a shabby attempt at empathy. "And he would be such a delightful addition to my show. I will pay a thousand dollars for Chaplin. And I'll continue talking to chef friends about using you as a vendor."

Extortion, Jenny thinks.

"A thousand dollars?! Why don't you just borrow him?" asked Marybeth.

"My show is *Annie's Farm*. It doesn't look right if we *borrow* a turkey."

"I don't think so," says Marybeth, looking at Duncan.

"Chaplin does love performing. Let's talk about it," he says.

"Yes," Annie says. "Talk about it. But not too long. I'll call you tomorrow. You should cut back those perennials."

As Annie walks back toward her Armada, Chaplin stands quietly. Jenny looks at Marybeth, who shakes her head. God, that woman is awful.

After lunch, Sadie agrees to a nap and gets under her comforter, already half-asleep. Marybeth kisses her daughter's forehead, then pulls down the shade. She sees the crayon drawing of Chaplin on the wall as she closes the door partway.

Marybeth finds Duncan out by his beloved celeriac, the Tom Thumb Erfurt Turnip Rooted Celery variety, which he'd describe to absolutely anyone at the drop of the hat. She found his enthusiasm for the root charming. "Celeriac at the top of its game. Roger Federer, 2006," he'd say. Marybeth had been skeptical that there would be a market for it but Duncan had insisted it would sell since virtually no one else in the country was growing it commercially. He'd been right. And Le Perroquet had been buying more than half of the crop for their celeriac soup, the restaurant's most popular dish.

"Checking for slugs?" she asks.

"And snails. So far, all clear," he says. "Sadie napping?"

"Yeah. What are we going to do?"

"Which problem?" he asks, going down on his haunches to inspect the next row.

"Chaplin."

He exhales, shaking his head.

"We can't do that to Sadie," Marybeth says.

"Venus and Serena will be bummed, too," he says. "We'll tell Sadie he's just going to live at Annie's for a while." He looks up at Marybeth. "We need the money."

"The Duncan I know would be the first to say that some things are more important than money."

"That's the Duncan without a child to feed," he says. "We've got to take care of our little girl."

"Okay," she says finally. "But I hate it."

She walks back quickly toward the house, unable to stop her tears.

Nothing and no one scared Aunt Doozy but she feels an unwelcome lurch of anxiety every time she lets herself into Emma Rose's house. For many months, she'd been caring for her oldest friend—once the little girl who lived next door, now the woman battling leukemia. Emma Rose's ranch-style house wasn't typical of Arnold Falls, but Doozy thanked her stars that it was all one level. As Emma Rose lost strength, it was a big-enough challenge getting her over the step into the shower every day. Still, Emma Rose had survived Dr. Jantzen's prediction by a year so far, a testament to her will to live and the fact that Dr. Jantzen, as Doozy frequently said, "should have been locked up in Arnmoor before they shut that loony bin down."

"Where's your blanket?" Doozy asks as she walks into

the living room. She looks okay, Doozy thinks, got makeup on today.

"I left it in the bedroom."

Doozy goes to get it. "Them Swedes made this . . ."

"Alda Nyqvist," Emma Rose says.

" . . . she made this just for you. She sells them hootchie-paps for a whole lotta money. But it don't do no good if you don't use it." She puts it around Emma Rose's shoulders. "How you feeling?"

"I'm doing fine, how are you doing?"

"So far, so good. Big crowd for breakfast," Doozy says. "I brought you strawberries from my garden. I think that's 'bout the last of them. Thank God I don't have to bend down no more to pick them since Sal gave me that grabber whatchamacallit."

"Thank *Sal*," says Emma Rose.

"You right about that. Did you have anything to eat?"

"I made some toast," Emma Rose says.

"Toast? You can't live on toast," Doozy says. "How many pieces?"

"One."

"You trying to kill yourself, Emma Rose? Death by toast? No, ma'am, that's no breakfast. I'll fix you an omelet and then I'll give you your shower.

"Is today the seventeenth?" Emma Rose asks.

"September 17, yeah."

"That's when Clayton and I had our very first date. In the park."

"How you remember something like that?" Doozy asks.

"Don't you remember your first date with Chester?"

"Naw. Well, come to think of it, I do. We was practically kids. Went to watch the sunset together. Held hands. But enough Memory Lane. Almost forgot. Here's today's *Observer* and the *Racing Form*." She gives Emma Rose the papers. "Now, you make your picks and we'll call in them bets to Dubsack. You want cheese in your omelet?"

"Yes, please."

"All right, cheese omelet coming right up for the pretty lady at table one." She places her hand on Emma Rose's shoulder and gives it a squeeze before walking toward the kitchen saying, "Sassy Little Lila's running Saturday at Belmont."

The golden hour sun is dipping between the branches of an ancient red oak tree in Benedict Arnold Park and illuminating the leaves. Bridget is seated on a bench next to her date, a brunette named Trudy Bettenauer.

She's stylish, Bridget thinks. Crisply stylish. Quite attractive. Jeebie will ask me if I behaved, so I will behave. She and Trudy had met on a dating website, months ago now, and they had been emailing back and forth since then.

"It's nice to finally meet you in person," Trudy says. "You're even prettier than your picture. The henna in your hair is just glowing."

"Thank you. You're too generous," Bridget says, reaching into her bag and pulling out a Thermos and two stainless steel cups. "Would you like some of my special tea?"

"That would be lovely. I have to confess, I haven't been on a *date* date in so long. They're usually so . . . I don't know . . . awkward and disappointing. Best left to the young."

"Truer words, and yet here we are."

Bridget considers, then thinks better of, telling Trudy about her last date, almost two years ago now, which had gone up in smoke. She had invited her date to the first preview of a first play by a promising client at a tiny off-off Broadway theater on the far West Side. The play was called *fog:fog* and the first thirty minutes involved characters stumbling around in a fog, both metaphorical and literal, the latter provided by a high-capacity, dry-ice fog machine. Rehearsals had gone well but when the tiny theater was full and the fog machine had run past the sixteen-minute mark (as the papers had reported), all that carbon dioxide in such a small space began to cause headaches and disorientation. EMS had been called, the performance canceled, and her date had fled, never to be seen again. And, she thought sadly, she had gotten house seats for Cherry Jones for that performance. Cherry hadn't spoken to her since.

It wasn't *her* fault, was it? Well, truth be told, yes, this sort of thing had been happening all her life. Yet it was hard to say was this sort of thing was, precisely: at times she was accident-prone, or accident-adjacent, even accident-inducing. At other times, tiny bombs of chaos trailed in her wake like cans tied to a wedding car, as if Mercury was always in Retrograde and she, Bridget, was Mercury.

Her sixth-grade teacher, Mr. Kotula, had been especially sympathetic to Bridget's jinx pheromones, and he had taught her his full of repertoire of sleight-of-hand techniques whenever Bridget had to stay after school in detention—which was often—to give her, as she later realized, a compensatory sense of agency.

Not only was she a natural at it, as Mr. Kotula frequently remarked, but legerdemain gave her a thrill that nothing else could match. Sadly, the Kotula tutelage was cut short when that kind man died after eating the wrong prickly pear. By the time she reached high school, she was determined to put her skills to use in the real world.

"Tell me more about being a theatrical agent. It sounds exciting," Trudy says.

"No," Bridget says, "not really. It's all contracts and egos. Here you go." She handed the tea to Trudy.

"You represent actors?" Trudy asks.

"Not just actors, I'll take my ten percent from anyone!" Bridget says, chuckling at her own cheekiness. "Actors, musicians, playwrights, directors . . ."

Trudy takes a sip. "Oh, that has quite a kick!"

"Yes, well, it wouldn't be special if it weren't laced with a little Clagger."

"What *is* Clagger, anyway? I've always heard about it but never tried it."

"I'm not sure myself. It's all very hush-hush. Everyone says antifreeze. Anyway, cheers. It's five o'clock somewhere!" says Bridget merrily.

Trudy looks at her watch. "Actually, it's five o'clock *here!*" and they both whoop and holler at this development, clinking cups.

When they settle down, Bridget says, "You're a private art dealer?" She begins to refill Trudy's cup but Trudy shakes her head. Bridget refills her own cup. Be good, she reminds herself.

"Yes," continues Trudy. "I had a gallery in the city for a number of years and when I moved to Blue Birch Corners full-time, I opened one here in Arnold Falls. But the overhead was too much and I didn't love all the looky-loos." Trudy's phone rings. "Oh, I am sorry, Bridget. This is my mother calling from Germany. It will only be a moment." She taps her phone. "*Hallo Mutti. Warum bist Du noch auf? Es ist doch schon spät. Ich kann im Moment nicht mit Dir sprechen. Ich ruf Dich morgen an. Ja, schlaf gut. Gute Nacht.*"

"Is everything okay?" Bridget asks.

"Yes, all's well. I'll call in her in the morning."

"More tea?"

"Just a little," Trudy says. "My mother's getting quite frail. Same at home: my pooch Delphy is eleven, and some days she's so lethargic that it breaks my heart."

"That's the catch with dogs," says Bridget. "They're never with us long enough. My dog Gussie is sweetness itself, though he does have a mischievous streak."

"Delphy's such a good girl. I've spoiled her terribly. But she has the most soulful eyes! You just can't resist them. Look." She reaches into her bag to get her wallet then pauses. "That's strange. I know it was here." Trudy continues to rummage. "Oh, I can't believe this!"

Bridget produces the wallet with a flourish. "*Et voila!*"

Trudy freezes, staring at Bridget. "You went into my *bag*? You stole my *wallet*?!"

"No! Well, yes, while you were talking to your mother. But I wasn't going to keep it. It's just this skill I have. Use it or lose it, right? Ask anyone, they'll tell you. Bridget is the best at sleight of hand."

"I'm not going to ask anyone anything. You're a thief!" Trudy stands up to go. "How would you like it if I went rummaging around your bag?"

Trudy grabs the bag lying in front of Bridget and proceeds to do so, pulling items from Bridget's bag and tossing onto the grass a bottle of hand sanitizer, a bag of Corn Nuts, a Magic 8 Ball, and a hail pail with "Return to Bridget" stenciled on it.

"Stop that!" Bridget shouts, putting the items back in her bag.

"You stole my wallet! This is your idea of a first date?!"

"What seems to be the problem, ladies?"

They both look up as Officer Wanda Velez strides over to them, determination packed into every inch of her wiry, five-foot-six frame.

"This *lady* stole my wallet!"

Officer Velez asks Bridget, "Do you have her wallet?"

"No. I gave it back to her."

"So you took it?" asks Officer Velez.

"I did," says Bridget. "I'm a sleight-of-hand artist, or I was when I was younger and I just like to keep up the craft. You're the triathlon champ, aren't you, Officer? That's hard to say. Tri-atthh-lon."

"Yes, I'm a triathloner." Officer Velez turns to Trudy, "Is any money missing from your wallet?"

"I didn't even check! Let me see." Trudy opens her wallet and peers in. "No, I don't think so."

"I never take *money*," Bridget says indignantly. "I'm a fingersmith. The thrill is the lift, you know? Being on the whiz. I could take your badge and you'd never know it."

"I don't recommend it," Officer Velez says.

"I could! Deputize myself. Just like that," she says, with a snap of her fingers. "*I shot the sheriff*," Bridget sings, "*but I did not shoot the deputy . . .*"

Officer Velez sighs. "Okay. That's enough. No one's shooting anyone. This isn't Elbridge Bartlett's Farewell Wassail. Let's take it over to the station. Come on, ladies."

"Whoa," Bridget says when she stands up, swaying. "Would you like some tea with Clagger, Officer? You know who you remind me of? A Rockette I once dated. What was her name? Something Rockette. They're used to precision, those girls. Very powerful high kicks. And you know what else? I have a very pleasing singing voice. Very pleasing to the ear." Bridget sings:

Hey! Give Me Some Clagger and a Bagger,

You haughty little, naughty little minx.
Bagger beggar, clagger kegger.
Spend some cheddar, ending better.
Everybody, everybody, drinks, drinks, drinks!"
Hey! Give Me Some Clagger and a Bagger
You haughty little, naughty little minx.
I'll be bossy, you be saucy!
Hopin' for some turny-tossy!
Everybody, everybody—

"That's enough, now," says Officer Velez, "with your pleasing voice."

"Isn't it?!" says Bridget. She turns to Trudy, "That's the first thing they teach first graders after the Plesh of Allegiance, the Arnold Falls' fight song. Iss in the cricclum."

"Very touching," Trudy says.

"Thass the esact word for it," she says, waving to Father Burnham across the street. "Hello, Father Burnham! Tootle-oo!"

Trudy represses a smile, but Bridget, even in her current state, spots it.

Bridget says to Officer Velez, "I like her."

"In that case, maybe you should have left her wallet alone," Officer Velez says as she holds the door of the police station for Bridget and Trudy to enter.

CHAPTER SIX

Truce and Consequences

J enny and I are across the street from Argos. It's dark
and we're mostly hidden by bushes. Dubsack's silver
Rascal is parked outside and we can see our mark
through the large picture window seated halfway down
the bar.

"Are you ready?"

"Let me just double-check the camcorder," I say. "Okay,
ready."

Jenny pulls out her phone and dials. We watch Sofia
pick up the receiver of the coveted powder-blue Princess
phone next to the cash register.

"Hi, Sofia, it's Jenny. Remember Hamster mentioned
that Dubsack is stealing my campaign lawn signs?" She
explains the rest.

Jenny waits a few minutes and then calls back,
repeating what I had suggested: 'Dub, it was fun but I've got
chlamydia. You should get tested.' Sofia dutifully writes it

down, hangs up the phone and hands the note to Dubsack. Jenny and I watch the silent movie unfold while I capture it on my videocam.

Dubsack stands up, throws a bill toward Sofia and storms outside. He kicks the bushes. He gives them a backhanded slap. He kicks them again. Then he starts kicking his Rascal, again and again.

I'm having trouble holding the camera still we're both laughing so hard. Sofia is peering out the window and the whole bar has become an audience of the Dubsack Show. And then the perfect, unplanned capper: Officer Wanda Velez walks into the scene and says something to Dubsack, who jumps onto the Rascal and hightails it out of there at top speed—eight mph—wheels not screeching.

"Come on, I'll buy you a drink," says Jenny when she catches her breath.

We emerge from our hideout and say hello to Officer Velez.

"What's up with Dubsack?"

"Karma," I say. "He's been stealing Jenny's campaign signs."

"Stealing your campaign signs? That's a misdemeanor. I'll keep an eye out for you."

"Thanks, Wanda," says Jenny.

"Anytime, Jenny. And good luck with everything."

We walk into Argos and Madora comes over to give us both a hug. Sofia applauds. We applaud back to her.

Susanne Nyqvist—she of the sprawling Swedish clan— says, "I'd binge-watch a season of that!"

Sofia says, "I told Dubsack there be might some burning during urination," as she brings red wine to me, Jim Beam to Jenny.

Susanne raises her glass. "To changing times," she says, and we all toast.

As Sofia and Susanne begin to chat at the other end of the bar, Jenny leans into me.

"Why don't you like Susanne?" she asks.

"Why do you say that?"

"Just a vibe."

"I do like her. It's just that whole family is so . . . talented and good-looking, and . . . I don't know."

Jenny rumbles out a laugh. "Jeebie, they're the nicest people!"

"Exactly my point. Way too much. I'd be happy, though, if the Nyqvist battalion wanted to work on the campaign."

"That reminds me," Jenny says. "I got an email from Lanelle Clark. She's the one who took over SOAR last year when Alice retired. Do you know her? She *does* want to work on the campaign."

"This town is too small," I say.

"Why? What's wrong with her?"

"She . . . never mind. Nothing's wrong with her. Questionable taste, that's all. Give me her email."

Jenny says "Maybe take her to lunch."

"Okay. And we've got to nail down a debate somehow. Rufus is going to put us off as long as he can get away with it.

"You're right," Jenny says. "Today's the eighteenth. How about we propose a debate for the third week of October and put it out on our Facebook page? He won't be able to ignore that."

"Good, I'll take care of it," I say.

Madora walks over chewing on the stale, pastel after-dinner mints Argos still leaves by the front door. "Hey, go check on Bridget. She's on the patio."

"Why, what happened?"

"Bad date. Turned into a court date."

That is a bad date, Jenny and I agree as we grab our drinks and walk out to the patio for the details.

Me: *Hello, Lanelle. You probably don't remember me but we met briefly at LST.*

She texts back: *You're G.B.*

Me: *Jeebie.*

She: *Well, you should know.*

Me: *Jenny said you want to volunteer for the campaign.*

She: *Yes.*

Me: *She wants me to take you to lunch.*

She: *That's not necessary.*

Me: *I don't want to either.*

She: *We agree on something.*

It goes on like this for a while.

We end up sitting at a picnic table overlooking Glencadia Creek. We're having a late Tuesday lunch outdoors at Darlene's, across the river, and we've got it to ourselves. It was only after singing the praises to Nelle of Darlene's, where she hadn't been, and especially of the Darlene burger, that she agreed to have lunch with me.

"We are *not* putting vinegar on those fries," Nelle says.

"I'm putting vinegar on *my* fries," I say.

"*My* fries? *My* fries. I thought we were sharing," Nelle says.

"No, I don't know you that well. We're splitting."

I grab a clump of fries and put them next to my burger. "And now the perfect fry sauce," I say, shaking the malt vinegar bottle.

She takes her first bite of the Darlene Burger and Nelle says, with her mouth full, something that sounds like, "Ohmygah, mih ih the beh bur I eh ha."

"I told you."

Funny thing: all it took was the drive from Arnold Falls to Darlene's for us to become fast friends. Nelle was born in Newark and moved to Brooklyn when she was seven, where she'd lived until she got the job as head of SOAR last year. She'd always done social work, focusing on mental health and substance abuse, but she was ready for a change of scene. So here she was. Motown aside, you couldn't help but love her. At least I couldn't.

"It's like they deconstructed a Big Mac," I say, "then built it back from scratch with the best ingredients, everything local and homemade."

"You've given this some thought," Nelle says.

"I like to know how things work," I say.

"I like to know how people work," Nelle says.

"How could you ever know that? Anyway, that burger makes me happy."

"What else makes you happy?" she asks.

"You can't just ask a question like that . . . just like that," I say.

"Why not?"

"Because we're talking about food, not, I don't know, that stuff."

"Boyfriend?"

"No."

"Why not?" Nelle asks.

"I like peace and quiet."

"Uh-huh. Okay. What does Jeebie mean?"

I take a sip of my coffee milkshake. "It's really Jeffrey, but my sister took one look at me after I was born and told everyone I gave her the heebie-jeebies. It stuck because my mother encouraged it. She thought it was cute."

"And were you really that freaked out that I like Jean Terrell better than your Miss Ross? Or were you just being dramatic?"

"No. Yes. Diana Ross *was* the Supremes."

"You're very invested in your point of view," Nelle says.

"Isn't everybody?"

"You know that song is about getting high, right?"

"What song?"

"'Up the Ladder to the Roof.'"

I snort. "*It is not!*"

"'We'll combine our thoughts and together we'll travel to the *fountain of loveliness?*'" Nelle asks incredulously. "Check Google Maps, Jeebie, so I can get directions to this Fountain of Loveliness. I hope there's a gift shop!"

I take a moment to consider this. "I never thought of it that way," I say.

"Exactly," Nelle says. "Though I suppose you could make the case that the song is about love. Or sex."

"Maybe it's about actually climbing up a ladder to get to your roof when your drains are clogged. Which reminds me . . ."

"You're the last of the romantics," Nelle says.

"I get that a lot."

After a moment, she says, "You have a nice speaking voice. Do you sing?"

I fill her in on my voice over and theater work.

"I'll bet you were a choirboy. Am I right?"

"Yes, as a matter of fact. Any other questions?"

"Musical instrument?"

"French horn," I say. "Your eyes are very merry at that. Why is that funny?" I ask. "It's not funny. Is it? It's not *that* funny."

"No, it's not funny. It's just so you," Nelle says.

"You can't say it's so me. You don't know me well enough yet." I decide the subject needs changing. "Do you sing?" I ask. "Your Diana Ross impression wasn't half-bad."

To my astonishment, Nelle looks out over the creek and sings: *"If I should write a book for you . . ."*

And holy moly, I get goosebumps from head to tail as she sings the first two verses of "Dedicated to You." I look straight ahead at the creek, too, and listen to the sounds and tone and phrasing and shading that she seems able to conjure effortlessly.

"Jesus," I say. "I . . . you should . . . what about doing a benefit for the campaign?"

"I don't like singing for a lot of people."

"We haven't raised much money yet and Rufus is getting a lot of support from Ivan Borger."

"The guy with the comb-over?"

"Yeah, our very own Mr. Potter. Or Mr. Burns. So, how about a benefit for Jenny at Traitor's Landing? Let's put on a show! Come on, Nelle. Do you have a show?"

She just looks at me, arms folded.

"Okay, translating here, yes, you have a show, but forget it, you've got stage fright."

"It's not stage fright. I like singing when I *need* to sing for myself, not when I *have* to sing for others."

"You don't like the performing part of performing.

Okay, I think we've definitively established that you, Nelle Clark, are a diva."

She shrugs.

"Far more Diana Ross than Jean Terrell," I say pointedly.

"Nice try."

"Well, what *do* you want to do for the campaign?"

"Whatever you need. Door-to-door stuff, phone calls. Like that."

"How about doing a show?"

"I'll think about it. But don't get your hopes up."

"I know Traitor's owner," I say. "He's a big fan of Jenny's. It could be great!"

"*Could* be? I don't do *could be*," Nelle says, reluctantly finishing her Darlene burger.

CHAPTER SEVEN

The Worst Sister City in the World

Bender is at his desk in his shop, listening to Keith Jarrett's *Paris Concert*, while his cat, Humboldt, is sprawled out across his feet. He's brainstorming on an oversized sheet of paper the latest in a series of imaginary places—cities, towns, countries—that he has created, first by hand and then using mapping software. Each locale has a history, governing style, landmarks, and notable citizens. Each follows its own rules and creating that internal logic is, for Bender, a large part of the appeal—it's occurred to him more than once that Arnold Falls' tenuous and intermittent relationship with logic may have spurred him on in this pursuit. His current map is of Lugubria and he's having trouble coming up with a list of Top Ten Things To Do there.

The door opens ("Wipeout!") and Humboldt darts to the back as Duncan walks in.

"Hey, dude," says Bender, setting aside his mapwork. "How goes it in Pluggyland?"

"Hi, Bender." They give each other a bro hug, which ends with two slaps (each) on the back. "New beanie?"

"Yeah," Bender says. "Did a swap with Grandma Nyqvist. She knitted this for me and I parted with my orange label *Astral Weeks*. How's the family?"

"Everybody's good."

"How's Chaplin?"

"That sucks. We sold him. Annie O'Dell paid a thousand bucks for him. She wants him on her TV show. Sadie's really bummed."

"A thousand bucks?! Well, you gotta eat."

"Exactly. Listen, I am hearing some crazy shit about Ivan Borger. Whoops, here's a quarter."

Bender says, "No one around, all good. You got the info from your City Hall spy?"

"Yeah. And it checks out. Have you heard anything?"

"No, man," says Bender. "What's Borger up to?"

"You're not going to believe this, but he wants to put a tire factory on the land he owns near the waterfront. That would be a fucking environmental catastrophe."

"Damn. Have you talked to anyone else in the Evergreens?" Bender asks.

"No, I thought I'd check with you first."

"That is seriously messed up. When do we meet next?"

"First week of November, I think," Duncan says. "That's too long to wait."

"Let's go to talk to McDufus," Bender says.

"He won't tell us anything."

"No. But we still might learn something. Let's go, dude."

"Is that Keith Jarrett playing?" Duncan asks.

"It is."

"*Paris Concert?*"

"Nicely done," Bender says.

"I think I want a beanie from Grandma Nyqvist."

"You have something to trade? She likes to barter with locals."

"I've got a boatload of celeriac."

"You never know," Bender says, turning the open sign around and locking the front door.

The first thing Duncan sees when he enters City Hall with Bender is Tishy Mustelle, Rufus's secretary. A heavyset thirty-one-year-old, Tishy is easily identifiable in the building by her wardrobe—comprised entirely of crafting experiments that have gone invariably, sadly, and sometimes horribly, wrong. Duncan takes in today's sweater, a harlequin pattern of colored felts, ineptly assembled, with the diamond-shaped pieces curling out, appearing eager to jump to safety. She'd babysat Sadie a number of times and he thought that Tishy, in her own way, rocked.

Tishy puts down *Harry Potter and the Prisoner of Azkaban* as Duncan and Bender approach her desk.

"Is he in?" Bender asks.

"Yeah," Tishy says. "I like your cap."

"Thanks, I like your sweater," Bender says.

Duncan winks at Tishy and she gives a flash of a smile in return. They go to Rufus' office door and see Rufus staring at his cell phone. Probably playing Candy Crush, Duncan thinks.

Rufus looks up and says, "Uh-oh, it's the eco-Nazis."

"Good afternoon, Mayor," Duncan says.

"Duncan, Bender. Have a seat. You here to support my campaign?"

"Next lifetime, dude."

"Or the one after that," Duncan adds.

"I'll put you down as a maybe," Rufus says.

Duncan cuts to the chase. "I'm hearing that Ivan is planning to build a tire factory on the property he owns near the waterfront."

"Are you looking for me to confirm that?" Rufus asks.

"Come on. It would make Arnold Falls uninhabitable," Duncan says. "Kids live here, you know that, right?"

"Yeah, yeah, yeah. Halloween is next month. Scare me then. Besides, he just wants to make rubber bands. He didn't say anything about tires."

Duncan and Bender look at each other and Duncan tries hard to keep a straight face.

Rufus realizes his mistake. "I guess I confirmed that for you. Doesn't matter, Ivan can do what he wants. It's zoned industrial, so what are ya gonna do?"

"He's just going to tear down the Dutch House? It's the oldest house in Arnold Falls and it's a landmark," Duncan says.

"Nothing to be done about that. Place can't be saved," Rufus says. "Unsound."

"Yeah, because Ivan hasn't done anything to fix it in years," Bender says.

"Why should he fix it?"

"Because he *owns* it," Duncan says. "Who else is supposed to fix it?"

"Some rich person," Rufus says.

"Like *Ivan*," Duncan and Bender say together.

"Look, how many jobs is a rotting old house going to bring in?" Rufus asks. "And *that* is the fly in the argument."

"Ointment," Duncan says.

"Ointment for what? Ivan doesn't want to make ointment. He wants to build a factory. Two hundred new jobs. Even you bleeding hearts understand jobs, right? Put your ointment on *that*!"

Getting up to leave, Duncan says, "Okay, Rufus. Thanks for your time. We'll let you get back to your Candy Crush."

"Angry Birds," says Rufus.

Duncan gives a wave to Tishy on their way out.

Once they're gone, Rufus shouts, "Tishy! Where'd my slushy go?"

"In your belly!" she shouts.

"Not in my belly!"

"Not in my job description!"

"Does Ivan want to make ointment?!"

"Rubber!"

Rufus repeatedly scratches the back of his head. He sighs, rubbing his hand over his mouth and chin as he rereads the letter that had arrived that morning from Mayor Haralambie.

Shortly after Rufus was elected in 2013, Haralambie wrote to him, explaining that he was the longtime mayor of Plopeni in Romania and that as Plopeni and Arnold Falls were roughly the same size, he was proposing that they become sister cities, fostering good will between the nations and perhaps spurring tourism between the two. Rufus had readily accepted. A sign was posted in front of City Hall touting the exciting Arnold Falls/Plopeni bond.

It wasn't long after the relationship was formalized by

letter that the first request came from Mayor Haralambie. He wondered if "Plopeni's dear brothers and sisters" in Arnold Falls could find it in their hearts to send a crate of potable water, of which Plopeni apparently had only intermittent supplies. Arnold Falls promptly raised fifteen hundred dollars for the effort and sent one thousand gallons to Plopeni.

The next year, Mayor Haralambie wanted to know if the town had extra guns they weren't using. There were plenty of deer around Plopeni, he explained, but without guns, many citizens couldn't provide enough food for their families. The Guns for Plopeni drive was a great success— 114 firearms were collected and dispatched in less than a month.

Now Plopeni's mayor said that Plopenians had all the venison they could ever want thanks to the guns from its sister city, but people were longing for vegetables—"some crunching, healthful vegetables"—rare as jewels since the soil was so arid. Could Arnold Falls please send ammonium nitrate for Plopeni to use as fertilizer, so children could grow up fortified by cabbage?

Who could say no to cabbage? The problem was, Rufus didn't want to ask voters to open their wallets before the election. In his latest letter, Mayor Haralambie was insistent that it was a matter of great urgency. "There is no crunching in Plopeni. Terrible tragedy."

Maybe, just maybe, he could use this terrible tragedy to help him win reelection.

"Tishy, can you come here?" Rufus shouts to his secretary. After a few minutes, he yells, "Take your time!"

She finally appears at the door.

"Ivan says I have to squish the blueberry," Rufus says.

"You told me that," says Tishy, sucking on a cough drop.

"I have a plan, Tishy."

"Uh-huh."

"Want to know what it is?" asks Rufus.

"Uh-huh."

"About Mayor Haralambie."

"Okay."

"It will help me win reelection."

"Ungh," Tishy grunts, cracking the lozenge.

"Plopeni needs ammonium nitrate, right? I'm going to send it to Haralambie, from me, on behalf of Arnold Falls. Find out how much I can get for two, three hundred bucks."

"Yuh."

"It's money well spent. Children get cabbage. Let's see Jagoda argue with *that*! What is Jagoda?"

"Blueberry."

"Right. Try Home Depot. Or better yet, try Amazon. We'll deliver it to City Hall in Plopeni. They must have a City Hall, right? See if we can get free delivery."

"Okay, Rufus. Ammonium nitrate, Amazon, Plopeni, overnight delivery."

"No, doesn't have to be overnight. But see if Amazon Prime has it."

"Yuh."

"Genius, right?"

"Ungh."

"That bird won't shut up. Reminds me of my sister."

Annie O'Dell is standing by the kitchen sink in her farmhouse, pounding an octopus, talking to her husband, Julius, who is reading the paper.

"He poops everywhere."

"You paid a thousand bucks for him," Julius says, without looking up. "Couldn't you have gotten one that doesn't poop so much?"

"Is that supposed to be funny?" Annie asks, pounding the octopus so hard that the mallet head snaps off.

"I think it's dead, dear."

"I know it's dead. I am trying to *tenderize* it," she says through clenched teeth.

"Put Chaplin in one of the coops at the other end of the farm."

"He just screeches when I do that. You can hear him from here."

"How's he gonna bring you ratings?"

"I don't know, people love him. He's a ham."

"Ham is pig," Julius says.

"You're Jack Benny today," Annie says, using a pestle to keep up her attack.

"Still alive?"

"I told you it's dead!"

"I meant Jack Benny," Julius says.

Slapping the octopus against the cutting board, Annie says, "No, they . . ." (pound) "are . . ." (pound) "all . . ." (pound) "*dead.*" (pound). "The octopus, Jack Benny, all of them. Anyway, Jack Benny died ages ago. Decades."

"I liked Jack Benny," Julius says.

"Everyone liked Jack Benny."

Chaplin starts yelping loudly.

"I am getting a migraine from that turkey."

"So cook him," Julius says.

"I can't cook—" Annie says. She wipes her hands on her apron and sits down at the table. "I *could* cook him. Farm animals have to serve a purpose. And this one's job is

Thanksgiving dinner. We'll do a pre-tape of his little act and then he gets brined."

"You might get some protests, though. Lotta kids are fans of that bird."

"Hm, I don't need the rabble blubbering on the local news. Let me think about it."

"You're all heart," says Julius.

"Clove, please."

Sadie scoops a garlic clove from a small Barkenshaw pail and hands it to her father.

"Thanks, chief," Duncan says.

Side by side with his daughter, both on their knees, Duncan looks at Sadie and sees so much of Marybeth, though when Sadie concentrates intently on a task, as she is doing now, he sees himself, too.

He places the clove in the soil. "Is this right?"

Sadie nods. "Pointy side up."

"And what kind of garlic is this?"

"Shezzstook?"

"Close! Chesnok Red."

His phone rings.

"Dude!"

"Hey, Bender," says Duncan, pushing the phone against his ear with his shoulder, putting his hand out to Sadie for another clove.

"Dude, dude, dude. Something has been bugging me about what McDufus said yesterday. He said Ivan's land was zoned as industrial. But it's zoned *light* industrial, I just checked."

Duncan says, "Wow, wow, that explains a lot. So . . .

Ivan is worried McDufus is going to lose reelection and that Jenny's appointees on the board won't change the zoning, and that would mean no tire factory."

"Exactly."

"So he's trying to rush through a change. When is the last zoning board meeting before the election?"

Sadie taps him. "Wrong way, Daddy."

Duncan rubs her head and adjusts the clove.

"November second," Bender says.

"Bender, you're a genius. We gotta get organized. Gives us about six weeks."

"I'd focus on the Dutch House," Bender says. "Ivan can't build anything while it's still standing and the preservationists will lose their shit if it's torn down."

"Right. I'll email the group explaining what's going on. Go wash your mouth out with soap."

Duncan hears Bender laughing as he hangs up.

"This town! Clove, please."

"I miss Chaplin, Daddy."

"I know, Sadie. I know." He does know. She's having a hard time thinking about anything else. "Come on, smells to me like Mommy's making banana bread. Let's go have some breakfast."

Taking Sadie's hand, Duncan leaves the pail and they walk to the house. They find Marybeth in the kitchen checking on the banana bread, and when she looks up, Duncan mouths "Chaplin" to her, pointing to Sadie. Marybeth nods.

"Sadie, I know you're missing Chaplin. We all are, sweetie. But we had to do what's best for the family," she says without much conviction, looking at Duncan.

"I hate Annie."

"No, Sadie, we don't hate people."

"I don't like her very, very, very, very much."

"Come here, honey."

"No, I don't want to."

"How about some peanut butter with the banana bread?"

"OK," Sadie says as she walks toward the side door and looks out through the bottom panes of glass.

"What do you want to do today? Should we —"

"Mommy! It's Chaplin!"

"No, Sadie. It's Serena or Venus."

"No, Mommy. That's Chaplin! It is! Serena and Venus are there, too."

Duncan looks out the window. "Son of a gun."

He opens the door and Sadie runs toward her pal. Chaplin gobbles.

Duncan and Marybeth look at each other.

"He must have escaped out of Annie's yard. She probably forgot that turkeys can fly."

"She probably forgot all about him," Marybeth says. "Sadie. He can't stay. Remember, he's going to be on television with Annie."

"It's too early to call," Duncan says. "I'll try Annie in a while and let her know Chaplin's here.

Venus and Serena walk into the yard to take in the latest developments.

"Do we have grapes for Chaplin?" Sadie asks.

Marybeth pulls off three grapes from a bunch in the fridge and hands them to Sadie.

Duncan sits at the kitchen table. "The banana bread smells good."

"Another few minutes," she says.

"Bender just called."

"Early for Bender," she says.

"He figured something out. Ivan needs to get the zoning changed if he wants to build his factory. The land, including where the Dutch House is, is zoned for light industrial."

"And he needs heavy industrial."

Sadie returns for more grapes.

"Right. That reminds me, I've got to send an update to the Evergreens about what he's up to. Uggh. This town."

"This town," Sadie echoes.

Sofia is up late, having binge-watched six episodes of the fifth *Dr. Who* season, from 1967, which she had somehow never seen. She's been restless for hours, since she got Duncan's email about Ivan. Fucking Ivan and his fucking scheme. What is wrong with people?

She washes her face in the bathroom, noticing a small pimple on the side of her cheek. What kind of joke is this? she wonders. I'm fifty-four. She thinks of her sister Lillie, ten years younger, off on her new adventure with Mac, in Wilmington. This strikes her as funny—adventure in Wilmington—but then she tears up.

"Goddammit," she says. She considers calling Lillie but remembers she and Mac are camping at some national park.

After she rinses her face again, the need to move, to walk, to *go* is overwhelming. It is physical. Her thighs feel jammed up. She resists and resists.

Another episode of *Dr. Who*? *Please Like Me*? *Mary Tyler Moore*? Not in the mood now.

Finally, close to three, Sofia puts on a coat and walks out.

Sofia didn't show up for work on Friday night and this morning, Saturday, Madora is at Sofia's house, a craftsman bungalow with brick and wood siding and a dogwood tree in front, which sits at the end of Benedict Arnold Way. She rings the doorbell again.

"Sofia!" She knocks loudly. "Dammit, Sofia!"

She pulls out her phone and tries calling her. Voicemail. She sits on the stoop and remembers the day Sofia first came in for a job, just a few weeks after Madora had opened Argos. That was seventeen years ago. Madora had loved how forthright she was and hired her on the spot. Her intuition had paid off—Sofia's ability to read people was uncanny and the bar started filling up with repeat business. Over the years, they had grown close. What to do? Madora is thinking when the front door opens and there she is.

"Oh, Sofia!" Madora says, standing up. "Are you okay?"

"I'm okay. Thanks for checking on me. Sorry I missed work last night."

"I was worried about you."

They hug.

"Sorry," Sofia says. "I need . . . some time."

"You don't have to be sorry. I'm glad you're all right. Is there anything I can do?"

"No," says Sofia. "But thank you."

"Call me if there's anything."

"I will."

"Promise me."

"I promise, Madora."

"You know you can tell me anything."

"I know."

They embrace again and Sofia goes back inside her

house. As Madora walks to Argos, she's sure there's more to the story, but she can't quite see it.

After days of ammonium nitrate shopping, Tishy walks into Rufus's office while he is playing Angry Birds. He makes her wait until he finishes the round.

I've kept you out of trouble so many times, she thinks, almost saying it out loud.

"Goddammit. Stuck on the Beach Volley level. What's the news?"

"Okay," Tishy says. "Amazon doesn't sell ammonium nitrate, but I found it on Alibaba and sent it to Plopeni's City Hall. Delivery was fifty dollars and takes two weeks. I charged it to your MasterCard."

"Did you put in a note?"

"Yeah. 'Best wishes to our sister city from the Mayor of Arnold Falls, Rufus Meierhoffer. Hope your "cabbage crop" will be booming.'"

"Tishy, you deserve a bonus!"

"I know."

"But you're not getting one."

"I know. You'll get yours," she says.

"Huh?"

She hears the Angry Birds theme music and hums along with it as she goes back to her desk.

CHAPTER EIGHT

Close Encounters

I'm at the Big Y, the supermarket-slash-philosophical conundrum, where I'm getting the ingredients to make a batch of maple chocolate chip cookies, from *scratch*, and drop them off at the office of Lanelle Clark. This is an effort to literally sweeten the pot, which, with any luck, will end with Nelle agreeing to do a benefit for Jenny at Traitor's Landing on October 24, which I might have booked for her with Traitor's owner at brunch yesterday, without her knowledge.

Not being a fan of the market's musical tastes, I have headphones on, listening to Yo-Yo Ma playing Ennio Morricone's film music, which, come to think of it, almost answers the market's existential question. Lost in my bubble by the brown sugar, someone taps my shoulder.

As I take the earphones off, I turn to see Will.

"Didn't mean to startle you," he says.

"How come you're not at the orchard?" I ask. This, it

occurs to me as I'm asking it, is an irrelevant, stupid question.

"I'm a free-range worker," he says. "Hey, how's everything at your house? After your 'major fire?'"

"Fine. All good now."

"You've got to be especially careful with Siretta furnaces. They clog a lot."

"Thanks. I'll be more—wait. So. Huh. How do you know what kind of furnace I have?"

"I saw it."

"How could you see it?"

"Jeebie, I was there."

"How were you—? You were —? You're a —?!"

"I'm a volunteer firefighter. Well, we're all volunteers."

I am at a loss for words. "Oh. Aha," is all I can think to say.

"Nice running into you," he says.

"Hey, Will. Thank you. You know, for the fire. I mean, not for the *fire*, but—"

"I got it. No worries. Glad everything's okay," he says. "Buying stuff for the firehouse right now. Cheers." He walks off but stops and turns. "Next time, Jeebie, don't forget to put on shoes."

Suddenly I have no idea what I'm looking for in this aisle or what I am doing in this store at all.

Somehow, in spite of this disturbance in the force field, I return home, bake the cookies, drop them off to reception at Nelle's office, and run to catch the eleven o'clock train into the city to do voice-over work for a small agency that uses me a lot. I was looking forward to viewing the parade of changing leaves and listening to a playlist I had put together of songs arranged by Thom Bell. (I won't take time here to explain Thom Bell; I'll just namecheck The Stylistics and

The Spinners.) I'd let Bell's strings wash over me along with his unlikely use of oboes, bassoons, even my (apparently amusing) French horn, right in the middle of classic seventies soul music.

"Is this seat taken?" someone says.

Without looking up, and resisting the temptation of a snappy comeback (which I didn't have at the ready, anyway), I say, "No, be my guest."

"You're Jeebie, aren't you?"

I look up. "Ah, you're the elusive Alec Barnsdorf."

"Well, I guess that's better than shadowy," Barnsdorf says.

"Shadowy is *le mot juste*," I say. "That's what I should have said."

"*L'esprit de l'escalier*," he says, sitting down.

"*Oeufs a la neige*," I reply, fresh out of French.

Alec Barnsdorf is a writer best known for his popular sociology essays in the *New Yorker* and his bestselling books compiled from those essays. He had bought a house in Arnold Falls in the spring of 2012, impressing the small slice of residents who regularly read the *New Yorker*. I am one of them.

Barnsdorf, in his early forties, is immediately recognizable by his tweed sports coats, frosty Einstein hair, and frostier mien. He is frequently observed around AF having coffee, accompanied only by a notebook and pen.

Two years ago, the first of the "Mischief in Merryvale" pieces appeared in the magazine. Merryvale is a fictional Hudson Valley town that bears some resemblance to Arnold Falls. There are more differences than similarities, but the denizens of Merryvale do drink a moonshine particular to their village called "Valley Dew," to which they attribute any misfortunes with the catchphrase "Valley

Dew done did it." A humorous declension, perhaps, in the fallow field of declension jokes.

Barnsdorf has also made use of Arnmoor, the crumbled ruins of the insane asylum at the northern end of Arnold Falls, now overgrown to the point of being nearly inaccessible, turning it into a lavishly renovated boutique hotel that maintains some of the ghostly spirits of its original tenants.

Even if few have met him, this has made Barnsdorf's relationship with locals complicated. On the one hand, it is flattering to think of one's community as worthy of fictional treatment and enjoyable to try and identify which actual townspeople might have inspired which Merryvale characters. On the other hand, there is a persistent suspicion that Barnsdorf is getting away with something: mining for eccentricities, repurposing stories and gossip, and profiting at Arnold Falls' expense, with the town receiving nothing for its end of the bargain. Those who do not see themselves in any of the characters or storylines are particularly aggrieved. Indeed, it is hard for many, when they are within earshot of the writer, to resist antic, emphatic conversations in hopes of intriguing the sphinx-like scrivener.

"How is the campaign coming along?" he asks. "Is she going to win?"

"Every vote counts. Are you registered here or in the city?"

"Up here," he says. "She's got my vote."

"Thank you! I'm glad you're following the race."

"Pericles said, 'Just because you do not take an interest in politics doesn't mean politics won't take an interest in you.'"

"Exactly," I say. I groan inwardly at the prospect of

having to chat with him for two-plus hours when he pulls a small pillow from his bag, closes his eyes, and promptly falls asleep.

Well, his loss. I put on my headphones and the train begins moving southward.

Later, as I'm heading to the back of the car to use the bathroom, I notice a young woman in business attire, typing away on her laptop, who looks familiar. It hits me after a few moments and when I'm returning to my seat, I stop and say, "I need a little Monica in my life."

She nods her head. "Always."

The spiders have begun turning up in my house in hopes of settling down before the long winter and I have taken matters in hand this morning.

My phone rings.

"What are you doing?" Nelle says.

"Discouraging spiders."

"You're not killing them?!" she asks.

"Of course not. Over the past hour, one at a time, I have patiently invited each to drop itself into the large mixing bowl I hold beneath it, followed by a toddle to the back porch as I attempt to keep the spider within, and then a gentle release into the wild, wishing him or her happy trails."

"Good. Thank you for the cookies. They're delicious."

"You're welcome."

"Did you go into the city yesterday?"

"Yes, and I sat next to Alec Barnsdorf on the way down."

"How was he?"

"Snoozy."

"You mean he fell asleep on you."

"Well, if you put it that way, yes."

"How was the gig?"

"Good. It was a Clydesdale commercial."

"For Bud?!"

"Yeah, six of us sang 'The Waters of March.' A bitch to get six people singing those lyrics with the same phrasing."

"How'd it turn out?"

"Okay, except butter-wouldn't-melt Carol Dilman insisted on singing 'And the river bank . . . talks' so she always kept a little for herself. It's 'the river bank talks.' No airspace there before 'talks,' Carol Dilman."

"That's evil," Nelle says.

"I know."

"What are you doing Saturday?" she asks.

"State your business," I say politely.

"Do you want to go on a hike with me? Easy hike."

"What do you imagine my answer would be?"

"Jeeeebie. Come on, Jeeeebie," she says.

"You sound like my house."

"Since when does your house want to go on a hike with you?" Nelle asks.

"It doesn't, yet. But it's constantly making plans for me."

"I'll help you take all those boxes we filled to Goodwill if you take a walk with me."

"I like 'walk' better than 'hike.' Okay, you're on. Are you going to do the show at Traitor's?"

"See you Saturday," Nelle says.

"Yeah, yeah, yeah."

"Smell the pine?" asks Nelle.

"That is beyond," I say.

"Aren't you glad you said yes?"

"To this hike? I will be glad or not glad at the conclusion, not before."

"Jeebie, shut up."

"Fair enough."

We continue in silence. I stop and take a picture of the rays of light splayed through the pines. Nelle keeps walking and I have to jog to catch up to her. Walking behind her on the narrow trail, I say, "You've got a big booty."

She laughs.

The path is taking us up the small mountain. After a steep, rocky incline, we emerge onto an open meadow.

"Wow, did not expect to see a meadow. So beautiful. Look, Jeebie! Yarrow. Good antiseptic. And there's Joe Pye Weed. The pink one."

"Joe Pye Weed? That's not a thing. You're making it up," I say.

"Says the guy named 'Jeebie'. When your sorry ass gets a cough right before you're booked for a voice-over, I'll make you some cough syrup with Joe Pye Weed and you can decide whether it's a thing or not."

"How does a Newark-slash-Brooklyn girl know so much about nature?"

"How does a white boy from Connecticut know so much about Motown?" she asks.

"*Gay* white boy. That's the key to that query. Ha, pun."

We rest on our haunches for a moment. I pull out a bottle of water from the side of my backpack and offer it to Nelle. She drinks and returns the bottle.

"So why aren't you in a relationship?" she asks.

"A, we weren't talking about that and B, you already

asked me that question at Darlene's," I say, punctuating my statements with a hiccup.

"You didn't answer."

"All right. I was in a long-term relationship, which lasted eleven years. It ended seven—no, eight—years ago. His name was Miles. Is Miles."

"Still a sore subject?" asks Nelle.

"It was. Not so much now."

"Did Miles spend time in Arnold Falls?"

"Not a lot.

"Why did you move here?"

"I used to visit friends downriver and in, let's see, 2003, I decided to rent an apartment in Arnold Falls. A refuge, I guess. In 2007, Eulalie, the much-loved AF drag queen, decided to head west to Palm Springs for his golden years, and put his house on the market priced to sell. Miles and I were going to buy it together, but he got cold feet. About everything. I bought it anyway. The house still needs a lot of work, but it's starting to feel . . . well, it's getting there. How about you? Relationship?"

"I was with Mateo for nine years. He's a great guy but we want different things, since we're doing the nutshell versions. Cold of Miles to bail on the house and you."

"Yeah, I'm practically Miss Havisham. But better than *after* we bought the house. And on the bright side, if I hadn't bought it, I wouldn't be taking a walk with you today. Should we eat?"

"I'm starved," Nelle says.

"Me, too. If you take the northern path over there, you'd come to what's left of Arnmoor. But it's so overgrown, it's really hard to see. And creepy. Let's walk over this way."

"Look, Jeebie! There's a little brook there. Perfect."

We find a patch of moss near the brook to sit and I begin

unloading my backpack. "I made grinders," I say, "and a beer for each of us. Plus, pecan pie from the Chicken Shack."

"Now I love you," Nelle says, opening the can and taking a sip.

"You know what this brook is?" I ask.

"What?"

"It's the fountain of loveliness."

Nelle does a spit take, nearly choking on the ale. "You're right, it is! It's the fountain of loveliness."

"So, um, Nelle."

"Yes, Jeebie?"

"Was just sort of wondering, what you were doing, say, Tuesday, October 24th, around, I don't know, eight-ish?"

"Why do you ask?"

"Because, remember when I said I know the guy who owns Traitor's Landing?"

"You mean Percy Tunnion?"

"Yeah, do you know him?"

"He called me."

"Uh-oh. Ready for a grinder?"

"It is not grinder time."

"Okay, okay. Nellsy, Nellsy."

"I'm listening."

"So I just thought that in case you decided to lend your voice to getting the first woman elected mayor of Arnold Falls, I would make sure there was a date on the calendar available to you. So what did you say to Percy?"

"I said you were a psycho who goes around pretending to represent singers and that Judge Harschly had issued a restraining order. That you weren't to come within fifty feet of me."

"Oh, my God, you didn't say that to Percy Tunnion!"

"I did. He said he always thought you were shady."

"Nelle, call him right now and tell him the truth!"

Then she cracks up laughing. "Serves you right for going behind my back."

I have to admit she has a point and has won this round handily.

"Mimi's playing the show," Nelle says for extra points.

"Mimi Unter der Treppe?! No way," I say as I hand Nelle her grinder. Mimi is one of the great rock 'n' roll guitarists. She moved to AF a while back to raise her family.

"Way. Percy asked her and she said 'absolutely.' We're gonna have, I think four musicians."

"I can't believe this! Who else?"

"So, Bill Folds is playing the piano. Mimi, guitar. Bass is Mac Devlin. And drums is Yurt. My friend Brenda is coming up to do backup vocals with maybe a couple of others."

"Yurt is gross," I say, taking a bite of the grinder.

"Yeah, he is gross, but he's a really good drummer."

"No one on French horn?" She ignores this. "Do you have your set list yet?"

"Ten or eleven songs. Under an hour." Leaning back, she says, "The sun feels so good."

"Will you tell me what you're singing?" I ask.

"No. I want it to be a surprise." After a moment, she says, "I wish we had a joint."

I go through my backpack.

Nelle says, "Seriously?! Now I really, *really* love you."

I take a joint out of an Altoids tin, hand it to Nelle, and produce a lighter. I say, "I haven't tried this. It's called . . . I want to say Count Chocula, but that isn't right. Argh. On the tip of my tongue. Bender says it's perfect for a picnic."

"He didn't say that."

"No," I admit.

Nelle sings, *"It was right on the tip of my tongue. But I forgot to say 'I love you.'* Group?"

"Brenda and the Tabulations."

Nelle high-fives me.

"Not Motown," I point out, "but who wouldn't want to be a Tabulation? Here Lies Jeebie, an Original Tabulation."

"The Whitest Tabulation," Nelle says. "Okay. This one's tough. Which background singers had a hit with 'Somebody's Watching You'?"

"They did background for Sly and the Family Stone. And . . . wait, they were called Little Sister and Sly's sister was lead.

"What was her name?" Nelle asks.

"Hmm. You've got me."

"Vet Stewart."

"Good one." After a moment, I throw down the gauntlet. "Best Aretha vocal?"

"Impossible. Too many," says Nelle.

There's a rustling of the wind.

"When Aretha wails after the word 'misery' . . ." I say.

"In 'Angel'?"

"Yeah," I say.

"Yeah," Nelle says.

We lay on the moss, sharing the joint, smelling the pines, gazing into the blue, blue October sky.

CHAPTER NINE

Prune Clafoutis Down

"You missed the first race," Emma Rose says when Doozy lets herself in. "Chickaboom Charlie by a nose."

"Shoot, I knew we should have bet that one," Doozy says. "Almost didn't get here. My Chevette acting up. Moody."

"Doozy, what year is that car?"

"'77, so what? Let me put the wings in the oven. Sal wanted you to have pecan pie."

"That was nice of him."

Doozy says, "He wants to fatten you up but he don't have to lift you into the shower."

"Our first horse is in the third race," Emma Rose says, closing her eyes, "so take your time."

When Doozy comes back from the kitchen, she sees Emma Rose, sitting under the blanket on the couch, with her eyes still closed. Doozy looks at her for a moment.

"Don't you go dying on me, Emma Rose. I got a beer for you, we got wings in the oven, and we got fifty each on Sassy Little Lila in the 7th."

Emma Rose opens her eyes, which are pink and cloudy. "If that's not a reason to live, I don't know what is. Next race is at 2:03."

"Them wings'll be warm in no time." Doozy sits on the chair with an ottoman and puts her feet up, sighing. They sit quietly.

"How old was Miss Georgia when she passed? Wasn't she ninety?"

"I can't hardly remember now. Could be," Doozy says.

"Hard to imagine your mother and my mother as young girls."

"Emma Rose, it's hard to imagine *you and me* as young girls."

"Oh, I can still picture you, Doozy. And Chester. You were the cutest couple in Arnold Falls, no doubt about that."

"True."

"What do you think would have become of you if Chester had lived?"

"I'd probably be sitting here right now, waiting for the race to start, talking to you. You on a nostalgia binge, Emma Rose?"

"Maybe a little," Emma Rose says.

"Meant to tell you. The sex museum?"

"The Red Light Museum."

"Yeah, the Red Light Museum. They want to do a whatchamacallit, a show."

"Exhibition?"

"Yeah, exhibition, about Miss Georgia. The lady there,

what's-her-name runs the place, came in for lunch and told me about the idea. I said fine with me."

"That's wonderful. I was thinking about my mother and your mother being friends all those years. People didn't mix so much then."

"'Specially not with the madam of a house," Doozy says.

"Miss Georgia was so elegant."

"She was. Yes, she was." Doozy stands up and farts. "Let me check on them wings." She opens the window next to the television and goes to the kitchen. Emma Rose reaches over to the drawer of the end table and pulls out a canister of Glade. She gives the room a long spray.

A few minutes later, Doozy pushes in a trolley with their lunch. She sets out the wings, opens the Pabst, and puts a napkin on Emma Rose's lap. "Eat whatcha want, thatcha don't want don't eat. Rufus come visit you?"

"Not lately," Emma Rose says.

"He got no business being mayor of Arnold Falls," Doozy says.

"That's for sure," says Emma Rose, making short work of a wing. "I like Jenny. She's smart and it's about time for a woman to run things."

Doozy says, "You got an appetite. That's good. Anyway, we do run things. We just don't get the money. Or the credit."

"Amen," says Emma Rose.

"Amen, amen," says Doozy.

"You think there's an afterlife, Doozy?"

"Hell no."

"I don't either," Emma Rose says.

"Some Catholic you are," Doozy says, sipping on the beer.

"Not much of a Catholic, that's true. Barely an ember. I

thought I might get more religious as I got older. But the opposite happened."

"Just as well if you ask me," Doozy says, "you sitting here with the gassy daughter of a whorehouse madam, drinking Pabst, gambling on the ponies." She laughs a *tss-tss-tss-tss* laugh.

"Are you ever going to tell me the secret to the fried chicken?"

"Naw. Maybe you come back as a blabby ghost," Doozy says and they both laugh.

"You remember Dubsack's great-uncle? Giovanni?" Emma Rose asks.

"Yes, I do."

"He was in the mob," Emma Rose says as she wipes her lips.

"All of them was. That whole family," Doozy says.

"What was the old woman's name? The matriarch? She was terrifying."

"Nezetta."

"Yes!" Emma Rose says. "Just hearing her name makes me shudder."

"Mm-hmm. A demon."

"Giovanni wasn't much better, but every year after Thanksgiving he decorated the big pine tree by the courthouse with real candy canes. Did it himself. That was nice," Emma Rose says.

"Nice, yeah, but them was stolen goods. Every year they hit the same candy factory in Troy."

"I never knew that," Emma Rose says. "Probably just as well. When do they want to open the show about Miss Georgia?"

"I think she said May."

They stop to consider this.

"You want more chicken?"

"Yes, please, Doozy. And a little more time."

"I can get you chicken," Doozy says quietly.

It's past four when they've finished the wings, the Pabst, and the pecan pie. They've both fallen asleep, Emma Rose on the couch, Doozy on the easy chair with her feet up. The TV is on and the announcer calls the 7th race. Sassy Little Lila wins by half a length and pays out 4-1.

Mateo, you should see the leaves outside my window in the morning light. So beautiful.

Nelle stares at the tree until the colors of the leaves blur together.

That's the view, sitting on the floor by my sofa, drinking coffee. I switched from Major Dickason's to Fair Trade, which is a local . . . what do they call it? Roastery? Good stuff. A few nights ago I finished the last bottle from that case of Chateau Lascombes. Nothing cures like time and love and Bordeaux, right?

Now you know everything I'm imbibing. Although, my officemate, Kera, drinks beet juice every day and she made me try it a while back. That is the single worst liquid in the world. I love veggies but spare me the veggie juice. Do you force that on your clients? LOL How's your work going? I met a physical therapist up here and he spent ten minutes telling me the best way to stretch my hamstrings. Sounded just like you :)

Finding SOAR very challenging but fulfilling—OMG there is so much need here. But launching these kids into adulthood is just an amazing feeling. At least when it all works right. Which it doesn't always. Sometimes the odds are just too long.

Haven't talked with you since, when? Early summer I guess.

"There it is," Nelle says aloud.

Anyway, I wanted to let you know that I'm performing on the 24th up here, a benefit for a woman who's running for mayor. You know how I feel about performing, but a friend of mine up here roped me into it. Brenda's coming up to do background. I'm kinda looking forward to it! I know, right?! Come to the show and visit this crazy place I live.

Yes, "Just a Little Lovin'" is on the set list.

Time to get ready for work.

Nelle

"Now we're at the point," Annie says, "when it's wheels up on our prune clafoutis! We're taking it out of the oven after eight minutes at 350 degrees and . . . look at *that*! So many good things ahead of you, young clafoutis. We take our bowl of *pruneaux d'Agen*, which, as I said, are the best prunes money can buy, and scatter the halves over the set batter. Just . . . like . . . that. We're going to sprinkle with sugar—my sweet tooth is telling me to be generous here and I *always* listen to my sweet tooth!" she says, winking to the camera. "And then pour the rest of the batter over . . . like so.

"Perfection. We're going to put this luscious prune clafoutis in the oven, still at 350, for somewhere between forty-five and sixty minutes. You'll know because the clafoutis will be golden-brown and puffy and just bewitching! Okay, happy baking! May the road *rise up* to meet you! And now we're going to take the prune clafoutis I made earlier out of the other oven to show you exactly how it should look."

She bends a bit to look into the window of the lower oven and freezes, then straightens up and turns around slowly, wearing a cryonic grin.

"*Who? Who murdered* my prune clafoutis?"

"Cut!" someone yells.

A shudder radiates through the room. The assistant director drops his clipboard.

"Has anyone here ever *been* in a kitchen before?" Annie asks slowly.

Silence.

"What is the leavening agent in a clafoutis? You, clipboard-dropper."

"Ben," he says.

"Ben. What is the leavening agent?"

"Erm, baking powder."

"NO! Any of you charlatans have the right answer? I didn't think so. There IS no leavening agent. The clafoutis rises, OR FALLS, because of STEAM or LACK THEREOF. And if you OPEN the DOOR during the BAKE it will COLLAPSE. As it HAS. It is now a DECEASED PITA to be interred with the WORLD'S MOST EXPENSIVE PRUNES. And speaking of expensive prunes, where is Louis?"

Karen goes to the back door and slips out, waving to the executive producer, who is on his phone in the yard.

"Is it any wonder that our ratings have gone down?" Annie continues. "This isn't a television crew. It's the Wreck of the *Hesperus*."

Louis comes rushing in. "What's happened, Annie? Can we salvage the clafoutis?"

"You do NOT salvage a prune clafoutis that has belly-flopped. If we're going to descend so far, why don't we just work with moldy bread and rancid hazelnuts and smelly chicken and BEANS with WEEVILS?!

"Why don't we shoot the Chaplin scene while the other clafoutis is baking?" Louis suggests.

"Where is that creature?" Annie asks.

"Right outside," Louis says. "Stacy, can you bring him in?"

The minute Chaplin is brought face-to-face with Annie, he starts yelping.

"We're taking a ten-minute break," Annie says. "*Shut this bird up.*"

Annie goes into her den, closing the double doors behind her. It's quiet and she sits at her desk for a moment before looking up a phone number and dialing.

"Jim Ebbens."

"Jim, it's Annie O'Dell calling."

"How are you, then?"

"Well, I've been better. I lost a prune clafoutis today."

"I'm sorry to hear that. What can I do for you?"

"I need you for a butchering job. Turkey."

"How many?"

"Just one."

"When do you need it?"

"It's for my Thanksgiving special, which we're shooting November ninth."

"You want it to age a few days before you cook it. November ninth is a . . . let's see . . . Thursday. Bring it over that Monday in the morning. That'd be November sixth. We'll tend to it."

"Thank you, Jim."

"Yup, see you then."

Jim puts his phone in his pocket and walks toward the poultry house, then stops and calls his sister.

"Morning," he says. "Listen, I just got a call from Annie O'Dell. She bought Chaplin from Pluggy's?"

"Yes, she did. She's a piece of work, that one."

"They got other turkeys there?" Jim asks.

"At Pluggy's?"

"No, I mean at O'Dell's," Jim says.

"Of course not. She's all hat and no cattle. And that's about the best that can be said for her."

"I don't know about hat. Giving her too much credit. Asshat, maybe."

"Jim!"

"Well, you're not gonna like this. She just asked me to butcher a turkey next month."

"She *what?!* She wouldn't serve Chaplin for Thanksgiving dinner." There is a pause. "Oh, God. She *would.* My first-graders will be heartbroken. Let me see what I can find out."

"Lemme know," he says.

Jim's sister texts her daughter who texts back immediately, *OMG, that is horrifying. We've got to stop her.*

Call your friend who works on Annie's show.

Will do it right now, Mom. She dials her high-school friend, Karen, who picks up after the first ring.

"Listen, I have a question for you. Is Annie planning on cooking Chaplin for Thanksgiving?"

There is silence.

"You're at work?"

"Yeah. On a short break. Clafoutis crisis."

"So is it true?"

More silence.

"Okay, I'm going to take that as a yes."

"Good, do that. Talk to Jesse," she says and hangs up.

It takes her a moment to realize what that meant. Bender's younger brother, Jesse, runs the animal rights group in Queechy County.

She texts: *Hey, Jesse. U know Annie O'Dell bought Chaplin, right? She's planning to cook him for Thksgvng. Wish this were a joke, but not.*

Jesse texts back, *Sicksicksick. I just texted Noly. She said she'll make an appeal on Monday at the Town Council meeting, start a Gofundme campaign, and get Save Chaplin t-shirts printed.*

Knew I could count on you. And Noly is the best! She then forwards the thread back to her mom.

Her mom looks at her watch. Total elapsed time: eleven minutes. Not bad. Good Lord, who would do that to Chaplin? Jim was right. She is an asshat.

Judge Lionel Harschly raps the gavel. "Good evening. The meeting of the town council will come to order."

The room does not get quiet.

"BUP-BUP-BUP-BUP!" says the Judge. "The way it works is *this*. I rap the *gavel*, you people *pipe down*. Is that so hard to remember? That simple cause and effect? And yet, it's the same thing *every* time, *every* month, *every* year —*yackety-yacking* after the gavel—while I continue to expect, continue to *hope*, in this Chamber of Dashed Hopes, for a different outcome. Which I am *well aware* is the definition of insanity."

At age seventy-one, Judge Harschly hasn't just seen all

it all, the felonies and the misdemeanors, he's also seen the sequels, spin-offs, and reunion shows. Not a lot to inspire optimism, but as he often says to his wife, recidivism put their two daughters through college. His owlish profile, bracketed by two tufts of side hair, gives him an air of gravity reinforced by a squint-scowl-and-peer, calibrated over decades, capable of freeze-framing gasbag lawyers and unruly defendants.

"I have kept strict order in my court room since I was a fledgling to the bench and yet, and *yet*, maintaining a sense of decorum in civic convocations is something that remains *disconcertingly elusive*. Do *not* test my patience and good-will further. Tonight, I have brought with me a *box* of *pins* and I will begin dropping them slowly. When I can hear *one* of these pins drop, we will proceed."

He pulls a pin out of the box, holds it up with a flourish for the spectators to see, and drops it. He scowls, peering straight ahead.

"Nope."

He takes a second pin and with a twist of his wrist, presents it to the crowd. After a dramatic pause, he releases it.

"Better."

He drops a third pin. Silence.

"This moment is the highlight of my civic life."

"You mean the *pin*nacle," someone shouts from the back.

Judge Harschly lets out a long, audible sigh. "Well, I enjoyed it while it lasted. Would have been happy for a few more seconds, but that's not the way the world works. Now, as I *started* to say, I am Judge Lionel Harschly, president of the *illustrious* Arnold Falls town council, and before we get to the Council's official agenda, we have a resident of our village named"—he glances down at his notes—"Noly Spinoly . . . Is that really your name?"

"Yes, Your Honor," Noly says.

"Get along with your parents, do you?"

"Yes, Your Honor. It's Victoria Nola Spinoly, so they just assumed people would call me Vicky."

"Life is full of surprises."

"You turned out to be Judge Harschly," Noly says.

He looks at her over his half-moon glasses. "Yes, so I did. So I did. Touché, Ms. Spinoly. Now, with these pleasantries behind us, I believe you have something you'd like to discuss with the Council. The floor is yours."

"Good evening," Noly says. "I'm here tonight to talk with you about Chaplin, the turkey beloved by everyone here that was recently sold to Annie O'Dell with the understanding that he would appear on her food show as a recurring character. Since buying Chaplin from the Elmores of Pluggy's Farm, Mrs. O'Dell has made it known that she intends instead to cook Chaplin for Thanksgiving dinner on her show."

There is murmuring in the room.

Judge Harschly raps the gavel. "*Nope*. No murmuring! You are *not* townspeople in a musical. You are to speak on the record or not at all, preferably the latter. Please continue, Noly Spinoly."

"Thank you, Judge Harschly. I am a member of Animal Alliance, which advocates for animal rights in the Hudson Valley. I exchanged emails with Mrs. O'Dell yesterday afternoon and she said she will not change her mind. So we would like to ask the Council to declare Chaplin the official mascot and a treasured resident of Arnold Falls.'

Rufus, who is standing at the back of the room, asks, "Is

that going to cost the town anything? I don't want this to be a burden on taxpayers. Our citizens pay enough!"

"Mayor Meierhoffer," Judge Harschly interrupts, "this is *not* a campaign event. Noly Spinoly is discussing the fate of Chaplin, a matter of great concern to this community. What you *want*, while no doubt *fascinating* from a psychological perspective, is of no relevance to the current proceedings."

"Judge Harschly—"

"Sit! Or I will hold you in contempt. My own *bountiful, personal* contempt." Judge Harschly gives Rufus a squint-scowl-and-peer and Rufus sits. With his hand the judge makes a zipping motion across his lips. Rufus makes the same motion and says nothing more. The judge gestures for Noly to continue.

"Animal Alliance would also like to declare Thursday, November twenty-third, Thanksgiving, to be Chaplin Day in Arnold Falls. We have interest in this story from CNN and local TV stations. To answer the Mayor's question, it will not cost the town anything: we have already raised $875 in a GoFundMe campaign and have printed these 'Save Chaplin' T-shirts, which we'd like to give to Council members."

Judge Harschly says, "Are you giving that to me in my capacity as a judge or Council president?"

"Council president, of course."

"In that case I accept, large for me, medium for my wife. Any of you council-type people care to make a motion—or do *anything* at *all* to demonstrate proof of life—before you take the swag?"

A motion is made on behalf of Chaplin and carried unanimously.

Judge Harschly says, "Ms. Spinoly? Godspeed."

CHAPTER TEN

Oktoberfest

Nelle wasn't dying to get up on Saturday and go to the greenmarket with me, but I reminded her I hadn't been dying to go on a hike with her, yet I did anyway without complaining. Or without complaining too much. And even if that isn't literally true, I was a good sport some of the time. And who brought the grinder? A *homemade grinder*? I ask you.

The market's hopping. I buy scallops, Swiss chard and cherry tomatoes; Nelle buys carrots and kohlrabi. We run into the Pluggy's gang—Duncan and Marybeth, and Sadie, my goddaughter—who are in line for breakfast tacos from Juan, who also plays trumpet in the Queechy Caliente mariachi band.

"Uncle Jeebie!"

Sadie takes a leap at me and I pull her up in one of those hug-'em-swing-'em-around moves. "Greetings, goddaughter."

Nelle puts out her hand and introduces herself.

Duncan says, "Nelle! I'm really looking forward to your show. Jeebie hasn't stopped raving about you."

"Jeebie's *never* wrong," Nelle says.

"Exactly. Duncan knows that. He and I have been friends since we were kids."

Duncan puts his arm around my shoulder, walks me away from Sadie, and gives me the latest on Chaplin.

"Annie is Freddy Krueger in an apron," I say with feeling.

"A plateful of hateful."

"Is that something I said?"

"No, I just said it," Duncan says.

"Well, it sounds like me."

"You're quotable even when you don't say it," Duncan says, knowing exactly how to flatter me. "Anyway, we're going to have to get Chaplin back. Can we meet up next week?"

"Of course."

Duncan also enlists my help in fighting the tire factory by writing some lyrics for a public service announcement he's working on with Giles Morris.

"Do you think Nelle would sing the track?"

"I'll ask her."

We rejoin the others and they head off to buy bread. Nelle and I stop for apples at Eiderdown.

"Hi, Will."

"Hey, Jeebie. You remembered your shoes. Good job."

Nelle looks puzzled. I introduce them.

"Are you going to Oktoberfest tonight?" he asks.

"Hadn't planned to," I say, and buy a half-dozen Macouns.

Nelle says, "I hear it's a really nice event. We'll be there."

"See you later then." Will says. "By the way, Jeebie, I did a monkey of you. Check it out on the site."

When Nelle and I get out of earshot she says to me, "What is wrong with you?"

"What do you mean?"

"Jeebie. You haven't mentioned Will to me?"

"Why would I?"

"Are you blind? He's very cute and very smitten with you."

"No, no. I don't think so. Really? He's a baby."

"Babe," Nelle says. "What was the comment about the shoes? And what does 'did a monkey of you' mean? Is that some new meme?"

"He draws monkeys. I hardly think he's smitten with anyone. Maybe himself." Nelle gives me the hairy eyeball and I capitulate. "Yes, all right, he's charming. And smart. But he's at least ten years younger than me and . . . come on, he draws monkeys. And he's a fireman!"

"What are you talking about?" asks Nelle.

I had told her about the fire but hadn't mentioned that I learned afterward that Will was one of the guys who came out that night. And that I had understandably forgotten to put on my shoes as I fled the raging inferno.

"You forgot to mention all that?" Nelle asks.

"Yeah."

Nelle actually harrumphs.

"I want to buy a bunch of those zinnias," I say, only to have her pinch my shoulder. "Ow! Duncan told me he needs your help with something." I brace myself to be pinched again.

"You and Duncan are childhood friends?"

"We are. He's my oldest friend," I say.

"Then whatever he needs, I'll do," she says.

"Thank you. Will you also have dinner with my parents and me on the twenty-seventh? Please?"

———

Oktoberfest is in full swing by the time Nelle and I walk toward Midden Park. Once the town dump, the green, ten-acre field has the best views of the Hudson in Arnold Falls. Oktoberfest is a scene out of Bruegel at his most pastoral, if you ignore the methane pipes.

The town had installed three fire pits on the crest of the hill behind the field, which are lighting up the dusk, and jack o'lanterns glow along the crisscrossing bridle paths. There's pumpkin carving, a pizza truck, a beer concession with pepperoni sandwiches, hay rides, kids roasting marshmallows in the fire pits, dogs scampering among the old families of Arnold Falls, hipsters, kids, and drag queens, while Theo Nyqvist ambles on stilts as "Don't Stop Believin'" comes out of the speakers. In short, Arnold Falls at its Arnold Fallsiest.

Just my luck, Bridget is the first person we run into. She seems in much higher spirits than the last time I saw her. I ask her for an update.

"Oh, that. Judge Harschly said if I behaved and stayed off the Clagger, he'd vacate the charge. And he's forbidden me to sing 'I Shot the Sheriff' in the presence of law enforcement. He was quite adamant about that."

"Bridget's a well-known talent agent," I tell Nelle.

"Oh, I don't know about well-known," says Bridget.

"Perhaps 'notorious' is a better word," I say.

"Jeebie, Jeebie. So funny, dear," she says, patting my

cheek. She turns to Nelle: "I hear you are quite the song stylist. Do you have representation?"

"No, I don't. But I have a career in social work that I really love. I don't see myself performing professionally."

"I'll get your number from Jeebie and we can talk. Well, no Clagger, but I'm sure a beer would be fine." And off she goes to join the beer line.

"What was that about Bridget and the judge?" Nelle asks.

I'm about to answer when Nelle runs over to greet Aunt Doozy, who is pushing Emma Rose in her wheelchair. I kiss Doozy on the cheek and say to Emma Rose, "It's nice to see you here."

Aunt Doozy says, "Nice for you, maybe. She's heavier than she looks. And six years younger than me."

"Doozy, you're a saint," Emma Rose says. "I wanted to see Oktoberfest again."

Jenny, wearing a "Jagoda for Mayor" sweatshirt, walks up with her young niece, Olivia, both of them eating cotton candy.

"What flavor?" I ask.

Olivia says, "Pina colada;" Jenny says, "Cool ranch."

"That is *disgusting*," I say. "I'm switching my vote to Rufus."

"Speak of the devil hisself," Doozy says, then calls over to Rufus. "Hey, Mayor, I've seen you pressing the flesh since I got here. You got a minute from all your jigamaroo to say hello to your own grandmother?"

Rufus, wearing lederhosen and a Tyrolean hat with a feather, walks over to Emma Rose, bends down, and kisses her cheek. "Hi, Grandma," he says. "Good to see you."

Doozy looks him up and down without a word.

Jenny says coolly, "Rufus, you promised to debate but

you won't get back to us. How about October twenty-third?"

"Well, I'd have to check on that. I, uh, have a lot of things on my plate."

"Emma Rose, I think your grandson may be a-skeered to debate," Doozy says.

"Doozy, I think you're right."

And then I see a side of Doozy I've never seen before: the Reverend.

"Can I get a witness?" Doozy calls out.

"Amen," says Nelle.

"Do you see this man here?" Doozy asks loudly, pointing to Rufus, who suddenly seems unable to move. "He's part man and part chicken. And he sounds like this: BWAK! BWAKBWAKBWAK! Can I get a BWAK?"

We all answer with "BWAK!"

"BWAKBWAKBWAK," says Doozy.

We respond in kind.

"If anyone knows chickens, it's Doozy. Ain't that right? He's TOO CHICKEN to debate Miss Jagoda. Ain't that right?"

"Yes, he is," "That's right," and "BWAK BWAK," we answer.

"Tell it, Doozy," Emma Rose says.

"Grandma! Not you, too!" Rufus says.

"Why'd the chicken cross the road?" Nelle shouts.

"To avoid a debate!" I yell back.

Doozy calls out to a little girl in a blue coat who is walking with Father Burnham of Our Lady of Lourdes. "Come on over here, come on. This is the mayor without the MCNUGGETS to debate. He ain't got no MCNUGGETS."

At the moment, Rufus looks stalled, like a video stream buffering.

"Rufus, I'm surprised at you," Father Burnham says. "Do you not have the McNuggets to debate?"

The girl in the blue coat says, pointing at Rufus, "I don't want to be like him."

That clearly gets to Rufus: he starts squinting and blinking rapidly.

"Care for more, Rufus?" Doozy asks.

"Stop! I'll debate."

Jenny jumps at the opportunity. "October twenty-third?"

"Yes."

Emma Rose says, "Get it in writing."

"I'm on it." Before Rufus can object, I'm recording Rufus with my phone.

"I will debate Jenny on October twenty-third," Rufus says.

"Louder," says Aunt Doozy.

"I will debate Jenny on October twenty-third!" Rufus says louder.

Jenny presses her advantage. "And I promise Dubsack and everyone else on my team will leave Jenny's campaign signs alone."

"We'll leave your signs alone."

"See you a week from Monday," I say. "Don't forget to practice."

Rufus stalks off and Emma Rose says "Attagirl" to Jenny. "And Doozy, you outdid yourself."

"That McDufus works my nerves," Doozy says.

We move on, sampling wares, trading gossip, and spending more time than I would ever have thought possible playing

hacky sack, until I check my watch and it's almost five to nine—
the closing fireworks should be starting soon. Nelle and I pick a
spot to sit near one of the fire pits on the hill because it's gotten
chilly. We watch a train pull out of the station, heading north.

Nelle says, "Doozy won Oktoberfest."

"She did," I say.

"Will didn't show," Nelle says.

"True. Maybe something came up."

"Maybe you're an idiot."

"Not that again," I say. "Are you going to pinch me?"

We look up expectantly to the night sky for the
fireworks. She pinches my shoulder.

"I'm still sore from this morning. Could you please
pinch me somewhere else, like nowhere? Could you pinch
me nowhere? Thank you. You look cold." I take off my scarf
and hand it to her. "Your show is a week from Tuesday."

"I know."

"How are you feeling about it?"

"Okay," she says, wrapping the scarf around her neck.
"Good." She hesitates.

"Spit it out," I say.

"Mateo. He gave me confidence about my singing.
Without him in the audience, it will be . . . different, I
guess."

"So invite him," I say.

"I did. Didn't hear back."

Nelle puts her arm around my shoulder. The first round
of the fireworks goes off. I look out over Midden Park and
see heads in unison, craning upward—a rare moment of
wonder in Arnold Falls. And I can't see the methane pipes
at all.

It turns out I'm a pretty good-looking monkey.

After I get back from Oktoberfest, I go to my computer. Will, I see, has drawn me in a tuxedo, a little younger and free of any gray hair. The face is clearly mine, though snub-nosed and with protruding canine teeth. I am smiling—roguishly, I would say.

The bio reads: "JAW-bone was sentenced to one-year probation by Judge Lionel Harschly for disrupting Vespers at the Chapel of Our Lady of Lourdes on Easter Sunday by throwing hazelnuts at parishioners. He enjoys starting fires, baking and having the last word."

Nelle has already texted me about the drawing: "I told you."

Did Will use the name JAW-bone because it includes my initials, J.A.W.?

Possibly.

CHAPTER ELEVEN

Eggs Benedict Arnold

Late in the morning after Oktoberfest, Will is still asleep. He had been fighting a fire that burned into the evening at a family home on one of the poorest blocks in Arnold Falls.

The events replay in his dreams: he and the other firefighters arriving at the Greens' house on East Gilbert, the pit in his stomach knowing it probably wasn't a battle they could win. Did they do everything they could to save the structure? They did, but it's cold comfort.

Will opens his eyes and checks the clock. It's almost quarter to eleven. He sits up and swings his feet onto the floor.

The house belonged to Luther Green, who works as a security guard at the courthouse; his wife, Elma, works in the hospital cafeteria. They have two young girls; the older daughter had been to the firehouse this past spring with her class. Everybody's safe, but it's clear that the house will have to come down. Will grabs his phone and checks the AF community board online. He's happy to see the efforts already underway, raising money and collecting food, clothing, school supplies and toys. And he suddenly remembers Hamster.

Will had been on a short break, standing near Luther, who was wrapped in a blanket, watching as the last of the flames were extinguished.

Hamster had walked over and said simply, "Luther."

"How do, Hamster."

"Don't lose this," Hamster said, handing him an envelope. "I won Pick 10 last week. Ten-dollar wager, got eight out of ten. That'll be three thousand dollars. Ticket's in there. Didn't know what to do with the money, anyway."

Luther looked at him. Hamster put up his hand and walked off.

Will gets back on his phone and pledges $25 to the campaign for the Greens. He calls the farm and lets them know he'll be in at noon. From a pile in his desk drawer, Will takes three subscription cards to different magazines and fills them out in the name of Ivan Borger. He makes coffee and is about to do his pushups, when he decides to skip them, sitting on the sofa while the coffee brews, strumming his guitar. After the machine beeps, Will pours himself a cup and takes a sip. He looks at his watch.

I've been awake, he thinks, almost twenty minutes and haven't thought about Jeebie once. Except now I've had a thought about not thinking about him and so the streak has ended.

Ivan Borger is at the customer window in the post office shaking a stack of magazines.

"I *didn't!*" says Ivan. "Why the hell would I?"

"Sir, can you please lower your voice?" asks the clerk.

Ivan continues, "Why would I want a subscription to the *Oprah* magazine? Can't stand her. Or *Soap Opera Digest*? *RV Life*? Something called *Aquarium Fish International* . . . Are you kidding me?"

"Just a moment, sir."

He waits impatiently while the clerk goes to get postmaster Lou Pastorella. As Lou walks toward him, Ivan curses at him silently. That's the goddamn eco-terrorist who started, what do they call themselves? The Evergreens! Assassins everywhere!

"Good morning, Mr. Borgia. How can I help?" Lou says.

"It's Borger. I'm getting these crazy magazines all of a sudden. I don't want them! I want them to stop! I never ordered them! Why would I subscribe to *Aquarium Fish International?*"

"To improve your aquarium?"

"I don't have an aquarium!"

"Well, where do your fish live?"

"I don't have any fish!"

"Do you have any enemies?"

Ivan glares at him. "Are you a postmaster or a prosecutor? Of course I have enemies."

Lou says, "I'm afraid someone has taken it upon themselves to subscribe you to these magazines, perhaps as a way to annoy you. Have you rubbered someone the wrong way recently?"

"Did you ask if I *rubbered* someone the wrong way?"

"I asked if you had rubbed someone the wrong way," Lou says.

"Who the hell knows," Ivan says. "I want this investigated."

Flipping through the magazines, Lou says, "Mr. Borgia, what someone seems to have done is illegal but it is very difficult to prosecute since it would be nearly impossible to trace the source. I suggest you simply unsubscribe to the ones you don't want. Although there was an article in *Oprah* recently on letting go of anger that you might find useful. Something to read in your RV."

"I DON'T *HAVE* AN RV!"

"No fish, no aquarium, no RV. A lot of negativity there. Something to think about. Next customer, please. Comb-over to window three."

Ivan, jaw twitching, starts back to his house to get the architectural drawings of the new tire plant and drive into the city for a one o'clock meeting with his Japanese investors, but the hail comes down and he's forced to make a dash for home. Out of breath, he grabs the drawings from his desk, and heads to the carport. That's when he sees that all four tires of his Lexus are flat. There is a note under his windshield that reads "Arnold Falls won't get tire-d."

A town full of assassins! Vipers! It may take a little arm-twisting for a demolition permit but he will put down this uprising.

———

Trudy isn't sure she's doing the right thing. But she's not sure she's *not* doing the right thing. either. What she's doing is waiting at a restaurant for Bridget Roberts for a second date, reminding herself that it couldn't be worse than the first one.

Bridget arrives, gives Trudy a kiss on both cheeks, and sits down. "I'm so glad you decided to meet me again," Bridget says.

"It was certainly not like any other first date I've had, I'll give you that. And I've thought about you," Trudy says.

"I have a certain something," Bridget says.

Trudy *had* thought about Bridget, trying to fathom how the pieces of an intelligent and kind woman fit with the unlikely bundle of idiosyncrasies, self-deception, and petty larceny. A second date went against Trudy's better judgment and yet at the very least, Bridget made her want to find out what would happen next. She was a mix, Trudy had concluded, of shaggy-dog story and page-turner. Trudy had been feeling for a long time that she needed to shake things up. Was dating Bridget overcorrecting?

"Have you been to this pop-up? They're only here another few weeks."

"No, I've wanted to try it," says Trudy.

The waitress comes over. "Here's our brunch menu. Can I start you ladies off with some coffee?"

"Yes, please. That's a lovely scarf, Trudy," Bridget says. "Hermès, isn't it?"

"Thank you. Yes, I love the pink roses against the aqua background. It was designed by Anne Gavarni."

"Just beautiful," Bridget says.

"It's not a pocket scarf," Trudy says. "So don't pocket it."

"I promise," Bridget says. "Though I could."

As they look at the menu, Bridget says, "I thought, if you'd like, we might take a walk at the sculpture park after brunch. And after that, if we're up for it, we could go see the documentary on Mary Oliver at Cinemania. There's a show at four."

"A great idea. I *love* Mary Oliver," Trudy says. She recites: "Finally I saw that worrying had come to nothing / And gave it up."

"Yes, Trudy! '*I Worried*' is one of my favorites."

"Mine, too." She looks up at the waitress. "I'll have a mushroom omelet, please."

"And I'll have the Eggs Benedict Arnold," Bridget says.

They chat companionably through the meal without the need for police assistance. On their way out of the restaurant, Trudy says, "Do you want to pick up Gussie for the walk? I would take Delphy, but one of her legs is bothering her."

Bridget agrees and Trudy is curious to see Bridget's home. Nothing, however, could have prepared her for what she sees the moment they enter: there is stuff absolutely everywhere. Not random stuff, not hoarded goods, but collections of stuff. The house is a collection of collections.

As Gussie greets Bridget with a friendly sniff, Trudy is trying to process the number of interests, styles, and levels of curious obsession on display. Souvenir buildings, lady head vases, dinosaur teeth, vintage glass insulators—the kind used atop telegraph and telephone lines—quack medical devices, Native American arrowheads. A House of Horror Vacui, Trudy thinks, with paintings, books (thousands of them), and framed letters forming their own collections.

"I get carried away by my interests sometimes," Bridget says.

"It's unbelievable!" is the best Trudy can do.

They drive in Trudy's car to the sculpture park with Gussie sticking his head out of the window the whole way.

She's still on sensory overload from Bridget's house. When they arrive, Bridget opens her door and Gussie springs out. The two ladies rush to catch up to him.

"Gussie! Stay with us!" Bridget says, catching her breath.

They are gazing at the trees in their peak fall colors when Bridget begins to show off her own Mary Oliver chops: "Oh do you have time / to linger / for ... Uh."

"What is it, Bridget?" Trudy asks.

Bridget walks swiftly toward the edge of the woods, dropping Gussie's leash, and goes down on her knees.

"Are you praying, Bridget?"

Bridget begins to vomit.

"Oh, no!" cries Trudy. "Gussie! Come here."

After putting Gussie's leash on him, they stand at a respectful distance as Bridget gets sick over and over. After a long while, Bridget stops and sits on her knees, shivering.

Trudy asks, "Do you think it was the hollandaise?"

Bridget moans at the word "hollandaise" and starts throwing up again.

After another twenty minutes of this, Trudy calls for an ambulance.

The next morning, when Trudy wakes up, she thinks perhaps Bridget becoming ill had been a dream. Then yesterday's events come back to her and she looks at the foot of the bed, where Gussie is snoring peacefully, lying on his back, right next to Delphy.

When the hospital decided to keep Bridget overnight, Trudy had assured her that she would enjoy caring for Gussie. And that had proved to be true, with the exception of one incident, early in the evening. Trudy had prepared a pork tenderloin, slicing some of the meat into the bowls for the two dogs. She called to them and when they didn't come, she went to investigate.

Trudy found Gussie in her bedroom, on the floor in the corner next to her reading chair, surrounded by the remains of her Hermès scarf. Delphy was on the chair, her face hanging over the armrest, surveying the damage.

Gussie had given her the most pitiful look and Trudy had said, "It's okay, Gussie. You're in a strange house and missing your mom. Come have your dinner. You, too, Delphy."

Trudy stretches with a little grunt, wondering whether or not she should tell Bridget about the scarf. She gets up and opens the curtains. The phrase from Mary Oliver floats through her mind: " . . . went out into the morning, and sang."

She starts Gussie's day off with a belly rub and then one for Delphy.

———

Madora has been keeping an eye on Sofia, who seems to be holding her own. Tonight, Sofia has the bar revved up with the Bingo variation she created one Christmas Eve called FUCKU! When you win, of course, you yell "FUCKU!", which turns out to be surprisingly satisfying for the winner even without the free drink that comes with it.

"C37 . . ." Sofia says. "U21 . . . F9 . . . C33 . . . U72 . . ."

"FUCKU!" says a young woman, to which most people reply "FUCKU, too," though some add their own twist: "and the horse you rode in on" or "and twice on Sunday."

Sofia looks at the game card. "And we have a winner! FUCKU all. What'll it be, hon?"

The next round of FUCKU! won't take place for a while, so the room levels off to a quieter buzz. Several people settle up and head out, Sofia relaxes for a few moments against the back of the bar. Manny brings clean glasses out from the kitchen as Madora sits with the Sunday *Times* crossword puzzle.

Sofia checks her phone and when Madora sees her tense up, she asks, "What's going on, Sofia?"

"Email from the Evergreens. Ivan Borger has been granted a demolition permit for the Dutch House.

"What an asshole," Madora says. "You gotta fight the good fight! He needs a big FUCKU!"

"Yeah, I guess," Sofia says, putting the glasses away.

The next morning, Madora and Manny arrive at Argos to find everything still locked up. Sofia was supposed to have been there since nine, opening for Sunday brunch.

"Not good. Anything happen? Something bad to set her off?" asks Manny.

Madora says, "She got an email last night from the Evergreens."

"About that house?" Manny asks.

Madora looks at him and nods. "Let me try calling her." She hands Manny her keys to open and calls Sofia.

Voicemail.

"She's gonna be okay, Madora," Manny says.

CHAPTER TWELVE

Winter Birds Don't Sing

Nelle and I are at Giles Morris' work studio on this chilly October afternoon with Giles himself, a twenty-five-year-old Arnold Falls native who has become an in-demand director after his indie film *Down The Rabbit Hole* hit big last spring. Giles is also a multi-instrumentalist musician, a wunderkind waif who is especially annoying because he's modest and gentle and deserves the success he's had. What he does not deserve is the beautiful, shoulder-length brown hair he currently has in a stupid bun.

The Evergreens had come up with an idea for a message about the health impacts of a tire factory, to be used in short public service spots run on Facebook and local cable, and that's what we're here to create today.

"How's the show going to be, Nelle?" Giles asks.

"Solid."

"Mimi said the rehearsal yesterday was amazing. Really

looking forward to it," he says, walking to the console. "So, I made the track a swingy, big-band sound to contrast with Jeebie's lyrics. You want to run through it, Nelle?"

"Let's do this."

After a few moments, Giles cues it up, an instrumental version of "Tangerine," Sinatra's song from the '60s. Nelle sings to the track:

Thanks, benzene. In our water streams.
At first, anemia
Then leukemia, sweet dreams!
Thanks, benzene. Cheers, styrene.
For lesions in my nose and elephantine spleen
Sight unseen, hey toluene
Makes your kidneys and your liver look obscene.
Yes, having a job is a thrill, but not when
you're mortally ill.
So thanks but say no thanks, benzene.

Giles says, "I think it's great, but I have one suggestion, Jeebie. I think the word 'elephantine' is too much. It's hard to understand."

"You're right, Giles. I'll fix it if you fix that man-bun, by which I mean undo it."

In spite of my petulance, Giles undoes his man-bun.

"Better," I say and go off into the kitchen to sweat out a new adjective. After a few minutes, I settle on "soon-to-rupture spleen."

They begin recording and Nelle nails it on the fourth take. Giles says, "I know just the place to run this, or a version of it. Let's get the Evergreens together on Friday and make it public on Saturday."

I'm curious to see what he comes up with.

Meanwhile, I race home for *another* meeting, this one for the Chaplin Squad, and get a nice fire going in the fireplace. (I did have my flue cleaned.) By the time everyone arrives, it's cold and dark outside and the fire feels good. The mood in the room, on the other hand, is grim.

"She can't kill him if she can't find him."

That's Noly Spinoly's comment and everyone nods thoughtfully.

At Nelle's suggestion, I bought a case of Pruneto Chianti and we're drinking that with delicious Riverwind cheese from Pluggy's. The Pluggies themselves—Duncan and Marybeth—are here, with Nelle, Noly, and Karen D'Angelo, the makeup artist on *Annie's Farm* and our very own mole.

Karen, Duncan and I are on the sofa, surrounded by a mass of blankets and throw pillows. Marybeth and Nelle are sitting on the floor, warming themselves by the fire.

"Are you all ready for your show?" Marybeth asks Nelle.

"We're good. How's Sadie been dealing with all this?"

"She heard at Pre-K what was going to happen to Chaplin and she's been inconsolable."

"We have until November sixth," Karen says. "Everyone on the show is sick about this, but Annie seems oblivious, convinced that her fans love her and nothing else matters. If I could find another makeup gig around here I'd quit tomorrow."

The fireplace crackles while we follow our thoughts. After a moment, Karen says, "She's still going ahead with the Halloween party."

"*Halloween party*?! She's out of her mind," I say.

"How can she be so oblivious?" Duncan asks.

"The crew will be filming Chaplin," Karen says, "and he does better with an audience. So, yep, party time."

"Anyone's invited?" asks Nelle.

"Yeah, she's expecting a big crowd," Karen says. "The happy, adoring townspeople of Arnold Falls."

Noly, who's been pacing this whole time, says, "Chaplin needs to disappear."

Nelle looks up. "Do you think Bridget could help make Chaplin disappear?"

"It's all about misdirection," I say, quoting Bridget. "Should we ask her?"

Everyone agrees, so I call her on speakerphone.

"Helloooo, Jeebie," she says in a low voice she reserves for the phone.

"I'm at my house with a group of people and you're on speakerphone. There's something we wanted to ask you. By the way, how are you feeling? I heard this date with Trudy ended up in the hospital."

"I preferred the police station," Bridget says.

"Do you think you could steal a turkey?"

"Of course," she says.

"I mean a living turkey."

"I am Bridget Roberts!"

I roll my eyes to the group. "Is that a yes?"

"This will be my greatest achievement!"

"Bridget!" I say impatiently.

"This is Chaplin we're talking about?" she says.

"Yes, of course. It's going down on Halloween at Annie's farm. We've got a chianti open," I say.

"The Pruneto?" she asks.

"Yes."

"I'll be right there," she says and hangs up.

We start planning the broad outlines of the caper, with Duncan sketching a map of the O'Dell farm. "Does this look accurate?" he asks Karen.

"Yeah, right on. One thing I was thinking. Annie is

doing hayrides in the big oval around the property . . . here," she says, tracing her finger over the map.

"If we can get Chaplin onto the flatbed," Noly says, "we could take a detour at the back of the property over to Our Lady of Lourdes. It's near the back of Annie's farm."

Duncan suggests, "We drop him off there to a waiting car."

"Hey, isn't this the plot of *The Sound of Music*?" I ask.

Duncan ignores me to ask Karen, "Are they using horses or a tractor for the hayride?"

"Tractor. Angus'll drive it," Karen says. "No one else operates that big thing."

Bridget appears in the den's archway, walks in, and helps herself to cheese.

"Good evening to you, Bridget Helen Roberts," I say. "Please come in, take off your coat. Won't you have some hors d'oeuvres while you greet your fellow travelers? You know, just for future reference, my house does have a doorbell as well as a knocker."

"Don't be so conventional, Jeebie," Bridget says with a mouth full of cheese and cracker. "Are you ever going to have the front hall finished?"

"Before I do that, I'm going to review security protocols around entryways. Can't have just anyone turning up here."

Bridget pats my cheek in that awful way she does.

"You are the worst," I say. "And I mean that from the bottom of my heart."

"Wait—did we finish the cheese?" Nelle asks.

Everyone says at the same time: "Bridget!"

She produces the cheese from her coat pocket wrapped in a tissue and hands it to me. "That's how we do it."

"Do what?" I ask.

"Chaplin," Bridget says.

"We put a Kleenex over Chaplin?"

"No, we take him in plain sight."

"The crackers, please," I say.

She gets the crackers, now somehow in a zipped baggy, from her other pocket and returns them. I give Bridget a cracker, which she eats. "Go on," I say.

"My mouth is dry," she says.

Marybeth goes to the kitchen to get Bridget a glass of wine.

"Also, it's getting so very chilly this time of year, Jeebie," Bridget says.

"Are you asking me to take the AC units out of your windows?"

"Furthest thing from my mind." When I raise my eyebrows, she says, "Maybe not the very furthest thing. It *is* almost November."

"Bridget, how many years have I helped you with your air conditioners?"

She mumbles something.

"I'm sorry," I say, "I didn't quite catch that."

"Several," she says.

"*Several?*"

"Several severals," she acknowledges.

"Fine, I'll come over first thing tomorrow," I say, looking at Nelle, who is clearly enjoying this.

"Not too early," Bridget says as Marybeth hands her a glass of wine. "Is it the Pruneto, dear?"

"Yes, it is," Marybeth says.

"Well, let's not dawdle," Bridget says.

We sit down and work on plans for a rescue mission until late into the evening. When we're finally done, everyone is exhausted and they head home. Everyone except Bridget, that is. I try to convince her that I don't have any more Pruneto but you can't con a con, so I end up giving her a bottle as a parting gift.

"You're a monkey!" my mother says early the next morning.

"Good morning, Mother," I say in a groggy voice. "It's seven o'clock."

"A perfect monkey!"

"Thank you, Mother. You woke me up to tell me that? I'm aware of our lineage."

"The monkey is you!"

"Could you please stop saying that?"

"Aunt Doris called. She saw it online. Whoever did it captured you perfectly. I know an artist when I see one."

"What are you talking about?"

"Go to the Jane Goodall blog."

"The . . . oh. Oh! I'm hanging up. See you on Friday, Mothership."

I jump out of bed and scamper over to my computer. The page loads and I see "JAW-bone" along with "Peaches" in her pearls and two other of Will's hinky monkeys: "Rex," a gibbon who is "the world's worst motorcycle driver" and "Penny-Penny-Plopeni," a gorilla who looks as if she shouldn't be trusted with a pillow in a pillow fight, much less the vast gun collection that surrounds her. There is a brief appreciation of Will's band of monkeys and a link to his Etsy site.

This might not have been the company I would have chosen for my fifteen minutes of fame, but I knew Will would be pleased with the recognition. I text Nelle, turn my phone off and go back to bed. I have vivid dreams—though the only thing I can remember is that Nelle and I were in a covered wagon, heading west. Nelle had a ridiculous bonnet on her head and she kept pinching me.

Word has gotten around about Will's monkeys being featured on the Goodall website and "Hey, Jeebie, want a banana?" is the witticism I hear most frequently as I walk into the high school auditorium for the mayoral debate. I tickle my underarms in reply. Nelle has saved a seat for me in the front along with the rest of Team Jenny. I'm happy to see Aunt Doozy a few rows back—she doesn't come to many political events. Seated in the front row on the opposite side is Rufus's wife, alongside Dubsack, and Ivan Borger, who is oozing malevolence. Even his comb-over looks spring-loaded.

At seven on the dot, Ginger Abrams walks to the table at the center of the stage and sits, tapping on the microphone in front of her.

"Good evening," she booms. She moves the mic back and continues. "I'm Ginger Abrams, Managing Editor of the *Valley Observer*, and I'll be moderating tonight's mayoral debate with incumbent Rufus Meierhoffer and challenger Jenny Jagoda."

Rufus and Jenny walk in from opposite wings, shake hands in the middle, and take their place behind their respective lecterns.

What can I say? It's a bit snoozy. Rufus rambles on about all the things he hasn't actually accomplished, offering a few talking points about low taxes (for which he gets applause and cheers) and a brighter future. Jenny hits her marks, discussing the need for improving the schools, affordable housing, job training. It gets very quiet while she talks about the need to safeguard the waterfront, making a concise argument about Ivan's tire factory and the Dutch House. I turn to scan the crowd's reaction and see Doozy shaking her head when Jenny says how much pollution the factory will bring. She also makes a plea to save Chaplin. The audience listens carefully to everything she says, taking her measure. Jenny sounds, to me at least, knowledgeable and competent. Ginger Abrams asks each candidate a few questions, but it looks like she's ready for supper.

As Jenny gives her summation—a clear, thoughtful argument about what she will do as mayor—I notice Rufus's attitude change. He begins to look like Chaplin in full strut, flapping his wings, bobbing up and down. Jenny concludes her remarks and Rufus begins. I brace myself for some kind of October surprise.

"I'd like to talk about something I'm very proud of. As you know, Arnold Falls has a sister city, Plopeni, located in the country of"—he glances down at his notes—"Romania. Since I have been in office, I have forged a lasting bond with Mayor Plompell . . . Lomplepu Larahambie . . . Wait, I'll get it. Pom-pil-iu Har-a-lamb-ie."

The audience cheers Rufus' stick-to-itiveness.

"Thank you. I've forged a lasting bond with . . . the mayor over there and we have made a real difference in the lives of our extended family members."

The room gets quieter as people try to assess where this is leading.

"As the Romanian saying goes, 'Lorem ipsum dolor sit amet,' which Tishy tells me means 'a friend in need is a friend indeed.' We sent our Plopeni friends one thousand gallons of water because they needed water. Last year, we sent them guns, 114 guns donated by Arnold Falls residents, so they could shoot deer and not go hungry. Yes, we did that! But what were they missing?! They had meat . . ."

A chucklehead shouts in a caveman voice, "Meeeeeat!"

Rufus continues, "They had water . . ."

"Shoulda sent Clagger!" another wag yells out, to general merriment.

"And so Mayor Haralambie sent me a letter recently saying that the one thing the good pleople of Popeni—sorry, *people* of *Plopeni*—don't have is vegetables. The stuff you hate is the stuff they need! Cabbage, am I right?"

A shadow falls over the room. People look at each other. Rufus feels it and he comes down with a sudden case of flopsweat, with little choice but to barrel on.

"No, we're not sending them vegetables, though I'm sure they would love the nutritious and delicious produce of Queechy County."

Instead of vocal affirmation of this desperate boosterism, it grows ominously still.

"With my *own* money—*not* the city's—but on behalf of the great citizens of Arnold Falls, I have sent one ton of ammonium nitrate for fertilizer to Plopeni's city hall!"

Then he hears it. It starts as a generalized rumble as the word "bomb" pops like champagne corks across the room, followed by a wave of chuckling, giggling, and chortling that eventually coalesces into one epic belly laugh, strung out as a slow-motion "Hallelujah Chorus" of mirth.

Jenny is doing a heroic job of holding it in. Ginger Abrams, however, is shaking violently. I see Ivan Borger slumped to the bottom of his chair. Nelle squeezes my hand while she laughs. The moment seems to go on forever.

Rufus is red in the face but in the end he joins in the Great Laugh of 2017 because it's his best option. I almost feel bad for him—or I would if he weren't such a jerk.

People are wiping their eyes, catching their breath, but there are a few additional ripples of laughter as the moment subsides.

Ginger decides it's time to wrap things up. "Thank you all for coming to this . . . this . . . this . . ." and she loses it for real, doubling over with laughter, shambling off into the wings.

The Executive Editor of the paper rescues the moment by getting to the mic and saying, "Thank you all very much. Remember to vote on November seventh. Good night."

Nelle and I walk over to Jenny and congratulate her on a job well done.

"How did you hold it together?" Nelle asks.

"I have no idea! What about New Years in Plopeni?"

"Have fun," I say.

"Can't wait for tomorrow night," Jenny says to Nelle.

"Fingers crossed," is all Nelle says.

———

Traitor's Landing was originally a warehouse next to the wharf where whale blubber was processed. For the past seven years, it's been a popular to place to see performers in an intimate setting—two hundred seats—and tonight, all of them are filled. *Tout*-Arnold Falls is here, full of anticipation, last night's debate debacle merely today's fish wrap.

When I went to Nelle's dressing room an hour ago, I was such a nervous wreck on Nelle's behalf that she had to make me lemon balm tea. She, on the other hand, after all that I-only-sing-when-I-need-to-sing business, was, to my surprise, imperturbability itself and did a wicked Adele impression to make me laugh. Will she pull it off tonight? I have high hopes.

I make my way to my seat, following a round of hugs and kisses, nods and waves with people I've seen repeatedly this week and every week. For a moment I think I see Will near the back, but it's the young attorney in Jewel Guldens's firm. The lights dim and the band kicks off with the first eight bars of Laura Nyro's "Time and Love." Nelle walks on stage wearing a black cocktail dress that accentuates her curves, a little makeup, and big hoop earrings. Completely at ease.

So winter froze the river and winter birds don't sing

So winter makes you shiver, so time is gonna bring you spring.

When the song ends, there's a whoop of applause and Nelle swings into "Heavy Makes You Happy" by the Staple Singers. She rips through it with propulsive pleasure. By the end, the backup singers have their hands up in the air as they sing those repeated "sha-na boom-boom yeahs." Nelle punches the notes to the back of the house, sprinkling the end of the song with quick runs, wooohs, and oh yeahs. It takes a while for the applause to die down.

"Thank you. I'm Nelle Clark and I'm so happy to be here. Sha-na boom-boom yeah! I have no idea what that song means."

The audience laughs.

"That's not true. I didn't used to understand it but I'm learning that it's exactly the things that are heavy and makes us blue, they're what we turn to music for. We find joy in them, make joy *out* of them. By singing, we *share* them. That's what we do with music and that's what music does for us.

"The world right now seems so broken, but, as Jenny

says, Arnold Falls doesn't have to be. We can find harmony here. And we can do that by electing Jenny Jagoda the first woman mayor of Arnold Falls."

Wild applause. The spotlight hits Jenny who gives a quick wave.

The musicians vamp the opening bars of the next song while Nelle says, "I was born in Newark, New Jersey, which is also the birthplace of my idol Sarah Vaughan. This is called 'Just a Little Lovin.' Dusty Springfield's version is classic, but I prefer Sassy's, which is a little looser."

Nelle sings it conversationally. I look around and see the same wonderful, dumb smile everywhere. Nelle has them, she does.

After that she says, "Bender Hubble, for those of you who don't know, owns the great record store in town called Long Strange Trip. He turned me on to this next song, 'Sailing' by Jo Mama."

"*Sail away to the sea of dreams,*" she sings, doing a rich, Sarah slide down the word 'dreams' and the room drifts along.

During the applause, Mimi Unter der Treppe switches to an acoustic guitar and Nelle and Mimi come downstage to the lip, sitting together in a single spotlight. Mimi strums as Nelle sings a kind of lullaby: *Ooh-oo Child, things are gonna get easier.*

Goosebumps.

At the end, silence and then a rousing ovation. Nelle thanks Mimi and introduces the musicians and backup singers. They shift into Stevie Wonder's "If You Really Love Me," which Nelle delivers as a perfect, pop-music sugar drop, followed by "Les Fleurs," a Minnie Riperton song about the wonder of flowers. Very Nelle.

Then. Then! Sondheim's "Move On" from *Sunday in*

the Park with George. The song every other theater song wishes it could be. Thrilling, profound, sad, wry, hopeful.

She gets a standing ovation and I see people with tears in their eyes. Nelle walks off-stage and returns for an encore.

"'Dedicated to You' is an Ella song that I'd like to dedicate to my auntie and uncle, Myra and Damon, who are here tonight from Brooklyn."

It is a grace note to a perfect evening. She bows again and exits.

Backstage is mobbed and it takes me a while to get to Nelle. I hug her and whisper in her ear, "I thought you said you had a show." Nelle roars with laughter and squeezes the hell out of me.

CHAPTER THIRTEEN

On the Move

Sofia has been missing for days. Her car is there but there's no sign that she's at home. Madora leaves Sofia's front porch with a sinking feeling and heads over to see Bender.

"I'm worried about her," Madora tells him. "She didn't show for work on Sunday and hasn't been seen since. Everything was fine on Saturday and then she got the email from the Evergreens saying that Ivan Borger had gotten the demolition permit for the Dutch House. Is that what's happening?"

"Pretty much. We're getting a temporary injunction but I don't know how long it will stay in effect. The house is in bad shape because Borger hasn't taken care of it."

Madora asks, "What's bugging her about this?"

"Beyond a tire factory that would destroy Arnold Falls?"

"That should make you mad, not disappear."

"Depression isn't linear," Bender says.

"You're right," Madora says.

"Try her sister."

"I did, she's off camping somewhere. Off the grid. The message said to contact Sofia and leave a message with her."

"Aren't Sofia and Susanne Nyqvist close?"

"Very."

"Call her."

"Okay." Madora pulls out her phone and has a brief conversation. When she hangs up, "Susanne thinks we should hang tight for a couple more days. If we haven't heard anything by Friday, she and I will go to the police."

Rufus had taken yesterday, the day after the debate, off. This morning, he's back at his desk, nursing a fierce hangover, reviewing the events. After the debate ended, Ivan had yelled and cursed at him for what seemed like an hour. Dubsack had said, "Well, boss, I guess you bombed. Get it?" His wife just shook her head.

He looks up to see Tishy in the doorway wearing her annual tribute to Halloween—an orange and black crochet jumble that was originally intended, perhaps, to be a sweater, with a plastic tarantula affixed to her shoulder. Locals understand that this is the season when one must exercise great caution if Tishy says, "Smell my tarantula," as it is connected to a tube pump that she will squeeze, causing the spider to spray water in one's face and Tishy to snort with laughter.

"Um. There's a guy here?"

"What?"

"There's a guy here from the FBI."

"What's he want?"

"He wants to talk to you."

"Do I have to?"

"Uh-huh."

"You didn't ask him to smell your tarantula?"

"Did," Tishy says.

A moment later, square-jawed Special Agent Ash Plank comes in and introduces himself to Rufus, shaking his hand.

"You look like a G-Man," Rufus says. "Have a seat."

"Thank you. Mayor Meierhoffer, we understand that Arnold Falls and the town of Plopeni, Romania have a relationship."

"Right. We're sister cities," Rufus says.

"And how did that come about?"

Rufus answers, "Well, their Mayor wrote to me and asked if we should be sister cities and I said yes."

"How much do you know about Mr. Haralambie?"

"Know about him?" Rufus asks. "Well . . . nothing, I guess. He's the mayor."

"I see. Did you send him guns last year? Over a hundred guns?"

"The Guns for Plopeni drive was a big success. We sent them 114 for the deer," Rufus says.

"For the deer?"

"To shoot the deer, so they can eat."

"So the deer can eat?" asks Special Agent Plank.

"No, so the Plopeni pleople—the Plopeni people—can eat."

"Did you recently send a ton of ammonium nitrate to Plopeni?"

"Yes, I did," Rufus says. "He said it was for fertilizer—they need vegetables. I'm thinking cabbage and carrots and sweet potatoes."

"Sweet potatoes are tubers," Agent Plank says. "Root vegetable."

"Root? Well, what's another regular vegetable?" Rufus asks.

"Spinach," Agent Plank says.

"No, I think that's a green," Rufus says.

"Pretty sure it's a vegetable," Agent Plank says. "A green vegetable."

"Hey, Siri! What is spinach?"

Siri replies, "Spinach is a green, leafy vegetable."

"Learn something new every day," Rufus says. "When the mayor over there asked for ammonium nitrate, I didn't know that people use that to make bombs! I mentioned it at the debate and everybody had a good laugh. Is that why you're here?"

"Sending firearms *and* materials used in bomb-making overseas are the kinds of things that are liable to come to the FBI's attention."

"Lotta thugs out there," Rufus agrees.

Agent Plank just looks at him.

"Oh, I get it," Rufus says. "You think *I*—I'm the *mayor*!"

Agent Plank says, "You wrote to Mayor Haralambie"—glancing at his notes—"'Hope your, quote, *cabbage crop,* unquote, will be booming.'"

"That was Tishy! She wrote the letter."

"Tishy?" says Agent Plank.

"You smelled her tarantula. I was trying to . . . trying to win the election."

"By sending bomb-making material to Romania?"

"Yes. *No!*"

Agent Plank pulls out Will's greeting card of Penny-Penny-Plopeni and shows it to Rufus. "Does this gorilla mean anything to you?"

"No! What the hell is that?" Rufus says.

"Okay, thank you, Mayor Meierhoffer. One other question. Has anyone from Plopleni sent any gifts to anyone in Arnold Falls, besides firearms and chemicals? Has there been any money exchanged? Anything the FBI might want to know about sooner rather than later?"

"No, I don't think so," says Rufus.

Agent Plank stands up and extends his hand again to Rufus. They shake.

"We'll be in touch if we have any other questions," Plank says and walks out.

Rufus puts his head in his hands.

Judge Harschly sees Luther in the Courthouse hallway. It's crowded and buzzing because it's the sentencing phase of a bank robbery trial.

"Say, Luther."

"Yes, Judge Harschly?"

"How are you getting on?"

"Day by day, Judge. We're taking it day by day."

"Terrible thing, a fire like that. Listen, yesterday I went with Elizabeth, the director of Queechy's Habitat for Humanity, to look at a house on Old Post Road that was just vacated. Call her and she'll take you down there to see whether it checks out with you. You're now at the front of the line for it if the paperwork doesn't kill you first. Stop in my office and Vera will give you her number."

"I can't thank you enough, Judge."

"That's what Habitat is there for. You let me know if you need anything else. Doozy!"

"Hello, Judge. Luther."

"How do, Doozy. Thank you again, Judge," Luther says as he walks down the hallway.

"Judge, talk with you about something?" Doozy asks.

"This is a first. Must be important. Come on, Doozy, let's go sit in my chambers."

Bridget had still been recovering from "L'Affaire Hollandaise," so Trudy had gone to the mayoral debate on Monday by herself. She had sat next to Kenny Winstian, owner of Winstian Antiques, and they'd agreed to get together for dinner tonight at Argos.

Kenny had originated the whole antique-dealer-from-the-city-to-Arnold-Falls movement when he relocated upstate in 1981 and was the last of the original dealers still in business. Trudy had always liked him. When she had her gallery in Arnold Falls, it had been only a few doors down from Kenny's and they had chatted together, usually on the sidewalk between their two shops, almost every day.

He arrives out of breath and gives her a hug.

"Sorry I'm a little late! I was looking for something and it took me a while to figure out where I'd put it." He pulls a small Hermès box from his coat pocket and hands it to her. "Here. I remember you always liked Hermès and I had no takers on this little pelican. Thought you might enjoy it. It's a key holder."

"Kenny, that's so sweet of you. Thank you!"

"I was thinking how much I missed our daily chats!"

"Me, too!" Trudy says.

Manny comes over, hands them menus, and takes their drink order.

"Why were you at an Arnold Falls debate, anyway?" Kenny asks. "Aren't you still in Blue Birch Corners?"

"I think I might be dating someone who lives here," she says.

"Who?"

"Bridget Roberts."

"Calamity Jane?! Well, good luck. You'll need it. Heart of gold but she's like the coyote in the Roadrunner cartoons. The anvil always gets her."

"So I've noticed," Trudy says.

Kenny laughs as she tells him about her first two dates. "Yup, that sounds about right."

When Trudy asks how business is, he tells her that he wants to sell his building on High Street—his store is on the ground floor and he lives over the shop—and do something related but not at the retail level.

"I don't mind the *idea* of retail," Kenny says, "But I just don't want to sell my stuff to the people coming in. I dread hearing the bell jingle when the door opens. They're so rude. Lately, whenever they want to buy something, even something small, I just say it's not for sale. So cash flow is tight. In January and February, nonexistent. Not much of a business plan. The building is five thousand square feet: I don't need all that space."

"Why don't you sell privately? That's what I did," Trudy says. "I've never regretted giving up the store and selling privately. Never once."

Manny returns with their drinks. Kenny and Trudy clink glasses and Trudy says, "So put your building up for sale."

"I could. But it might take a long time to sell. I feel like I'd be in limbo."

"Do you still own that carriage house near the Dutch House?"

"I do. Good memory!"

"I always loved that building," Trudy says.

"Me, too."

"You could stay where you are until the building sells, and then move to the carriage house. Show the antiques by appointment. Could you live upstairs or is it too small?"

Kenny says, "I think it would be big enough. As long as Ivan doesn't build his fucking tire factory in the neighborhood."

"You'll know soon enough, won't you?" Trudy looks down for a moment and then says, "Kenny? I just had an idea. Why don't we work together? I have art clients, you have antiques clients. Could make for one big, happy family. Don't you want to shake things up? I do."

"Huh," Kenny says. "Are we in the shake-things-up stage of life?"

"I think we might be! We could call it Bettwins," Trudy says.

"What's that?"

"Our two last names together, Bettnauer and Winstian."

"I could live with you having top billing," Kenny says.

"Bridget would kill me if I didn't have top billing."

"You really like her."

Trudy sighs a what-are-you-going-to-do sigh.

It turns out to be a lovely evening and when Trudy gets home, the first thing she does is put her keys on the pelican.

CHAPTER FOURTEEN

Merryvale Strikes Back

Since Judge Harschly is finishing up a trial, he's not at tonight's town council meeting; neither is the Mensa crowd, apparently.

It feels like we're about to adjourn when the majority leader, sitting in for Judge Harschly, makes the fatal error of calling on Petalia Jijanova.

Petalia launches in: "I heard that they want to turn the Loomworks Street Garage into an art museum. I live across the street from there and no one asked *me* about that. We have so many galleries—why do we a need a museum, too? Just more strangers milling about. This town needs more parking. And affordable housing."

Someone I don't recognize says, "I agree with Petalia. There's nothing to buy on High Street—it's all antiques and fancy food."

"Why can't they get the streets plowed quicker when it snows?" another person calls out.

One of the Council members makes the point that with or without the garage, there's plenty of street parking.

"But then we have to shovel off the snow and move our cars for street cleaning!" Petalia says.

The tiresome Phil Fleck chimes in, "Are they still going to call it the Loomworks Street Garage? I don't think they should be able to change the name. It's the name I grew up with. Everyone knows it's the Loomworks Street Garage and that's what the museum should be called. I don't blame Petalia. I wouldn't want to live next to a museum. Too much traffic."

Before anyone can point out the errors of logic here, Alec Barnsdorf raises his hand and is recognized by the majority leader.

"Good evening, I'm Alec Barnsdorf. Uh, the plan to turn a garage into an art museum? That's in Merryvale."

"Where the hell's Merryvale?" asks Phil Fleck.

"I made it up," Alec says.

"You made the whole thing up?" asks Petalia. "Why would you do that? That's really disgusting."

"What I mean is, Merryvale is fictional," Alec says, "I write for the *New Yorker*, and the idea of turning a garage into an art museum was part of the Merryvale series that was published last week."

There is absolute silence for a few moments while the room tries to process this puzzling turn of events.

Phil Fleck asks Alec, "Can't you get the snow cleared faster?"

"No," Alec replies. "I'm afraid I can't."

Phil tries again: "If you're making things up, could you make up lower taxes?"

"The sidewalks are terrible," says a woman who, just moments before, had been fast asleep. "And the tap water tastes like chlorine. Also, pizza. Can't get a decent slice to save your life."

She does have a point about the pizza.

Sensing that no good can come of this conversation, the majority leader asks if there's a motion to adjourn, which is made, seconded, and carried. Alec Barnsdorf comes up to me as people lumber out and asks if I have any more "Jenny for Mayor" buttons. I pull one out of my coat pocket and give it to him.

Nodding toward the room, I say, "Merryvale strikes back" and I get something close to a smile.

While she's waiting for Susanne inside the police station, Madora thinks of the morning in early spring that she, Sofia, and Susanne went to Kendricks Farm, a sanctuary for old and unwanted horses. They had ended up staying there for hours, stroking those mysterious and beautiful creatures, even the ones that weren't beautiful at all. Especially them. Feeding them carrot after carrot.

Susanne comes in wet. "Cloudburst," she says. "Rain, at least."

They hug. "Thanks for meeting me," Madora says.

"Of course, of course."

Madora wonders if Susanne's level-headedness comes from being part of a large family like the Nyqvists. The eye of the storm. In any case, she's exactly the person you want by your side in a storm.

"Can I help you?" asks the officer at the window.

"Is Wanda . . . Officer Velez in?"

"Let me check. Can I have your names?"

"Madora Kosta and Susanne Nyqvist."

A minute or so goes by and Officer Velez comes into the lobby. "Hi, Madora, Susanne. What's going on?"

"Sofia," Madora says as her throat closes and she suddenly tears up. "Don't know where she is."

"Hey, hey, it's okay, come on, come on back and let's talk," Officer Velez says.

They sit by her desk and explain what they can.

Officer Velez says, "So just to get the timeline straight, Sofia got an email that upset her on Saturday night and then she didn't show up for work Sunday morning. Radio silence since then but her car is still here. Today's Friday. She went missing for a short time last month. And this is something that's happened in the past. She suffers from depression. Is that the gist of the situation?" When they agree, she adds, "Do you think she might try to harm herself?"

"I don't know," Madora says.

"Susanne?" asks the officer.

"I don't think so."

"Why don't we give her a little more time? She bounced back last month," says Officer Velez. "I have faith in her." She writes something on a card. "Here's my cell phone number. Don't hesitate to use it."

When Madora and Susanne get outside, it's stopped raining. "I'll check in with you later."

"Thanks, Susanne. We should go visit the horses again," Madora says.

"We will," Susanne says. "Listen to me, Madora. She's going to be okay. I don't know what she's going through right now, but Sofia is tough. She'll get through it. She said to you she needed time. Let's give her that time and be waiting with open arms when she's ready. Okay?"

Madora nods.

CHAPTER FIFTEEN

A Charming Mess

We're back in Giles' studio at a special meeting of the Evergreens. Giles is saying, "Ivan's plan to build a tire factory near our waterfront is preposterous on its face and yet it could happen. Arnold Falls being Arnold Falls."

He's referring to the farrago of narrowly thwarted bad ideas, bad intentions, and bad luck, otherwise known as development proposals for Arnold Falls over the years. They have included a roller derby/outlet mall, the Girl Scout Cookies debacle, Elbridge Bartlett's secession plan, an Olestra factory, a Bitcoin mint, an artificial waterfall, a Winter Olympics bid, a preppers' underground city called Plan B, the Redlight Redux Initiative, designs for a Museum of Spontaneous Combustion, a proposal for a Perchloroethylene factory (the carcinogenic chemical used by dry cleaners) with the jaunty name PERC UP!, the monorail fantasy, Panty Raid Fest, and so many more it's hard to remember them all.

Duncan says, "I understand there are other groups who've already started, let's say, expressing their displeasure to Ivan, so we'll leave that to them, but whoever's sending him magazine subscriptions deserves a prize. For our part, I asked Jeebie to come up with lyrics for a song that will communicate how dangerous a factory like this is. If there's one thing we've learned from all the pitched battles over the years is that Arnold Falls likes arguments boiled down to the essentials."

Giles plays the video, which goes over well. He's invited people for the debut of an alternate version of the video at the Dutch House tomorrow night.

It's getting dark when we finish and Nelle and I head to Argos for a quick drink, determined to destroy our livers in a manner of our *own* choosing before dinner with my parental units.

As we're walking, Nelle says, "I love October nights."

"Me, too. How does it feel to be the talk of the town?"

"Because of my show?"

"Of course."

"Feels like a long time ago already. It was fun."

"I'm sorry, what?"

"I said it was fun."

"Ha!"

"Except that Mateo didn't show. On the *other* hand..."

"Go on."

"Nils Nyqvist introduced himself afterwards. I could barely look him in the eyes. Those blue eyes."

"Too busy looking at his blond tresses?"

"No, I got the gist," Nelle says.

"Absolutely gorgeous. The whole family is. But too

much talent. Too tall. They should have been Animatronics." I swing Argos' door open for Nelle. "Well, I suppose you could do worse."

"He wants to talk with me about something."

"About what?"

Nelle shrugs her shoulders.

We have a six-thirty reservation at Pumphrey's. The restaurant is mostly empty when Nelle and I sit down, so Nelle asks for a quick rundown on my parents.

"My mother took up painting in her forties and she's had a successful career. I know I'm biased but she's really good. One of her recurring motifs is showing a house from the outside, when it's dark, or getting dark, or rainy, and contrasting the warm light from within. It might sound sentimental but you'll see she doesn't have a sentimental bone in her body. The paintings say someone lives here and it's home. That is, it's someone's home, but not yours. You're an outsider looking in. When I lived in New York, she painted quite a few brownstones in the Ellen Walker manner, as I think of it, and they're some of my favorites. My father was an ad exec and still thinks it's the nineteen-fifties, but not so bad for that type."

My parents arrive and I make the introductions.

"Did you drive straight here?"

"Oh, no," my mother says. "We stopped for lunch in Lakeville with the Maxwells and then we went for a walk at Bash Bish where they have an actual waterfall."

"She always brings up Arnold Falls' lack of a waterfall," I say to Nelle.

My father is looking around at the room. "Are the owners named Pumphrey?" he asks.

"No," I say, "John and Isabel Pumphrey were Quakers who opened Arnold Falls' first house of prostitution."

"Very resourceful of them," my mother says approvingly.

I turn to Nelle. "That's me ma!"

"Is the HVAC fixed, Jeebie?"

"Yes, good as new."

"Don't let it go so long," says my father.

"Funny because people call him Mr. Fix-It," Nelle says.

"*Jeebie?* Really?" asks my father.

"Yes, dear father. I have many skills of which you are unaware."

"If you say so."

"Have you spoken with Daphne?" my mother asks.

"You know my sibling is not big on the whole communications thing."

"We're going out to visit her for Thanksgiving. You should book a ticket," my father says.

The waiter comes over to the table in the nick of time. "Good evening, Walker family. Nelle, your show was amazing."

"Thank you!" Nelle says.

"Hi, Davis. Davis is an old pal of mine," I explain to my parents, "from our cater-waiter days in the city."

"I have menus for you and a wine list," Davis says.

"Do you still have that wonderful Gigondas from Domaine du Pesquier?" Nelle asks Davis.

"We do," says Davis.

That was it. From that point on, my dad is smitten. Nelle can do nothing wrong.

"You know your wines," says my father.

"When I was at NYU getting my masters," Nelle says, "I worked nights at a restaurant and got very interested in wine. I even considered studying to be a Master Sommelier."

My dad spends much of the evening talking wine with her. I keep an eye on things, but Nelle seems to be enjoying it.

I ask my mother what she's working on and she tells me she's got a new series of houses in Maine, where they visit in the summer.

When my dad finally gives the wine talk a rest, the conversation ranges from his days as an ad executive to Nelle's show. While we polish off the second bottle of Gigondas, we have an extended discussion about movie performances we've loved, which leads me into a story about making a complete fool of myself when I met Kathy Bates at a party. I stop mid-sentence.

"What's the matter, Jeebie?" my mother asks. "You've gone white."

I see Nelle figure it out. Will has come in and sat down with a square-jawed guy I've never seen before. "No, nothing. Where was I?"

We finish dessert and after wrestling over the check (my father insists), we make our way out. I catch Will's eye and nod. After we get our coats on and say our good nights, Nelle links her arm in mine and walks me home.

"Don't," I say.

"I'm not. I wouldn't."

"The guy's handsome," I say.

"He's not you," Nelle says.

"Come with me to the farmer's market tomorrow?"

"No," she says, "that's something you need to do without me."

She hugs me and goes on her way, leaving me standing in front of my house, outside looking in.

The morning is chilly but sunny and clear, in that late October way, so I take my cup of coffee, phone, and the paper to the back porch, along with a throw—one of Grandma Nyqvist's most beautiful designs—and sit in the Adirondacks chair.

Last night.

No, I don't want to think about it, and so I peruse the day's headlines instead. The food was good. Nelle more than held her own with my father. What did my mother call the Pumphreys? "Resourceful," wasn't it? For opening a brothel. I put the paper down, pick up my phone and call Davis.

"Hey Davis, it's Jeebie. Lovely evening."

"Hey, Jeebie. Glad to hear it. Did you leave something at the restaurant?"

"No, I need some intel."

"Sure, what do you want to know?" Davis asks.

"You know apple-boy Will," I say.

"Yeah, yeah, works at Eiderdown. He was having dinner with G. I. Joe."

"What do you know about that?" I ask.

"What I heard was G. I. Joe, who's actually an FBI agent from the Albany office, was asking around about McDufus sending illegal stuff for bombs to the town in Romania—what a moron that guy is. Anyway, G. I. Joe went out to Eiderdown because apple boy had done the cartoon with a gorilla and guns that talked about Plopeni. And then somehow a few days later they're having dinner."

"Huh. Doesn't sound very professional," I say. "It was a date?"

"I guess so. Seemed like it. Are you interested in apple boy?"

"I'm . . . not *not* interested."

"You're a mess, Jeebie."

"Yeah. Yup. Thanks for the info, Davis. Talk to you later."

No farmer's market for me today. Nope. I dabble my fingers on my lower lip. After a moment, I call Duncan.

"Hey, Duncan."

"What's up, Jeebs?"

"How are things going with the Chaplin rescue?"

"We're good to go on Tuesday. That's not why you called."

"No. So, you're my oldest friend."

"I am," Duncan says.

"Would you say I'm a mess?" I ask.

"Of course," he says.

"No, I'm serious," I say.

"So am I," he says.

"Okay, okay, but when you say *mess*, do you mean a *big, old* mess? A *hot* mess? A *sloppy* mess?"

"How about a charming mess? What's going on, Jeebie?"

"Well, do you know the tall guy who sells apples at the farmer's market?"

"You mean Will, who has the huge crush on you?"

"What makes you say that?" I ask.

"*That* question, Jeebie, is exactly what makes you a charming mess. Do you need me to elaborate?"

"All ears," I say.

"Okay. Well, you're one of the most perceptive people I know. But sometimes . . . how can I describe it? Something happens to your perception after it goes through the whirl of your brain, and you sometimes draw the wrong conclusions or miss the point. You see but you don't see. Does that make sense?"

"Yeah, in a way. I need to mull it over."

"We can talk more about it whenever you want," he says.

"Would Marybeth say the same thing?"

"Absolutely."

"Thanks, Duncan."

"Love you, bud," he says. "And don't mull too much. That's kind of the point."

It occurs to me I'm becoming quite the activist, fighting for an historic house tonight, a charming turkey a few nights from now. And for Jenny! Three campaigns. Arnold Falls does strange things to you.

I arrive at five in front of the warehouse across the street from the Dutch House. Giles come up to me and gives me a hug, saying, "I love you, Jeebie, even if you hate my man-bun." What on earth is one to say to that? I fear for this next generation.

Giles's work on the public service announcement we're using on Facebook is, to my eye, straightforward and effective. But he hasn't shown us this version. There are about three dozen people gathered, including the NBC local affiliate from Albany.

The chairman of Historic Preservation starts things off with a few remarks about the significance of the Dutch House and its grounds. There is applause when he tells the crowd that Judge Harschly granted us a temporary injunction yesterday. Then he turns it over to Giles.

"I'm Giles Morris, thanks for coming out. I was born and raised in Arnold Falls and I care deeply about this community. That's why a group of us got together to make this video. Arnold Falls needs to reject a tire factory, protect our environment, and save an important piece of history from the wrecking ball or further neglect. And the time to act is now."

He turns our attention to the front facade of the Dutch House, onto which the video is projected. It begins with a pristine landscape done by a Hudson River School painter of the exact area where the Dutch House is located, not far from the Hudson itself, and we start to hear the sound of someone trying to breathe with emphysema.

Nelle singing "Tangerine" (with my lyrics) begins, accompanied by a collection of medical x-rays and images of the effects from chemical exposure, including bright red spots on arms (with the word "leukemia" stamped on the image) and an enlarged spleen that looks like a horror film animal ("styrene") begins to cycle. Following that there's an overhead sequence he must have gotten with a drone.

The final shot echoes the painting at the beginning, but he's used a photograph of the same area and Photoshopped it so that the air is clouded by particulates. Nelle's cheery vocal and the big-band orchestration only make it more macabre. The video will play on a loop after sunset every day, projected onto the Dutch House, at least until the Zoning Board meeting next week.

Giles has done a good job of sounding the alarm. Will it make any difference?

———

The last Sunday in October is Hail Pail Day, which most people assume goes way back because you're supposed to offer a pail to friends and strangers with the archaic request, "Prithee accept my hail pail."

Hail pails, you'll remember, are said to be essential equipment in AF owing to the random and sometimes malevolent hail storms that are a meteorological part of life here. But even kids don't want to wear milk pails anymore, because they look ridiculous; they would, sensibly enough, rather wear their bike helmets.

But the tradition does *not* date back to the early Quakers as is commonly supposed. Instead, it was the idea of Otts Barkenshaw and his brother, "Barky" Barkenshaw, who owned an aluminum factory in Troy. One day in 1949, following an afternoon of sensual pleasures, the brothers were preparing to return from Arnold Falls to their city when a particularly fierce hail storm met them on their way to their car, giving Barky a concussion and Otts an idea.

With the help of Dubsack's uncle Giovanni, the brothers dreamed up an allegedly Quaker tradition of milk pail day for Arnold Falls, a day that celebrates—well, it's not exactly clear what is being celebrated, but the important thing is that hail (a.k.a. milk) pails are gifted and re-gifted freely. And the much more important thing is that the pails be authentic Barkenshaws, produced in their Troy aluminum factory.

Even if adult use of hail pails never quite became fashionable, the holiday turned out to be a keeper. To this day, children are encouraged to carry a small hail pail to and from school, farmers in the valley still dutifully buy Barkenshaw pails for their farms. Otts, Barky, and Giovanni made out well over the years.

So that helps to explain why I am pulling a little red wagon laden with milk pails behind me as Jenny, Nelle, Bridget and I go canvassing house-to-house for the mayoral race.

We start on Shippen Street at the top of the hill, knocking on the door of Dr. Emil Jantzen, the Chief Medical Officer of Queechy General. After a few moments Dr. Jantzen himself opens the door, says "tongue out," and places a tongue depressor on Jenny's extended tongue, peering into her throat.

"Hello, Jenny. Who have we here?" he asks as he examines the rest of us. Jenny introduces us while Dr. Jantzen completes the throat exams and pulls out an otoscope to check our ears. Jenny talks about her campaign, her hopes for Arnold Falls, and then asks for his vote.

"I have great plans for Q-Gen," Jantzen says of his hospital. "I am determined to make it the number one care facility in the state."

This would be a surprising turnaround since it is currently ranked 127th.

"I like your henna," Dr. Jantzen says to Bridget. "Interesting plant that we get henna from, *Lawsonia inermis*. Been in use for three thousand years. Maybe more. Medicinal as well as cosmetic use. Also called the mignonette tree. Nothing to do as far I can tell with the mignonette sauce that goes with oysters. The good news about oysters is that they're making a comeback in the

Hudson. Indeed they are. Do you know what baby oysters are called? Oyster spat."

He pauses for a moment and seems to realize that he is not alone.

"Not entirely sure how I got to oyster spat. The mind is so fascinating, is it not? By the way, if no one else wants it, perhaps I could use the Dutch House as a clinic. A clinic never before seen in the western hemisphere!"

Jenny cuts in before the free association can kick into high gear. "That's an interesting idea for the Dutch House. I'll keep it in mind. I know how busy you are, Dr Jantzen, so we don't want to take up any more of your time."

"So many doors to knock on," Nelle says.

"Yes, of course, of course. The Ancient Greeks had door knockers. 10 Downing Street has a lion's head door knocker. But I don't suppose that's on your list today."

For some reason, he guffaws at this as we head back out into the sunlight. Nelle looks at me.

"He's a renowned infectious disease specialist and probably certifiable."

"He was right on about *Lawsonia inermis*," she says.

"If only we had been there to discuss anything related to henna."

"Or door knockers," Jenny says.

"Or oyster spat," Bridget points out.

"We forgot to give him a hail pail," I say.

I knock on the next door—a much smaller house than Dr. Jantzen's—and a woman opens it, dressed in a faded navy housecoat sporting cream-colored gardenias. I have the thought that a necktie made out of that fabric would be very fetching. I'm surprised to see her smoking a corncob pipe, but I'd be surprised to see *anyone* smoking a corncob pipe.

"Good afternoon, madam," I say.

"What?"

"Are you the madam of the house?"

"Those days are over, buster."

I hear in her raspy voice the plangent tones of Boodles.

"Are you Mrs. Benedetta Liverwurst?" Nelle asks, looking down at the voter rolls on her clipboard.

"Yeah, Miss Bunny Liverwurst. End of the line for the Liverwursts."

"Miss Liverwurst, prithee accept my hail pail," I say.

"Nah, I don't believe in that crap."

"Hi, Miss Liverwurst, my name is Jenny Jagoda. I'm running for mayor of Arnold Falls."

"Why in fuck's name would you want to do that?" she asks, laughing heartily. "That's batshit, is what that is."

"Well, I grew up here . . ." Jenny begins.

"I know who you are. You're all right. I doubt Meierhoffer can spell his own last name. And he can't be bothered to lift a finger for Arnold Falls but sends that crap to Romania. Who's this riff-raff you're with?"

Jenny introduces us.

"Well," Bunny continues, "you three aren't doing your friend any favors." She blows out a stream of smoke. "Like in the movies, when you're in a haunted house, get the fuckingfuck out. Don't dillyfuckingdally waiting for Jason to turn up with a machete, if you know what I mean."

"I think I can make things better around here," Jenny says.

"Hope so," Bunny says. "Not sure where your optimism comes from, but you got my vote, honey."

Nelle makes a note on the clipboard and we're on our way.

"Watch out for machetes!" Bunny Liverwurst yells to us with good cheer.

We walk down Shippen Street knocking on doors. Some answer, some don't, some give us pledges of support, some are rock-solid for Rufus. As we're going through our voter rolls, who walks right up but Nils Nyqvist? He says hello and kisses Nelle on the cheek. Bridget's eyes widen, Jenny cocks her head, and Nelle steps backward and manages to stumble a little.

"What are you doing in these parts?" Jenny asks.

"I'm going to see Bunny Liverwurst. I visit every few weeks with a bottle of Aquavit and a cake from my sister. Just to check on her."

Nelle emits the tiniest of sighs.

"Well, good luck on the campaign trail," Nils says, looking at each of us, Nelle last, then walks up toward Bunny's house.

We make an immediate, unspoken pact to ignore what just happened, although I can tell Bridget is dying to ask Nelle questions.

"Let's see," Jenny says. "31 Shippen. Margaret Croce. That's Jim Ebben's sister."

The door opens and before we can say a word, Margaret says, "Jenny. *Please!* Please do something. You have to save Chaplin. My brother is supposed to do the butchering but he's all torn up about it. And my first graders will be heartbroken, just heartbroken."

"We're on it, Margaret," I say. "Tuesday night at Annie's Halloween Party. Are you going?"

"Not in a million years," Margaret says.

Bridget says, "Well, I'm sworn to secrecy. But—"

"*Bridget,*" I say.

"Let's just say," Bridget continues, "that a one-night-only, standing-room-only road company will grace the party for a performance involving exuberant songs, immersive time travel to Salzburg, and a coup de théâtre that will be the frisson of all frissons."

"Nice underselling, Bridget."

Jenny says, "Margaret, these guys won't let you and your first-graders down."

I realize Jenny has just made her first promise she may not be able to keep. We continue canvassing until the afternoon light runs out.

CHAPTER SIXTEEN

Murder Most Fowl

D ear Auntie,

Thank you so much for your birthday call today and thank you again for coming up to see my show. They both meant so much to me. As you know better than anyone, celebrating my birthday always seems so complicated, so I am giving myself some time to reflect. I'll be forty in the blink of an eye. Three years.

It is 9:30 in the evening, I am sitting at my kitchen table, listening to Sarah Vaughan, of course. And because I know you'd ask, she's singing "The Long and Winding Road," which is way too on the nose for a birthday reverie. Sarah's voice sounds like the road itself—tarry, undulating, endless, bidding.

Yes, I am having a glass of wine or two, a Sauternes that's sweet and fancy and from 1980, just like me :)

You know how much I love you and Uncle Damon. How grateful to you I am every day. Don't tell me to hush.

I'm glad you liked the show. I was happy with it, too. We raised over four thousand dollars for Jenny, which, up here, is a lot of money. A woman came to the show named Bridget Roberts—she's a talent agent—she's been trying to convince me to sign with her. I love music and I love singing, and, yeah, I'm good. But working for SOAR, I see the real difference I can make in people's lives. That's not something to toss away. And there's a lot of need here. Bridget told me I was a healer. No one has ever said that to me before.

I miss being in the same room with you. You asked about Mateo when you were here but I didn't get a chance to really answer. I thought he might come see the show but he didn't. Anyway, he's good. We still talk once in a while. I think he's seeing someone—he hasn't told me but I can tell. You're wondering if I made the right choice. I wonder, too. I think I did. He wants kids in the worst way and I can't see bringing a child into the world right now. He'll be a great dad.

I was thinking about my dad today. I have no real memories but I feel a connection to him. Maybe from the photos, especially the ones where he has that wide, goofy grin. Sarah's scatting through "Sometimes I'm Happy" and I'm grinning myself, because what else can you do? Some of the stuff she does is impossible, but she does it anyway. You said Sarah was his favorite, too. My dad, the happy, gentle, brown bear. He was so young when he died. Five years younger than I am today. I try not to think about the circumstances of his death, but sometimes I can't help it. What could be lonelier than a heart attack, by yourself, in a big rig? I always thought sometime I would drive that stretch of road in Indiana, though I don't remember any more what town he was passing through, just that it was I-80.

There's an older woman here named Emma Rose. You would like her, Aunt Myra. She's suffering from lymphoma and she wants to stay at home, but her family does nothing for her. A friend of hers, a ninety-three-year-old woman—six years older than Emma Rose—takes care of her when she can, bathes her every day, out of friendship and loyalty. It's beautiful, in a way, but how does it make sense?

It sounds like I'm blue but I'm really not. Just thinking things through. Anyway, something happier. Do you remember me introducing you to my friend Jeebie? I think I finally got the brother I always wanted. We have an intense connection. Sometimes I could kill him, which I guess is how siblings feel. I worry about him, too. It's a little hard to explain. Mostly, though, we have a really good, easy time together and we laugh a lot. That was nice of life to send him my way.

Do you want to come up for Thanksgiving?

All my love,

Nelle

P. S. Keep your fingers crossed for the election!

Dubsack thinks Rhonda is a knockout, but that voice—straight out of her nose—total buzzkill. He's hoping she won't be at the front desk of the Arnold Home for the Aged (AHA) but there she is, a sight for sore eyes, blackboard chalk for the ears.

"Hi, Dub. Where ya been?"

"Rhonda, how ya doin'? Ya know, here and there."

"Such a kidder. Evelyn, look what the cat brought in."

Rhonda's colleague pokes her head out of the staff room and gives him a wave.

"Remember poor Mr. Egan? Yeah, had his AHA moment last week."

"Duke? Sorry to hear that," Dubsack says. "Listen, I've got ballots for next week's election. I'll just go room to room to see who's up for voting."

"So civic-minded, Dub. What's got into you? Haaa!"

"Good one, Rhonda. Catch you later."

"No hail pail for me?"

"Next year, I promise."

Dubsack hurries down the hallway.

He walks into Mrs. Corthouts' room first. "Mrs. C! It's your old friend Dubsack. Mrs. C!"

She opens her eyes from a mid-morning nap and sits up. She's wearing an oversized Save Chaplin t-shirt.

"Remember I used to deliver your newspaper?!"

"In the bushes."

"That's right, I was no Sandy Koufax! It's almost November, Mrs. C. and that means it's time to vote. I brought you a ballot."

"What's this for?" she asks, taking the ballot.

"For the mayor's race. Rufus Meierhoffer is running again to remain Arnold Falls' mayor."

"Meierhoffer? I know them," she says.

"So you just fill out the dot next to that name and sign at the bottom."

"Not the idiot grandson?"

"No . . . that's another Meierhoffer," Dubsack says.

"I should hope so."

She signs her ballot and hands it to Dubsack. Before she can finish saying, "And don't let them kill that turkey!" Dubsack is off to the next room.

Julius is on his way back from the city and Annie is making

brisket for him. He's had a good year, she thinks, but he usually does, possessing a knack for turning distressed companies into big profits for the hedge fund. Worth a brisket now and then.

While the meat is braising, she prepares two bunches of kale for sautéing in brown butter. The TV is turned to CNN but she hasn't been paying much attention until she hears this:

Thanksgiving dinner or murder most fowl? That's the choice ruffling feathers in one New York town where a beloved turkey may be on the chopping block for the holidays.

Is his goose cooked? Chaplin, the Narragansett bird who nests in tiny Arnold Falls, was recently sold to chef Annie O'Dell to be cast as a recurring character on her TV series. But then the chef decided a brined version for the holiday was more to her taste.

That has laid a turducken with Arnold Falls' children. This five-year-old boy is practically in tears: "I love Chaplin and I am very sad!"

"Boo-hoo," Annie says out loud.

A stringy woman in the background is holding up a sign that reads No Museum! Save the Loomworks Garage.

But Chef O'Dell says if you can't stand the heat, don't be a butterball: "Farm animals must serve a purpose and this turkey will bring a group of us together to eat in peace and be thankful for our blessings."

Next time no interview until she's had a chance to check her makeup.

The chef's plucky critics cluck that she's out of her gourd and are beating the drumsticks to save the little tramp. Protest organizer Noly Spinoly is talking turkey: "Chaplin was just declared by our town council to be Arnold Falls' official mascot and this Thanksgiving has been proclaimed

Chaplin Day. We intend to have Chaplin as part of our community for many years to come."

The whole town is gobbling. "Brine Annie!" *suggests one resident, pounding his breast.*

Wattle happen? Will Arnold Falls have to quit Chaplin cold turkey? Is it really turkey lurkey time? Stay tuned to find out if the town gets its wish . . . or just a wishbone. Jeanne Moss, CNN, New York.

The news anchor chuckles as Annie clicks off the television.

The next morning, as Ivan is watching the CNN story on his office computer, he thinks that as long as they're talking about the turkey, they're not talking about tires.

But then he sees he's gotten dozens of emails with the same subject: "Arnold Falls Won't Get Tire-d." They're letters sent to New York State's Department of Environmental Conservation expressing concern about the proposed tire factory and CC-d to him. He flips through them and sees they've been prompted by a Facebook page called "Won't Get Tire-d."

Ivan goes to the page where he is greeted by a public service announcement.

This is trouble. Time to shut this down once and for all.

CHAPTER SEVENTEEN

Layee Odl, Layee Odl, Lay-ee-oo

It's Chaplin night and it is game on. Ha! You missed one, Jeanne Moss.

We decided to meet at Noly Spinoly's dad's house because he's a sympathizer, of course, and one who owns a flatbed.

If you remember, I had remarked that whisking Chaplin away from certain death to a nearby chapel sounded like the last part of *The Sound of Music*. After equal amounts of discussion and chianti in my den, we went all in, Rodgers and Hammerstein-wise, in ways that, I'm sure, the R & H organization would sternly disapprove.

We're warming up our vocal cords and looking at each other to reassure ourselves that this enterprise is a reasonable one for adults to be undertaking, a.k.a. just another night in Arnold Falls.

Nelle, in a bit of nontraditional casting, is Maria. Duncan is Captain Von Trapp, and I'll admit he looks more dashing than ever. Marybeth is the Baroness. Sadie is Gretl. Bridget and Trudy are both nuns—Trudy is Sister Margaretta, while Bridget insisted on being the Mother Abbess. Noly Spinoly will be driving the flatbed, or I guess now that it has some lovely Alpine mountains painted by Theo Nyqvist on it, we're more of a parade float. I am dressed as a Nazi.

We might look like any old *Sound of Music* coterie out for a good time on Halloween night but thanks to my friend Preston Davis, a Broadway wardrobe mistress, we've got a trick up our sleeve, or more precisely up our nuns' backsides.

Preston has created two tunics for Bridget and Trudy and two scapulars to go over them. But the back of the scapulars are connected by Velcro. So as long as the nuns stay side by side, there should be plenty of room for Chaplin to enter into their antechamber, as we're calling it, and remain shrouded from view until we make him disappear. Magic.

The bell of Lourdes strikes six o'clock (aka as five fifty-five) and that's cur cue to hit the road to Annie's Farm. Our makeup mole, Karen, is working the party, and she's tipped the cameraman to record our set piece rather than Chaplin. I look fondly at our ragtag troupe as we bounce along into enemy territory, our timpani on board. Giles had one lying around his studio, as one does, and we thought it could help add to the wall of noise we'll need to create if Chaplin starts acting up. No one else could handle the timpani, so Giles has been a good sport and stepped in. He's dressed as a nun.

By the way, I'm not just any Nazi, I'm a Nazi with a French horn, which will be used to herald our arrival. Everyone else has tambourines or maracas.

Nelle is twirling around like Julie Andrews on the hills

—I'd say she has a rare case of nerves—and Marybeth is working through the details of the antechamber with Bridget and Trudy. I could have sworn I smelled Clagger on the Mother Abbess' breath just now but I'm going to put that out of my mind. Duncan is double-checking the sound system as we are only a couple of minutes away from Annie's Farm. When he's satisfied with that, he commands a group hug, just like a proper Captain Von Trapp.

I've cleared out the spit valve of my French Horn three times. I have a pit in my stomach as we round the corner that leads to the entrance of Annie's Farm. We're about to pass the azalea bushes, which is where Karen told us to start the show.

Duncan nods, Giles gives a drum roll on the timpani. I play a hunting call on the horn. And now we're beyond the garage on the ring road of the property, exactly where we want to be. As we emerge by the party area, a big crowd comes into view and I see Annie standing at the back with Julius and a couple of sycophants.

The karaoke track of "The Lonely Goatherd" begins, as loud as it will go, and we're off singing at an equally preposterous volume. Still, the crowd immediately gets into the oompah rhythm and Nelle leads the call-and-response. We keep do-si-do-ing around the float to create distracting movement while Bridget and Trudy stand upstage center, ever the placid nuns, remaining *in situ* so that when Chaplin arrives, care of Noly's friend Jesse Hubble, he can immediately be led up the ramp into the anteroom.

The song quickly deteriorates into a goulash of "layee odl, layee odl, lay-ee-oos," with the audience joining in, as we'd hoped.

Out of the corner of my eye, I see Jesse guiding Chaplin

toward the back of the float. Someone whispers something in Annie's ear, which spooks me a little, but so far, so good.

Duncan and Marybeth have said that once Chaplin is in place, he should be fine; he loves riding in the back of a truck and he also happens to love music. It's the moment of transfer—up the ramp, onto the float and into the antechamber—that will likely be the most fraught. We'll need to cover any noises Chaplin might make, and there's only one possible song from the movie to do that: "Climb Ev'ry Mountain."

During our strategy session, Nelle pointed out that when you want the loudest version of something, as a rule you want Shirley Bassey. We all love us some Shirley, but she is not the kind of performer to leave any rafters unshaken, if you know what I mean. One listen to her cut, swirling strings, a passel of backup singers, and Shirley going full tilt (the only tilt she knows), well, it was an easy call.

As the song plays, Nelle matches Shirley note for note, and all the rest of us over-sing the song loudly, piercingly, shamelessly At the two-minute mark, I can tell that the moment has begun and Chaplin is walking up the ramp.

"Every day of your life, for as long as you live," we sing as Chaplin makes his way into the antechamber. My peripheral vision tells me that Chaplin is where he needs to be. Jesse hitches the Velcroed scapulars together and heads back down the ramp.

"Climb Ev'ry Mountain," we bellow.

But right before we get to "ford every stream," Bridget howls, "WOH!"

Then, instead of "Follow every rainbow," Bridget yells, "OH HO HO HO WOO WOO," and God bless her, whatever Chaplin is doing to her at that moment, she manages to turn it into a contrapuntal run—"WOO WOO WOH WOOO AH HA HA HA HA"—that perhaps doesn't comport with the dignity of the song but gets us through "til you find your dream."

I scan the area where Annie and Julius were standing but they're not there. Where are they?

We swing right into our final song, "Do Re Mi," performed, I have no doubt, at the loudest volume and greatest intensity that that ditty has ever been rendered. At this point, Bridget seems frankly deranged, jolting her body around as if she is receiving frequent electric shocks. Her upper body remains in a diva pose, with her hands clasped demurely together and a frozen smile on her face, while her bottom half seems as if it were on a mechanical bull ride. I glance over and see Trudy looking at Bridget with concern, but also admiration.

I spot Annie walking toward the float just as we get to "golden sun," and apparently so does Noly because she speeds up the driveway toward the back of farm as we're finishing the number. We make the turn toward Lourdes.

When we're well out of sight and earshot of the party, we give a whoop and there are hugs all around.

Bridget announces, "Chaplin and I are engaged to be married."

We arrive in the courtyard outside Lady of Lourdes where Bender is waiting in his car with the motor running. All of a sudden, Annie's voice cuts through the air.

"Chaplin! Chaplin!"

Chaplin hears her, too, and freezes, then takes off into the forest.

"Chaplin, no!" we hiss as he disappears out of sight.

"Don't!" Duncan says when some of us start after him. "We can't have Annie see us looking for him there. That gives away the whole game. It's only a mile to our farm and Chaplin made that trip before on his own. Let's get out of here and wait for him there."

"I have a drone with a night-vision camera," Giles says. "I'll get it and bring it over to Pluggy's."

Of course Giles has a night-vision drone. Just of course.

We arrive at Pluggy's a deflated bunch, changing out of our costumes, except Bridget, who seems to like her Mother Abbess duds.

Duncan gets off the phone and says, "That was Jesse. The party's still going on at Annie's," he says to us, gathered around the fire pit that Marybeth is lighting. "If Chaplin's in the forest, settling in a tree, we won't find him until morning. Sadie, why don't you go upstairs and get in your PJ's?"

"I want to look for Chaplin," she says. "He's my friend."

Marybeth says, "Go get in your jammies. We're going to use a drone to look for him so we'll be right here." When Sadie goes upstairs, Marybeth sighs. "Oh, why did we—"

"Don't," Duncan says. "I know. You were right. Well, help yourself to wine, everyone. On the kitchen counter."

"I already did," says Bridget.

Giles walks quickly up the driveway, carrying his drone in a satchel. "Let's get this thing in flight. We can add an iPad for screening so we have two sets of eyes looking for him."

I get the first chance of being Giles's second mate, and we go to the backyard to stare intently at our screens as the others gather around quietly. Marybeth brings blankets out and starts wrapping them around our shoulders. She is a good egg, that Marybeth. If I haven't said that before, I should have.

The drone is already up over the forest and, as Duncan feared, it's not easy to see beyond the dense tree cover. There are just a few openings in the canopy and while at one point we spot several deer, if Chaplin has bunked in for the night, we're not likely to see him.

After a while, Giles moves the drone past the forest and we start a slow sweep over the rest of Arnold Falls, up High Street, down Hester Biddle, past the courthouse, over the cemetery. Giles checks the side streets and the back alleys. Even though it's Halloween, it's gotten quiet except for the bars on High Street. Few people and no Chaplin. It's stressful keeping such focus and when Nelle offers to relieve me, I hand her the iPad and head for the wine.

"I'm going to go back to the forest," Giles says, "and then we can check out the waterfront and the warehouses."

Duncan's cell phone rings and he says to us, "Annie." Duncan is at least able to respond to her, truthfully-ish, "I wish I knew. I'm sure he'll turn up. Keep us posted."

After a bit, Giles says, "I'm going to fly toward the waterfront."

Sadie comes out in her pajamas and a parka and snuggles up next to me. She's got two grapes in her tiny hand.

"Can I have a grape?" I ask.

"No. They're for Chaplin when he comes back."

"Got it," I say. "Good plan."

Giles says, "There are so many crevices around the waterfront and the warehouses and the containers."

It's very quiet. It's like we're collectively willing Chaplin to appear. Minutes tick by.

Nelle says suddenly, "Giles, did you see that?"

"You see him?" Giles asks.

"No, but there was a shadow that moved. In the Dutch House."

"*In* the Dutch House? Probably some kids getting high."

"Can you go back?"

We crowd around the screens, concern etched on our faces, our outlines framed by the glow from the fire. A fitting Halloween tableau.

Giles guides the drone back toward the Dutch House, where his video is playing on the front facade.

"In the back. The window on the right." Nelle says.

"Upstairs or ground floor?"

"Upstairs."

It's very faint, as if there's a small candle lit and nothing else. But there is a light and it is flickering.

"How the hell did you spot that, Nelle?" I ask.

"I don't know. It's the only thing that's moved on the screen the whole time."

Giles positions the drone at a distance from the window, then moves in slowly. "I don't want to get too close. Whoever's in there could hear it."

Suddenly, there's a silhouette at the window.

"Oh, my God," Nelle says. "Sofia."

We're stunned for a moment until Nelle says, putting on her coat, "Call Madora. Have her call Sofia's sister. Bender, can you drive me there?"

"Yeah, of course, dude."

"Giles," Nelle says. "Can you keep the drone flying until we get there? In case she leaves?"

"Sure thing," Giles says.

"What about Chaplin?" Sadie asks.

Marybeth says, "You and I'll wait here for him, honey. Nelle, where do you want everyone else?"

"Stay here, please. Tell Madora to come down there."

Minutes tick by as we watch the two screens. Madora is already waiting outside when Nelle and Bender arrive.

The front door and the downstairs windows are barred by planks of wood, so they have to find whatever entrance Sofia used. That turns out to be an old coal chute that looks to have been widened by vandals. Nelle goes feet first, followed by Madora and Bender.

For several long minutes, we stare at the screen, completely silent, until Bridget blurts out, "This part could use some tightening. Maybe a dream ballet here."

"Look! Bender's coming out," Marybeth says.

We watch him pull up Sofia, then Madora and Nelle. From this vantage point, Sofia looks okay. As she and Madora walk off, presumably back to Sofia's, Nelle calls.

"She's okay," Nelle says.

"Wait. Let me put you on speakerphone."

Nelle continues: "She's okay. Madora is going to stay the night with her. Sofia didn't get into the details but she has a family connection with the Dutch House. I'm sure Madora will get the rest of the story. She seemed completely rational. Just sad. Pissed off, too, at you, Jeebie."

"At *me*?!"

"Yeah, you. She said your lyrics to 'Thanks, Benzene' are—I think the expression she used was 'so fucking annoying.' I'm heading home."

We say our goodnights to Nelle and move inside to warm up.

"Well, there go my dreams of winning Eurovision," I say wistfully.

CHAPTER EIGHTEEN

Out of the Woods

Sadie watches the grownups come back inside. She sees that the side door is still ajar and knows just what to do. Sadie pulls the stool over to the kitchen counter, climbs on it, grabs hold of the pack of sunflower seeds, and climbs off the stool. The grownups are talking with themselves, so she slips out into the enclosed area, opens the gate, and continues to the edge of the woods. An owl hoots.

"Hey! Hey, Chaplin. Come here. Chaplin! I know you're there."

She listens carefully but hears nothing.

"Come on, Chaplin. *Please.*" Sadie removes the top of the jar and eats a couple of seeds. "Mmm. Delicious! Chaplin."

Nothing.

"It's me. Sadie. You're safe."

Nothing.

After a moment, she says, "Chaplin! I miss you!" fighting back tears.

She hears a twig break and holds her breath.

"Chaplin!"

He walks his bow-legged walk out of the woods, showing off his feathers and gobbling.

"I knew it!"

She gives him a hug and he nuzzles his head into her neck. "Chaplin, you're home!"

CHAPTER NINETEEN

Doozy Lets Loose

I hear "Chaplin, you're home!" from my goddaughter and realize that Chaplin is out of the woods.

"MB, I think Chaplin's back. Sadie's outside."

She looks at me and flies out the door. Duncan, Bridget and Trudy follow.

Marybeth kneels down and strokes the turkey's head. "Chaplin, I missed your caruncly face."

Sadie hugs him again.

Headlights suddenly illuminate Chaplin and Sadie.

"Cheese it. It's the po-po!" Bridget says.

Not quite out of the woods.

Bridget says, "Hold my wine," handing her glass to Trudy as Officer Velez gets out of the cruiser.

Marybeth and Duncan walk toward the officer with Bridget. As they do, Chaplin spots Bridget and lets out a cackle, racing toward her.

"So nice to see you again, Officer Velez," Bridget says,

pushing her hand behind her back to keep Chaplin away.

"Good evening. Annie O'Dell's turkey, Chaplin, has gone missing. Anyone here know where he might be?"

Chaplin spreads his feathers.

Officer Velez notices Bridget's outfit. "Are you taking your vows?" she asks.

"Just . . . kicking the tires," Bridget says.

"I see," Velez says. "This wouldn't be Chaplin, by any chance?"

Chaplin gobbles.

"Isn't he at Annie's farm?" Bridget says.

"We got a call. Seems he escaped."

"I hope someone finds him," Bridget says.

"Uh-huh. You're sure that you haven't seen him?" Velez says, glancing at Chaplin.

"They found Sofia," Bridget says quickly. "Safe and sound."

"That's great news," Officer Velez. "Where was she?"

Marybeth explains as Bridget puts her arm around the officer, walking her to her vehicle. For once, I think Bridget has been flawless, but no. As Velez starts the cruiser, Bridget returns the officer's badge.

"Okay, okay, all right. Settle down, you people." The judge raps a gavel. "The meeting will come to order. Order! I'm hearing chatter from the back. As most of you know, I'm Judge Lionel Harschly and I am the President of the Arnold Falls Town Council. I am *also* the chairman of the Zoning Board, the hat I am wearing tonight. *Lucky, lucky* me."

Judge Harschly is in rare form, I see. I'm still recovering from Tuesday's Chaplin escapade but Jenny and I are here to add our voices, as needed, before the Zoning Board takes its vote about Ivan's land.

"We are in my courtroom because this location gives us enough room for you people to sit down; most of you, anyway. Nothing I can do for all of you standing. But this is a *kindness* on my part to use my courtroom and you will return the *kindness* by letting us do our work without comments from the peanut gallery unless we open the discussion to you. And when I say peanut gallery, I don't mean that literally. There is no food allowed in here. For the few of you who have not been brought before me, the esteemed county of Queechy has not seen fit to trust me with windows, justifiably concerned that I would defenestrate at the slightest provocation even though we are on the ground floor. So it is *infernally* and *eternally* close in here. If you eat so much as a bite of a Snicker's bar, we will all be thinking about Snicker's bars. *Don't* try it.

"The meeting is being recorded so you can watch the best bits again and again in your living rooms on a snowy January evening. Please do not invite me over for that." The audience laughs. "I was not being funny. This is a municipal meeting, *not* open mic night.

"Now, the matter before the Zoning Board this evening is concerning the land owned by Ivan Borger . . . Was that *hissing? Hissing?!* You hissing people, do you want me to come over to your office and hiss you into next week? Because I will do that. I will *make time* for that. Trying again . . . the matter before us is whether the property owned by Mr. Borger"—he pauses to listen for hissing, then, satisfied there is none, continues—"currently zoned for light industrial use, will be rezoned for heavy industrial use. Mr. Borger would you like to make a *brief* comment?"

"Thank you, Judge," Ivan says. "I will be brief. This

factory, which will make parts for automobiles, will employ one hundred people when it opens and two hundred people when production is at capacity. This will be a boon to Arnold Falls and the whole county. We have submitted all the paperwork requested by the Zoning Board and I urge the board to do what's best for the people of Queechy County and vote to rezone the area from light to heavy industrial. Thank you."

There is murmuring in the audience.

Judge Harschly says, "I've told you there is no hissing. *Murmuring* is also *out* of the *question*. Do I have to go down the entire list for you people of what constitutes unacceptable behavior?"

"Go for it!" someone says.

"Who said that?" He scours the room. "One more sound—and I'm including coughing, clearing your throat, and cracking your knuckles—and you will rue the day. Now. Let us continue. Lou Pastorella, founder of the Evergreens environmental group, wishes to make a statement."

Pastorella stands. "By parts for automobiles, Mr. Borger means tires. A tire factory. And a tire factory means poisoning our air and water and disease and death."

He lays it out succinctly, spelling out the chemicals Arnold Falls can expect to breathe or ingest and the consequences to each of them and their families, neighbors and friends. Lou takes less than three minutes and the room listens intently to every word.

"Anyone who can move away, will. Anyone who can't, will suffer," he concludes.

"Thank you, Mr. Pastorella," says Judge Harschly. "A sobering set of facts. Next, speaking on behalf of the efforts to preserve the Dutch House, is Sofia Vass."

Sofia stands and addresses the Zoning Board.

"My name is Sofia Vass." She pauses. "It's not easy for me to do this."

Susanne reaches up and squeezes Sofia's arm.

The room is silent. She takes a deep breath.

"My grandmother was a Van Dalen, a descendant of Ambroos Van Dalen, who built what everyone now calls the Dutch House in 1795, before Arnold Falls was even founded. One way or another, it stayed in my family until 1979. A great deal of my childhood revolved around that house and the two-and-a-half acres behind it. It was a happy place.

"But as these things go, it became increasingly difficult to maintain such an old house and eventually, when my grandmother died, it was left empty. That was deeply embarrassing to our family and perhaps most of all to my sister and me, since we were the only family members who still lived in Arnold Falls. And now it's just me. Not to be able to take care of the house and grounds, modest as they were, was something my family and I will always regret deeply. And for years, no one wanted to buy the house. So, to my shame and to my family's shame, it sat there and fell apart.

"About a decade later, in 1990 I think, Ivan Borger tracked my father down and made him an offer for the property and the taxes owed, which my father accepted after Mr. Borger promised not to raze the house. I don't know if that was ever in writing or not—both my parents are deceased—but I know the promise was made.

"I would like to see my family's house saved. I would like to see the oldest house in Arnold Falls, a true piece of history, become a home again, or a museum or even a bed and breakfast. Something, anything, with *life* in it. I would like Mr. Borger to honor his commitment, not to mention respect our environment.

"Look, as a community, we need to value our past as a part of our future. It's going to take money to restore the Dutch House. And a leap of faith. But people who come after us will want to know how it was in centuries gone by. Not just words, but something they can see, touch, walk in. Breathe in the air. *Clean* air. The Dutch House was built eight years after the Constitution was signed. We should honor it. Please work with Historic Preservation to save the Dutch House. Thank you."

"Thank you, Ms. Vass. Movingly put."

Way to go, Sofia!

Judge Harschly looks at his watch. "Before we get to the vote of the board, I believe we have one more speaker for the evening. Is she here?"

Heads swivel to the back of the courtroom and the doors swing open. After a moment, Aunt Doozy strides through them, dressed in a pale blue church outfit and a wide-brimmed black hat with a large, purple flower made of ribbons. She drops her overcoat onto the hand-railing. Pinned to her lapel is Chester's Bronze Star and a button that says "Stay Woke, Don't Get Tire-d." Jenny and I look at each other, unsure of what is coming next. Before she turns toward the room, I see her wink at Judge Harschly. He gives her an almost imperceptible nod.

The room is quiet. Turning around, Doozy says, "I ain't got time for speeches. You want to poison the air and the water with this nonsense about a tire factory? What planet you on? What planet you going to? What about your kids, your grandkids? You think you could live with the poisoned air? Lemme tell you somethin'. I had three-bean chili for breakfast and kielbasa with sauerkraut for lunch. I need to spell it out for you? Doozy's about to rock your world. You strap yourself in this room here about, I guess, three minutes from now. Then you sit there and tell Aunt Doozy how you want to live in Arnold Falls when the air and water is all poison. Gonna revise my estimate. Two minutes and counting. Nine on the Richter scale. Maybe a ten. And I ain't movin' an inch."

It takes a moment for all of this to sink in, after which the room erupts into a loud buzz that Judge Harschly does nothing to discourage. He is, in fact, raising his own voice: "No, Aunt Doozy, no! My courtroom has no windows!"

"Can't be helped," Doozy says loudly.

The temperature in the room rises as people scramble out of their seats.

"Please, Aunt Doozy! Think of the children!" pleads Judge Harschly.

"Tell it to Krakatoa!" exclaims Doozy.

By this point people are power-walking to the exits. Members of the Zoning Board join the crowd surging toward the doors at the back. Judge Harschly pulls the fire alarm on the wall behind his desk and reaches down for the bullhorn in the bottom drawer of a file cabinet. As the alarm bell rings, the exodus speeds up. Judge Harshly shouts through his bullhorn:

"I AM JUDGE LIONEL HARSCHLY. THIS MEETING IS ADJOURNED. FOR YOUR SAFETY PLEASE LEAVE THE BUILDING IMMEDIATELY AND DO NOT RETURN. BUPBUPBUP! *DON'T* RUN! WOMEN AND CHILDREN FIRST. AND HAPPY HOLIDAYS."

Sofia turns around to look at Aunt Doozy before walking out. Doozy remains expressionless.

"Let's get outta here," Jenny says to me, smiling.

CHAPTER TWENTY

The Room Cleared

The room is clear, leaving only Judge Harschly and Aunt Doozy. Doozy leans against the hand-railing, watching him turn off the alarm, then the lights.

"Fire alarm was a nice touch," she says.

"A bit theatrical, but had to be done," Judge Harschly says, putting on his trench coat. "Krakatoa was good." He barks out a laugh, then sighs. "Tire factory! Miss Jagoda better get herself elected or we're all doomed," he says, wrapping a scarf around his neck.

"Should we wait for the fire department?" Doozy asks.

"No, no, I told them there would be an alarm around seven forty-five and to ignore it."

Judge Harschly helps Doozy on with her overcoat, puts his arm around her shoulder, and walks her to her car, giving her his hand as she gets seated.

He leans in and says, "Job well done, Doozy."

"You want a compliment back from me? Told you I liked the fire alarm. Don't push it."

After four tries, the Chevette starts and Doozy drives home.

CHAPTER TWENTY-ONE

Signed, Sealed, Delivered

It's almost noon on the Saturday before the election and a rally is about to start in front of the Red Light Museum (*Where People Come to Honor the Past*®) on Hester Biddle Street. The museum is centrally located and its front lawn is a popular place for gatherings. There's a strong turnout, easily one hundred people, many with brussels sprouts stalks and Swiss chard from the farmer's market sticking out of their bags.

Even though Aunt Doozy may have helped us dodge a bullet, Jenny wanted to hold the rally anyway. It looks like a friendly crowd, except for the six guys in the back wearing USW sweatshirts. Google has just confirmed that United Steelworkers is the union for tire factories.

We get started and the head of the local Dems introduces Sofia, who says more or less what she said at the Zoning Board meeting two nights ago. The audience, including our USW friends, listens attentively. I admire her for speaking out—it can't be easy.

When Jenny gets to the podium, I feel the energy change and I can tell that so does she. But she's ready for it.

She starts with this question: "Has anyone here had a family member or friend with leukemia?" A few hands go up. She points to a woman with her hand raised and asks, "How would you describe the experience?"

"Horrible," the woman replies.

Jenny nods sympathetically. "My uncle developed leukemia after working for twenty years at a tire factory in Akron. I wouldn't wish that on anyone."

"We need jobs!" shouts one of the Steelworkers.

"I'd love to see two hundred jobs created in Arnold Falls, but I'd like to see most of those jobs go to people who *live* in Arnold Falls. Do any of you gentlemen live in Arnold Falls? I haven't seen you around."

No response.

"I didn't think so. And that's one of many things that my opponent won't be upfront about: the two hundred jobs that this tire factory is promising won't be Arnold Falls jobs. They'll be *county* jobs. But all the pollution, most of the environmental effects and the terrible health toll, *we* will take the brunt of it. It will be especially hard on our . . . on our children."

"Why do you hate unions?" one of the USW guys shouts.

Jenny was waiting for this.

"What's your name?" she asks.

"Paul."

"Hi, Paul. So, here's the thing. I don't hate unions. I come from a long line of union members. My family has fought for unions and workers' rights all our lives."

Paul starts to interrupt.

"Hang on a second," Jenny says. "I'm a union member myself. NewsGuild of New York Local 31003, Communications Workers of America. I was a correspondent for the website Journo until NewsCorp bought it last year. So let's be clear: I am *pro* union. I am *pro* jobs. I am *anti* a tire factory in the heart of Arnold Falls that will destroy the health of residents and the town itself. And the developer needs to destroy Arnold Falls' oldest house to make room for this local death star. So this is what we're talking about, guys. We're talking about destroying our past so that we can destroy our future. All of that for some jobs in the present. I would call that a really lousy collective bargain."

Loud applause and cheers.

"This morning, I received an email from Governor Klingman, who asked that it be read aloud at today's rally.

Dear Friends in Arnold Falls:

Your town, like many others in New York State, is undergoing many changes, some of which you see, some of which you feel, and some of which you may fear. We must summon up the best in ourselves, a full complement of wisdom, to address these often difficult issues.

You will need strong leadership and I enthusiastically support Jenny Jagoda in her run for mayor of Arnold Falls. I know she will make you, and all of New York, proud.

You will also need to build on the great strides your town has made in recent years, protecting both your historic legacy and the beautiful environment afforded by the Hudson River and the Hudson Valley. I urge you to find a way to preserve the 1795 "Dutch House"—a tangible and beautiful piece of the past—as you safeguard your community for future generations. Common sense tells us that building a tire factory in such a thickly settled, environmentally sensitive area is an idea to be rejected. Listen to your common sense. Honor your common purpose.

Finally, it is our responsibility, all of us, to protect the most vulnerable among us. It is in that spirit that I grant a full pardon to Arnold Falls' newly designated mascot, Chaplin, the beloved Narragansett turkey, that he may remain a joyful connection to all God's creatures for the Arnold Falls community, and his many admirers near and far.

Warmest regards.

Sincerely,

Nancy Klingman

Governor

"I thank Governor Klingman for her endorsement, I appreciate her insightful words about our community and I pledge to you that if I am fortunate enough to become your mayor, I will work my butt off so that future generations can enjoy Arnold Falls the way we and those who came before us have. Please remember to vote on Tuesday."

"Where is Chaplin?" someone shouts.

"I am told that Chaplin is safe."

"Um, excuse me?"

Oh, no. Petalia Jijanova.

"Personally, I'm not for a tire factory but why do we have to have a museum where the Loomworks Street Garage is. Why can't it stay a garage?"

I catch Jenny's eye and run my finger across my neck.

"Loomworks will remain a garage. There aren't any plans to change that, Petalia. Okay, we'll wrap things up here. Thank you all for coming."

Lots of huzzahs for Jenny; even Paul, the union guy, shakes Jenny's hand, although he'll still vote for McDufus.

At the end of the rally, Darnell from the Red Light Museum, whose drag name is Hester "Chesty" Biddle, emerges from the building dressed as a beige store mannequin, and walks around the lawn, passing out Hershey's Kisses leftover from Halloween and condoms. He calls out, "Kisses and condoms, kisses and condoms."

Nelle had mentioned a book to me called *The Auberge of the Flowering Hearth* from the early seventies about an inn that was located in the Chartreuse Mountains of the French Alps, run by two women who lovingly prepared French food. It was written by a fellow named Roy Andries de Groot and it sounds right up my alimentary canal, so I'm headed to the library in search of said tome.

You may be surprised to learn that Arnold Falls has a library at all. I know I was.

When Andrew Carnegie was on his library-building jag at the start of the 1900s, Arnold Falls said yes to Carnegie's generous offer until people realized they'd have to foot the bill in perpetuity for a librarian, at which point they were a firm no. The library, such as it was, opened its doors just seventy-seven years later.

The town had made do with a modest collection of books in a two-story Colonial house with clapboard siding built in 1810. What it lacked in actual books it made up for in charm and coziness, enhanced by a working fireplace in the main room where people were free to curl up and expand their horizons.

The current librarian, Juliet, in her late twenties, has been making strides increasing the depth and breadth of the library's collection. A passionate evangelist on the power of books and the importance of reading for digital-age kids, Juliet often begins a conversation with an indifferent child by pointing to one of the tattoos on her arm, the one that quotes Thoreau: "What I began by reading, I must finish by acting." They might not understand it but it makes them curious. "Books change us," she says.

It's a chilly morning and I'm looking forward to sitting by the fireplace and perusing Nelle's recommendation. As I round the corner to the building, I spot Juliet on the porch, gathering up the jack o'lanterns.

"What rule is it that jack o'lanterns must be removed within a week after Halloween? Why do you hate jack o'lanterns, Juliet?"

"I don't hate jack o'lanterns, Jeebie. I just feel it's time to move on to dried corn."

"Well, I suppose there were no jack o'lanterns at the first Thanksgiving dinner, so you may be on firm historical footing. Although I'm going to go out on a limb and say they didn't serve marshmallows on their yams, either."

"I think we've sorted things out nicely," Juliet says in that agreeable way of hers. "How's Jenny going to do on Tuesday?"

"I think it'll be close. I'd say there's more resistance to a woman for mayor than you'd think at this late date."

"I'm sure you're right," Juliet says. "Plus, Rufus and his goons will do a lot of very sketchy stuff to win."

"No doubt about that."

"Are you looking for anything particular?" she asks.

"I am. Do you know off the top of your head if you have *Auberge of the Flowering Hearth*?"

"Actually, I think we do—it would be with the food books. I've got the fireplace going if you want to read here. But you'll have to share it."

"I may read a chapter or two to see if I want to borrow it."

Heading inside, I turn left where the food books are, and after considering whether it would be filed under the A, D, or G of the author's name, I find it under D. I can smell the burning wood and I head to one of the comfy chairs in the main room.

In my favorite chair is Will. He looks up at me.

"Hey, Jeebie. I hear you've been busy rescuing turkeys."

I can't tell if this is supposed to be a snarky comment or not. Snark isn't his thing, but for some reason it rattles my famously even keel.

"Yes, word gets around," I say. "How about you?"

"Finishing my application for Cornell. It's due December first," he says. "I'm going for my Masters in Conservation Biology."

"I didn't know that you . . . Anyway, that's great. Saving the planet is good," I say and wish I had not. A stupid comment. "I like my monkey," I add, making it worse.

"I'm glad," Will says.

"Everyone says what a handsome monkey I am," I say, unable to stop myself.

"Since the Goodall blog ran the photos of my drawings, I'm having a hard time keeping up with orders. JAW-bone is one of the most popular."

Even in this awkward conversation, part of me is delighted at the popularity of my simian counterpart. "Go JAW-bone!" I say, punching my hand in the air. Please let the earth open up and swallow me whole.

Juliet walks in and says, "Sit and stay for a while, Jeebie."

"Oh, well, I couldn't find the book I was looking for," I say.

"Isn't that the de Groot book in your hand?" she asks.

I gawp at the book. "I was looking . . . for the other de Groot. Book. His other book. Not the other de Groot. If there is one. I mean, his father was Mr. de Groot, too. Stands to reason." Kill me.

"Didn't you ask me for *Auberge of the Flowering Hearth*?"

"Did I? Yes! I did, I did. But I've changed my mind. Because I read it. Ages ago. Good. Good story. Excellent. Lots of . . . French food. Oeufs a la neige! Eggs of snow!" Out of the corner of my eye, I note Will looking at me quizzically. My forehead is sweating from the fire. "People come in for one book and decide on a different book. That must happen all the time. Occupational hazard."

"Yes, all the time, Jeebie. We have plenty of books to choose from," Juliet says in a tone you would use with an elderly relative who has gone for a walk in their bathrobe.

My fight-or-flight response is now off the charts and *flight!!!* is the message surging through every synapse in my nervous system.

I hand the book to Juliet and say, "Don't forget to vote on Tuesday. Very important." I look at Will and say, "You, too, um . . ."

"Will," he reminds me.

"I know, I know. Gotta boogie."

I have never said "gotta boogie" in my life.

This the central point I keep coming back to as I review the sequence of events this morning at the library.

What *happened* in there? I wonder if there was an issue with carbon monoxide from the fireplace. Although Will didn't seem affected by it. Can firemen develop some kind of immunity to carbon monoxide?

I hear Duncan saying to me, "Don't mull too much. That's kind of the point." But maybe the library has sick building syndrome. Although . . . I would have noticed it before. Dust mites? I consider calling Nelle to discuss this but then I think better of it. She can be very single-minded.

It's all so vexing. I'd like a distraction—too bad I left the library without the *Auberge* book. I decide to do some deep-breathing exercises, but it's hopeless. All I can hear in my head is A Taste of Honey's "Boogie Oogie Oogie."

Argos is hosting our election night party. The place is already packed with people waiting for the nine p.m. poll closing and we should know the winner not long after that.

I was with Duncan and Marybeth, but they've sat down at a table for a bite. Nelle's en route. Jenny has been mingling, dressed in the black cocktail dress we picked out together. Sofia and Madora are both behind the bar. Our opponents are almost certainly at the Elks.

Darnell from the Red Light Museum is appearing as his alter ego, Hester "Chesty" Biddle, saying "Five minutes 'til polls close" into her mic and tossing out jokes.

"Hey, Manny," Chesty says. "I've got one for you."

Manny stops on his way to the kitchen as someone shouts "I bet you do!"

"That is *high*-larious," Chesty says. "A laugh riot. So, Manny, what happens to old *mayors*?"

"I don't know, Chesty. What happens to old mayors?"

"They get put out to pasture!"

The groans don't faze her at all. "A play on words, folks. You can handle that. This election, we've rocked the *vote*. And now Jenny Jagoda is going to rock the *boat*!" She hits the button on a boom box and lip-syncs to Beyoncé's "Run the World (Girls)."

People turn back to their conversations but there's a lot of glancing down at watches and phones. It's been almost a year since Jenny announced her campaign and the room is eager for the tallies. My wineglass is empty and there's a crush of people waiting for drinks at the bar. I spot Bridget's henna signaling to me like a beacon and make my way over to her.

"Bridget. How's your Clagger stash at the moment?"

"I see your cup runneth dry. Here," she says, producing, from nowhere discernible, a jumbo flask.

"Thank you. The suspense is killing me," I say. "Where's Trudy?"

"Last I saw her, she was out in the patio, plotting with Kenny Winstian."

"How are things going with you two?"

"She's the real deal. A lovely soul."

I'm about to tease her but Bridget looks so happy talking about Trudy that I give her a hug instead. "Don't fuck it up," I add. We clink glasses.

"Backatcha!" she says, which is odd, even for Bridget.

Nelle appears, complete with glass of red wine and a small box of popcorn.

"How'd you get served so fast?" I ask, grabbing a handful of popcorn.

"Connections," Nelle says.

Another fifteen minutes goes by and conversations feel anxious and strained. The air in the room seems fraught. Finally, there's tapping on glasses, shushing, and the music suddenly goes off. Jenny stands on a chair with her cell phone to her ear. She says, "A few more seconds."

Everyone draws a breath.

Jenny's listening intently to someone on the phone. "Okay, okay."

She says to the room, "These aren't certified. There are still absentee ballots to come in and some ballots may be challenged."

To the phone: "Okay."

To the room: "Hey! We got this! We got it! 1,858 for Rufus and 2042 for us! We did it!"

Chesty Biddle cues up Stevie Wonder's "Signed, Sealed, Delivered (I'm Yours)" and everyone in Argos is instantly up and dancing. She follows it with Harry James' "Back Beat Boogie" and I decide the gods are toying with me.

Later, when Jenny and I are dancing to "Waterloo," Jenny shouts to me, "Thank you for everything!"

I shout back, "Nothing at all. The downside is now you have to be mayor," and her laugh is louder than ABBA.

CHAPTER TWENTY-TWO

Fika

After they heard about Governor Klingman's pardon for Chaplin, Marybeth had sat Duncan down at the kitchen table and made him write out a check to Annie for a thousand dollars, while she wrote a note that said:

Annie:

Chaplin has returned home. Our family has learned a lesson the hard way about what makes a home a home. We wish you and yours a peaceful new year.

Duncan and Marybeth Elmore

"I'd drop it in her mailbox today, Duncan."

"Yes, m'am."

"That's more like it. And I had an idea," she says.

"What's that?" Duncan asks.

"Well, since the Council agreed to declare Thanksgiving Day 'Chaplin Day', wouldn't it be fun to have a parade with Chaplin as Grand Marshal?"

"Great idea!" Duncan says. "What do you think, Sadie? Wouldn't Chaplin like to lead a parade?"

Sadie says, "Yes. But don't leave out Venus and Serena."

"We'll have to get a permit from the town, but that shouldn't be a problem," Duncan says. "How about a walk from Argos to Benedict's Inn?"

"Perfect. What music are we going to have? I doubt we could get the marching band at such short notice. Those kids will have vacation plans."

"What about Queechy Caliente?" Duncan asks.

"A mariachi band for Thanksgiving? Why not! I wonder if people might be in the mood this year to be together for dinner. I'll bet they might."

Nelle admires the colorful Swedish-style double doors of the Nyqvist headquarters and then knocks.

A man with a long, pleasant face, aquiline nose, and sandy-gray hair opens the door and says with a twinkle, "Oh, Good Lord, not another Nyqvist."

"Yes, I'm the black sheep."

"Come in, glorious Nelle, come in, come in. Your show was one of the best things I've seen in years."

"Thank you," Nelle says.

"I'm Trevor Aitken," he says, extending his hand. "Nils just texted that he'll be right along."

"What a beautiful room!"

The office part of Hulla, the Nyqvist brand, is a spacious, all-white kitchen with a big window at the back, including one brick wall painted white and a white ceiling with white timber beams.

Nelle says, "Clearly I am here for contrast."

"I knew I would love you. I just knew it. Take off your coat, sit. Nils has fika planned."

"Fika?"

"It's the Swedes' idea of afternoon tea. Don't let them fool you," he says.

"You're British, I'm guessing?"

"Yes, born and raised just outside London. When the Nyqvists were performing regularly in the circus, about fifteen years ago, I was put in charge of caring for them during their London engagement and I never left. The worst case *ever* of Stockholm Syndrome."

"I can find a safe house for you, Trevor," Nelle says.

"That's just it! They're talented, beautiful, kind. Insufferable, really."

"That's what Jeebie said," Nelle says.

"Ah, that Jeebie's a smart fellow. Very fond of him."

Nils comes in with a pastry box. "Sorry I'm late. Thanks for coming, Nelle." He shakes her hand.

"Trevor has been very entertaining."

"I'm sure he has," Nils says. "Complaining about the Nyqvists?" He grabs a plate and opens the pastry box while imitating Trevor: "They're *insufferable*, the whole lot of them."

"Amusing, Nils," Trevor says. "So many comedians hail from Sweden. Now sit down and I'll take care of the so-called tea."

He walks into the pantry. Nelle shifts in her seat, trying not to look too long in Nils' eyes. What am I even doing here?

"Congratulations on Jenny's win," Nils says.

"Thanks," Nelle says. "But I didn't have much to do with it."

"Except blow everyone away with your show," Nils

says. "By the way, I hope you like chaga. I harvested it myself in the Adirondacks. And my sister has just made *kanelbullar*, like a cinnamon bun."

Nelle says, "I do like chaga, although I'm just learning about medicinal mushrooms. I've studied a fair amount about medicinal herbs."

"We'll have to go foraging sometime."

"Here's your *chaga*," Trevor says, bringing a small tray to the table. "Mushrooms for tea! If that isn't a sign of the apocalypse, I don't know what is."

"Traditionally, we should be having coffee for fika," says Nils.

"And here are the buns," Trevor says. "I'll be in my office. Yodel if you need me."

"Swedes don't yodel, Trevor."

"Not for lack of trying!" Trevor says and goes into his office.

As Nils strains the tea into a cup for Nelle, she takes a bite of the bun. "Mmm, that is amazing."

"Thanks, I'll tell Stella. Do you know much about what we do as a family business?"

"A bit," Nelle says. "I know the circus, of course."

"Yes, Hullabaloo Circus was how it started. We all used to perform but as we got older, we started performing less and hiring outside the family. Susanne and Martin, my parents, still live in town, as does Theo, my brother. Susanne makes jewelry . . ."

"I have a pair of her earrings," Nelle says. "I love them."

"I'll tell her. Dad runs the circus, Theo paints, and my sister, Stella, is a chef and baker. My grandmother knits hemp sweaters, caps, blankets, stuff like that. There are more of us. My suggestion is don't try to keep everyone straight. It can't be done. And in spite of what Trevor says, we all have massive flaws but we love each other and we love what we do. So we're incredibly lucky."

Nelle is sipping her chaga, looking at Nils' full lips moving and realizes she's missing a lot of what he's actually saying. She hears "massive flaws" and thinks "flawless skin." He's got a nice voice, too. Beautiful hands. Did he just ask a question?

"Sorry?" she says.

"Do you like your work for SOAR?"

"I love it. Sometimes we really and truly help people out of the cycle and into something much better. When we see that happen, it's incredibly gratifying."

"What about your other gift?" Nils asks.

"Music? I don't know what to say about it. It's a big part of who I am."

"Let me get to the point," Nils says. "I've had some success as a music producer. The family has talked for a few years about building a recording studio here. We think we could create something special that would work not only for me, but would attract musicians from all over the Valley and from the city. We'd like this facility to remain the laboratory of what we do and we'd like a place on High Street to be the showcase for it, starting with a space selling Stella's sweets. So, those are our grand plans."

"They sound great," Nelle says.

"More chaga?"

"Yes, please."

"Since I saw you perform," Nils says, "this is what I've been thinking: *get the studio done now*. What I'm asking you is, would you consider recording? I would love to produce for you or you can use the facility with another producer, but if I knew you were interested, it would be a great motivator to get it done. Everyone in the family agrees."

"Well, wow. Very surprising and very flattering. I don't want to tour, I know that. But recording is a different thing. I think I might love that opportunity. I'll give it some serious thought."

"You have serious talent," Nils says.

Trevor comes in, taking his cellphone off the counter and says, "Has he asked you yet? Give it a go, Nelle."

"I'll think about it. I'm going to need some time to process the idea. Well, I should get back to my day job."

"Can I walk you?" Nils asks.

"Yes, of course."

"It was so nice meeting you," Trevor says.

"You, too, Trevor."

Nelle and Nils head outside and take the more scenic back road, where there are still maples and oaks showing off brilliant colors. They're engrossed in conversation as they walk past the Dutch House and notice a piece of construction equipment in the yard. But they're talking about Dusty Springfield and then the moment is gone.

And the chance that went with it.

At seven a.m. the next morning, a truck arrives at the Dutch House and the guys deposit a giant container on the front lawn.

Half an hour later, Ivan Borger arrives with his project manager, a demolition contractor, and an excavator operator.

By lunchtime, the Dutch House is history.

CHAPTER TWENTY-THREE

A Temple of Delight

We swoop in on Sofia.

After word got around about Ivan's despicable act on Thursday morning, we quickly arrange a trip on Friday to Saranac Lake in the Adirondacks. Madora insists that Sofia take the time off and Sofia agrees without much resistance. One directive for all: meet at Saranac Lodge by the fireplace for drinks at eight.

Susanne Nyqvist and Sofia are driving up together, Nelle and I are taking my car, and Madora called Sofia's sister, Lillie, who is driving up from Wilmington.

I'll spare you our car cabaret, but Nelle and I have a blast singing to my playlists. One highlight: Nelle asks me to teach her something from Motown that she didn't already know.

"Love found or love lost?" I ask.

"Found."

"How about 'Bless You' by Martha Reeves and the Vandellas? Do you know it?"

"I don't think so."

"Google the lyrics."

While Nelle Googles, I say, "Hey Siri, play 'Bless You' by Martha Reeves and the Vandellas."

It takes Nelle about two seconds to join in, adding background vocals, handclaps, and a perfect imitation of Martha Reeves. We crush it. By this point, we've passed Schroon Lake and decide to give our vocal cords a rest.

"Pee stop?"

"No, I'm fine," she says.

"We should be there in a little over an hour."

"Any Will updates?"

"No! Nope, nope. Nothing. What kind of updates could there be? He's probably drawing me as a honey badger."

Nelle looks at me and says, "Jeebie."

So I give her a blow-by-blow account of my performance in the library and she, of course, laughs at me.

"Jeebie, you're a grown, middle-aged man."

"WHAT!?! *Middle-aged?!* Get out of this car. Right now. I'm serious. Out. Jump. Scoot."

"*Jeebie . . .*"

"I know. I know . . . No, I *don't* know."

"Don't know what?" Nelle asks. "How you feel?"

"*Why* I feel."

We think about this for a bit.

"What do you want?" she asks.

"No wonder your clients are so depressed when all you do is pester them with personal questions." I glance over at her. "Okay, okay, okay, okay. I wouldn't have turned into a blithering idiot at the library if I didn't feel something. For Will. I feel something. Okay? Happy now?"

"Can you be more specific?"

"No, I can*not* be more specific. My feelings don't sort neatly into specific boxes. Yes, he's attractive. But an apple seller who draws monkeys?"

"*And* a volunteer fireman," Nelle adds.

"Yes, and applying to grad school."

"He's applying to grad school?"

"That's why he was at the library. He was working on an application to Cornell for a Masters in Conservation or something."

"You're right, Jeebie. The guy's not good enough for you."

"I believe sarcasm is my bailiwick," I say.

"Go out with him," Nelle says.

"He's dating G. I. Joe."

"You don't know that."

"You make it all sound so easy," I say.

"No, nothing's easy," Nelle says. "'Stop worrying where you're going . . .'"

"*Oh, no you don't!*" I say. "*My* car. No quoting Sondheim to make your point."

"Okay, who am I allowed to quote?"

I think about this. "Charo."

"You mean María del Rosario Mercedes Pilar Martínez Molina Baeza?"

"Is that her real name?"

"Yep," Nelle says.

"How do you know that?"

"I just do," she says. "Okay, so, in the words of the great María del Rosario Mercedes Pilar Martínez Molina Baeza, also known as Charo, give cuchi-cuchi a chance."

"Thank you, Nelle. Give cuchi-cuchi a chance. I'm going to remember that always."

We get to the lodge around seven thirty and, after freshening up, head down to the bar. I order a bottle of Sardinian cannonau and Nelle gives me a thumbs up.

Nelle was so busy in the car asking me annoying questions, she hasn't checked her phone since we left. As she does that now, I give a long stare at the fire. Her back is to the doorway but I can see out into the lobby as Sofia and Susanne arrive. With surprise guests.

"Nelle, what was the line you quoted again?"

She glances up from her phone and says, "Stop worrying where you're going . . . "

"No, not that one."

"The Charo?"

"Yes, the Charo. Remind me how it goes."

"Give cuchi-cuchi a chance," she says, a tad warily.

"Give cuchi-cuchi a chance," I repeat. "So beautiful. So true."

"What are you up to?"

"Nils is here."

"Funny," she says.

"Turn around."

She turns around and then snaps her head back. A sound like "cchhhhhhohhhh!" comes out of her mouth. "What's he *doing* here?"

"Nelle, you're a grown, middle-aged woman," I say, throwing *that* back at her. "Susanne probably told him she was going and he decided to come along. I'm sure the fact that you were going to be here played *no part* in his decision. Has he built the music studio for you yet?"

"I hate you."

"Don't be like that, my little cuchi-cuchi. Let's go say hello. Come on, Trevor's here, too."

We have a lovely dinner at the Lodge. Sofia seems in fine spirits, considering the circumstances. Her sister, Lillie, arrives just as we're sitting down. Nelle and Nils sit next to each other though they have the good manners not to get into the sweet-nothings business.

Trevor keeps us laughing during the meal—he's a natural storyteller, a talent I envy. He worked many years ago as an assistant director on a play in the West End with Maggie Smith and has us howling with his uncanny impression of the Dame.

After dinner, we have more wine and digestifs nestled around the fireplace. We talk about the walks we'll take tomorrow, who wants to snowshoe or go cross-country skiing, what books we're planning to start over the weekend.

Lillie is sitting next to Sofia. You can tell they are related—same large, brown eyes—although Sofia is more Mediterranean-looking.

After a pause in the conversation, Nelle turns to Nils and says, "You're sure it's okay?"

Nils replies, "Of course, you must tell her."

"Sofia, I need to get this off my chest."

"Spill it," Sofia says.

"Nils and I walked by the Dutch House on Wednesday. We saw a piece of equipment, heavy equipment, parked behind it. We were talking and it just didn't register until later what it meant. We might have been able to stop it."

She takes that in and says, "No, no, no, don't do that to yourselves. If we had somehow stopped Ivan from razing it, he would have just torched the place later. I knew the house was going. I could feel it in my bones. Some kind of . . . weird, collective memory from the future. I sound like a fucking nut. Well. Whatever. That's why I needed to spend time there. Ivan behaved like Ivan. And as sad as it is to admit, we didn't give up claim to the house when my father sold it to Ivan. We gave it up when we didn't care for the house all those years. Just because that's hard to accept doesn't make it any less true. You take your lumps."

"I'm truly sorry for your loss," I say. "I'm also sorry about 'Thanks, Benzene.'"

"What's 'Thanks, Benzene?'" Lillie asks.

"Jeebie's created a new form of torture," Sofia says. "I'll explain it to you later. We're good, Jeebie. All good. You're safe for now."

"But I *am* going to lock the door to my room tonight."

"Push the dresser in front of the door, too," Sofia says.

"Okay, ha. Right? Ha ha?" I ask.

"Anyone else feeling contrite about something?" Trevor asks.

Susanne says, "No. I'm feeling grateful."

"Those Nyqvists are so full of optimism, but *why?*" he says, giving the "why" the long Maggie Smith nasal diphthong. "'Ay, in the very temple of Delight/Veil'd Melancholy has her sovran shrine.'"

"You can keep your Keats, Dame Trevor Smith," Susanne says. "We're here, in one of the world's prettiest spots, with good friends, wine, a roaring fire, warm on a chilly Adirondacks night. Can you really ask for more? The loss of the house is a terrible one. Terrible for you, Sofia, and your family, but terrible for all of us, too. The question is, what are we going to do about it?"

"Do about what?" Sofia asks. "The house is rubble."

"Yes, my dear friend," she says, squeezing Sofia's hand. "It is. Rubble and dust is the end of most human endeavor. So Keats does have a point, Dame Trevor. Terrible loss *is* in the temple of Delight. But would it even *be* a temple of Delight without loss? I suppose that's something for philosophers and poets to sort out. We can't bring the Dutch House back now any more than we can the lives lived there. Only our perspective can change. The future is even less certain. Will the Pyramids still be there in another thousand years? Five thousand years? Will anyone remember Shakespeare? In two hundred years, will the earth even be habitable? We cannot know those things and we must not grieve for what we do not know, for a future as yet unwritten. The wine *has* got me talking.

"So, that brings us to today. And tomorrow. And next month. If we can only explicate the past, we can *cultivate* the future, to borrow from Voltaire. Perhaps that's what we mean by hope. We have choices. Not limitless choices. But *some* choices. We now have Jenny leading the way in our little dot on the map. I *am* feeling grateful and optimistic. But to merely observe is a failure of duty and imagination. What matters is what we *do*. What we *cultivate*."

Susanne looks around at the group.

"All right, end of speech," she says.

"Hear, hear! Mamma," Nils says.

"Thank you, Susanne," Sofia says. "Yes, yes, yes."

Nelle taps me and says quietly, "Where are you, Jeebie?"

"Here. I'm here. Just thinking. Must be the mountain air."

The bartender buys us all a round and the mood becomes more playful.

"Want to sing something, Nelle?" Nils asks. "Piano's right there."

"I couldn't get my fingers on the right keys at this point," Nelle says.

"I play," Nils says. "Name a song."

"Come on, Nellsy, I say, "Don't be a diva."

She gives me a look, of course.

"Okay, just one," she says. "How about . . . Nils, do you know 'I Wish You Love'?"

"'I wish you bluebirds in spring'? That one?"

"That one."

And then, just like that, he plays it and she sings it. Oh, man. It is dreamy. Heaven.

It's past midnight and people are starting to think about bed. It turns out no one has plans to sleep alone.

In the morning, we'll learn who ended up where: Nelle with Nils, Sofia with the bartender, whose name she can't remember, I hook up with Trevor, and the normally hetero Lillie and Susanne with each other.

We all gave cuchi-cuchi a chance.

There are no walks of shame: everyone seems pleased by their time so far at Saranac Lake. After breakfast, we hike Ampersand Mountain which is a deceptive bit of nature. It starts easy, and then gets pretty steep, yet I remain a good sport, in my opinion, the whole way. In two hours, we've made it to the top, amply rewarded by the views. I can't stop humming "I Wish You Love."

It's cold up here, but the sun is shining, so we unwrap the baguettes filled with ham and Brie that the lodge packed for us. Nelle sits down right next to me and looks out at the view as she munches her sandwich.

"Maples, birches, aspens, pines," she says.

"Verb? Adjective? Direct object?"

"Nope. Just appreciating them. Thinking about what Susanne said."

"Me, too. Duncan thinks I'm a charming mess," I say with a mouth full of Brie.

"Duncan is a doll."

"Your comment doesn't follow logically from my statement."

"I can live with that," Nelle says.

"Falling asleep with someone was nice," I say.

"Nicer when you want to wake up with them. What's the universe telling you?"

"The universe and I don't have that kind of relationship. It tells me surprisingly little. Trevor's a lovely man, but it was just a lark. For both of us. He's already planning three weeks of debauchery in Majorca over the holidays."

Nils calls us over. He's pulled out a thermos, paper coffee cups, and a small bakery box from his backpack. "Stella baked these ginger cookies yesterday," he says, then pours coffee for everyone.

Trevor walks over, ending a phone call he's been on, and says to us eagerly, "Okay, here's a question: What's the opposite of a tire factory?"

We shake our heads.

"A *park!*" he says. "Van Dalen Park! I've been thinking about what you said, Susanne. I was just on the phone with a friend who works for the governor and Klingman is *livid* that the house was destroyed. My friend's going to see what can be done from their end. The state *can* take land for a public improvement—it's extreme but eminent domain is at least a remote possibility. Anyway, I have a feeling that won't be necessary. Arnold Falls is too small for Ivan to prevail."

"How do you figure that?" Sofia asks. "God, those are delicious, Nils."

"In a big city, money can insulate you from contact with your community. Here, we can make damn sure the pressure against him is too much. He hasn't got a lot of allies that I can see. How will he walk down the street? Meanwhile, we will cultivate a park."

"He'll sue," Lillie says.

"He'll lose. I hate to bring this up, but the temporary injunction against demolition was still in effect. My Klingman contact checked."

"*He just did it anyway*?!" Lillie asks.

"It seems he did," Trevor says.

Nelle says, "He must have figured that a board with Jenny's appointments wouldn't change the zoning so he just thought, 'Screw it' and got the process started."

"Asshole," Sofia says.

"Indeed," Trevor says.

After our coffee, Sofia yells "FUCKU!" several times to the valley below and I feel the world righting itself, just a bit.

The next morning, we're in the courtyard of the lodge, packing up the cars. Nelle and Nils are going back with Sofia and Susanne, I'm with Trevor. He offers to drive and I hand him my keys.

As we make our way toward the highway, I tell Trevor that I think his idea made a huge difference to Sofia. We chat for a while and then leave each other to our own thoughts. The classical station we're listening to is playing Dvořák's "Serenade for Strings," a warm bath if there ever was one.

I stare out the window, thinking about the weekend, Susanne's thoughts about what we cultivate, and about my conversation with Nelle on the way up. Why we feel. Could life even be a temple of Delight without loss? As the trees blur past, I hear Nelle singing "I Wish You Love."

Saranac Lake has been the loveliest of idylls but it's time to get back to reality, inasmuch as Arnold Falls is any kind of reality. Dvořák works his magic and I close my eyes.

CHAPTER TWENTY-FOUR

The First Lady

OoOO child, a lot has happened since you were here. But first, thank you again, Brenda, honey, for coming up and doing your thang with me. Nobody does backup like you. Just nobody. I owe you big time. And Jenny won! Who rules the world?!!

How are rehearsals going? What's Lin-Manuel like to work with?! Don't tell me he's a nice guy, too. I hope he's a monster LOL.

About that gorgeous Swedish guy, remember? Nils. Nils Nyqvist. Some surprising developments. So the family company is called Hulla and I go to their office, where everything is whitewhitewhite and we have a chat. And—I'm not kidding you—he says, "I want to build a recording studio and produce an album for you." Craziest thing I ever heard. He's produced albums for a bunch of people and they're good, but I mean, come on! The whole thing seems nuts but *that's Arnold Falls for you. You just go with it. So I said maybe.*

Then. A bunch of us go up to the Adirondacks—long story—and he shows up. And all of a sudden it's midnight and he wants to sleep with me. So I said yes. Should I have said yes to recording and maybe to sex? I hear you laughing right now, Brenda.

I invited Mateo to the show last month but I didn't hear back. Have you talked with him? Have a feeling he's seeing someone. Which is good.

Gonna draw myself a bath now and think about what I would sing if I recorded an album. At least fun to think about. There's an agent who lives here named Bridget Roberts, have you heard of her? She's been on me about becoming her client. You think things are complicated in the city?! LOL.

Love you.
Nelle

Gussie doesn't like wearing the blue-and-white striped sweater that Bridget puts on him when mornings are as cold as this. There were several inches of snow, but it's sunny now, so they've braved a walk.

As usual, Gussie leads the way, following his nose, which manages to pick up all kinds of scents, the freezing weather notwithstanding. As they pass by Winstian's, Gussie starts to pee at a favored spot in front of the antiques shop, but Bridget pulls his leash to stop him. Since Trudy is talking with Kenny about joining forces, there's no point in doing anything to irk him.

They turn left onto Ledyard, with its especially pretty

cluster of buildings. The street is deserted and it is utterly quiet now that they're off High Street. Halfway down the block, Gussie stops to sniff, and Bridget glances at the parked car next to her. Its roof is covered with snow, which has cascaded onto the windshield.

But the side window is clear and through it Bridget sees the shocking sight of a woman with white hair, perhaps ninety years old, sitting in the passenger's seat, her face partly covered by an oxygen mask. She has no overcoat, just an unbuttoned cardigan. The car doesn't look used since the snow fell, so she may well have been there overnight. Bridget fears the woman is not alive.

She knocks frantically on the window anyway. "Hello! Hello! Are you all right?"

The woman is non-responsive. Bridget tries the door, which is locked. She takes out her cell phone and calls the police department. "Hello! I am on Ledyard by the church and a woman has frozen to death in a car."

In no time at all, Officer Velez pulls up, lights flashing.

"Where is she, Bridget?" Officer Velez asks. Bridget points to the car.

Another police car arrives and Officer Mills jumps out with a window punch in his hand.

Before breaking a window, they try rousing the woman, knocking on the glass, shouting to her, testing all the doors, to no avail. Finally Officer Mills takes the tool and drives a punch into the center of the back side window. It shatters and he's finally got access.

After a moment, he says, "Grandma's not with us. But she never was." He gets out of the car and stands up, smiling. "Dummy."

"Dummy?!" Bridget says.

Looking over Mills's shoulder, Officer Velez says, "My guess is Grandma's friend is approaching."

The red-faced lunk is not happy. "What the hell are you doing?! Why did you break the window?"

"Sir. This is your car?" Velez says.

"Yes!"

The officer continues, "You have a very realistic-looking elderly woman locked in your car in frigid temperatures, using an oxygen mask, wearing nothing but a cardigan. What did you think would happen?"

"She's a CPR training device. The Martha Washington model. I work for the company that manufacturers them. Who's gonna pay for my window?"

"Maybe Martha will kick in a few Georges," Bridget says.

"Oh, that's so funny," the guy says. "Who are you?"

"Bridget Roberts. I found Martha and called the police," Bridget says as Chief Williams and the EMS truck arrive. "That's no way to treat anyone, certainly not Martha Washington."

"You people are all whacked."

Officer Velez says, "Sir, you have to admit that any reasonable person might draw the same conclusions as Ms. Roberts."

While Officer Mills takes pictures of the car, they explain the situation to Chief Williams who is trying not to smile. He says to the car owner, "You're with Martha?"

"Yeah. Who's going to pay for my fucking window? You had no right to do that. Stupid asses!"

The Chief is no longer almost-smiling. "Let me tell you something," Chief Williams says evenly. "If you leave Martha or anyone else in your car again overnight, in any temperature other than sixty-eight degrees *exactly*, the Arnold Falls police are going to smash *all* of your f-ing windows and escort Martha into the station for a nice cup of hot cocoa while we come up with something to charge you with."

Martha's companion gets into his car shaking his head.

Bridget yells after him, "And get her a nicer sweater! My *dog* has a nicer sweater!"

───────

The next morning, Trudy is having coffee, reading the *Times*, when her cellphone rings.

"Hope I'm not calling too early," Kenny says.

"Not at all."

"I'm glad Bridget saved Martha Washington! It's in the *Observer* this morning. Martha looks very realistic."

"I saw it. It could only, *ever* happen to Bridget."

"What could only ever happen to me?" Bridget asks, walking into the kitchen in her bathrobe.

"It's Kenny. He thinks you're a hero for saving the mother of our country."

"I took her wallet."

"Bridget! You didn't! She wouldn't have a wallet!"

"She did and I did. From her purse. There was a handkerchief in there, a Bible, and Afrin. I left those and gave her a few of my Corn Nuts. Serves the man right for dressing her in such a shabby sweater," she says, pouring herself coffee.

"Did you hear that, Kenny? You're laughing so I guess you did. I don't know what to do with her."

"Fuck, marry, or kill," Kenny says.

"Kill, for sure," Trudy says.

"Yeah, probably your best choice. So, anyway. The reason I called is, I was thinking about our plan."

"You're not bailing on me?"

"No, not at all! Just something I've thought about for a long time. I would love to offer an internship, a paid internship, to someone young, maybe a student, to teach them about antiques and we could expand that to the art world. What do you think?"

"Love it," Trudy says. "Love that idea."

"What idea?" Bridget asks.

Trudy waves her away.

"Then let's make that part of the plan," Kenny says. "I think we're ready to come up with a partnership agreement. Don't you?"

"I do. Do you want to use Jewel Guldens?"

"Works for me," Kenny says.

"I'll give her a call and let you know what she says."

"Sounds like you're moving ahead with it," Bridget says after Trudy puts down her phone.

"Seems that way."

"Any doubts about it?" Bridget asks, sitting down next to Trudy.

"No, not really. I mean, you never know how a partnership will work out but I've known Kenny for so many years now."

"I think it's a great idea," Bridget says.

"You do? You haven't said that before, so I'm glad to hear it."

"Let's have him over for dinner. In fact, let's have him to my house."

"We could do that . . . "

"I've done some clearing out in the past few days. You'll see. Much airier."

Delphy and Gussie walk into the room together. Delphy curls up under Trudy's legs and Gussie sits near Bridget, waiting for a treat. From places unknown, she produces a biscuit in her hand and gives it to him.

Luther walks over to Judge Harschly as he enters the Courthouse.

"Judge?"

"Morning, Luther."

"I wanted to thank you from me and my family. We're moving into the house on Old Post Road this weekend. And we are grateful to you, Judge."

"That's happy news. Glad to hear it."

"Elma made you her cinnamon crumble apple pie— okay to leave it in your office?" Luther asks.

"Thank you, Luther, of course. That wasn't at all necessary but very kind. Please thank Elma for me. It's still the best pie in the world. Leave it with Vera, but tell her she will be terminated if she takes a single bite of it."

"Elma made one for Vera, too."

"Then make it clear to Vera that only *one* pie—and I suggest you hold up your finger to reinforce the concept of one, not two—is for her to take home. Vera is slippery."

"I'll let her know, Judge. One pie to a customer. One for Hamster, too."

"Oh?"

"Night of the fire, Hamster walked over and handed me a lottery ticket he won the week before. Three thousand dollars. How about that?"

"The human race is a complete mystery to me, Luther."

Will is in the orchard when his phone rings.

"Good morning, this is Caitlin Krumpe, an editor from Burgess Books in New York. I'm trying to reach Will Shaffer."

"This is Will."

"Hi, Will. The reason I'm calling is I've seen your Hinky Monkeys series and I love it. Have you ever considered turning it into a book?"

"A book?! No, to be honest, I haven't." He crouches down and strokes Parachute, the cat that likes to follow him around the orchard.

"Is it something you might be interested in?"

"I've never written a book before," Will says.

"Nobody's written a book before they have," Caitlin says. "And my sense is that both your writing and illustrations would make a wonderful book. If you wanted to just illustrate it, we could pair you up with a writer. Or maybe you have someone to collaborate with. I just wanted to see if it's something that might interest you. By the way, I adore Peaches."

Will chuckles. "Thanks. I have no idea what to say to this."

"Would you give it some thought?"

"Yes, of course. I'll call you after Thanksgiving. Should I call you back at the number you called from?"

"That's perfect. I really think it could be a book that brings a lot of joy."

"Thanks, Caitlin. I will think it over. Thank you! Thanks for calling."

Will sits down on the ground crosslegged and Parachute immediately curls up in his lap. He pulls out his phone to check the call log. Not a prank: the call was from Burgess Books. He's trying to decide what to do when it comes to him. He knows just who he should ask about this, so he starts typing her a message.

———

Chester Jordan was killed on November 13, 1944, outside of Obreck, France. He was part of the Black Panthers, as the 761st Tank Battalion was known, and only days before they had become the first black armored unit in combat.

November 13th had been a Monday and Doozy got the news from Chester's family on Wednesday afternoon. She took Thursday off but was back to work at the Chicken Shack on Friday. Appearances hadn't mattered to her, even at the age of twenty, even if she was racked with grief, as indeed she was. Nothing would ever change how she felt about Chester, she thought at the time, and nothing ever did. She simply understood that no amount of fuss would bring Chester back.

A year later, when his family asked if Doozy wanted to meet them at Chester's grave on the anniversary of his death, Doozy made it clear that "hoo-hooing over a piece of stone" wasn't going to do Chester any good and that she thought about him every day, not just once a year. Instead, she went to the Oyster Bar in Grand Central.

The Oyster Bar tradition had started because one of Doozy's lifelong pals, Ruby Winter, who had worked briefly for Miss Georgia, knew that it would be good to get Doozy out of Arnold Falls on the anniversary of Chester's death. And Doozy loved oysters, so that was that.

They kept doing it every year, missing only a few along the way, always ordering the same thing: a half-dozen oysters each and a bottle of champagne. Sometimes they'd split the oyster pan roast, too. Afterward, they might go shopping or to a Broadway matinee, or back to Ruby's place. Ruby lived in Hell's Kitchen in a large, rent-controlled apartment, and when they hadn't seen each other for a while, they'd go there and talk for hours.

It's another November 13th and Ruby, a stylish figure who could pass for someone twenty years younger, is sitting at a table in the Oyster Bar, wearing a navy blue turtleneck dress and a colorful wrap that only partially covers her dark hair. Her lipstick is bright red. Doozy walks in to the restaurant and spots her right away.

"How you still ain't gray?" Doozy asks as they embrace.

"Your eyes are going, Doozy. There's gray in there. How is Emma Rose?"

"Heavy," Doozy says.

"How is she really?" asks Ruby.

"Not good."

"You two still betting on the horses?"

"'Course," Doozy says.

"She eating?"

"On and off. When I'm there to remind her. How you doing, Ruby?"

"No complaints," Ruby says. "Still walking every day in Central Park. At least when it's not too cold. You remember Alvin Peters?"

"Yeah. Handsome. Why? He die?"

"No! He called me up a few months ago. Living now with his son in Jackson Heights. He asked if I wanted to go to the movies. He just wants company. Sometimes we walk. Sometimes we go to a museum."

"Nice fellow," Doozy says.

The waiter comes over and they order their champagne.

"Got things on my mind today, Ruby."

"Say your piece."

"Emma Rose. Got me thinking about things. And her family. They don't do nothing for her. She has me and a few others, too, looks in on her. Getting to the point where she can't do for herself no more."

"Can't she afford someone to stay with her?" Ruby asks.

"She can. But she stubborn."

Ruby looks at Doozy. "Did you just call someone *else* stubborn?"

"Tss-tss. Me, stubborn! Tss-tss-tss-tss."

"How's your health? You feeling okay?" Ruby asks.

"So far, so good. Naw. The other thing is . . . well, 'bout money."

"You need help, Doozy? Just tell me what you need."

"Not like that! Although thank you, Ruby. No. Something I ain't never told you."

The waiter comes over with their champagne. After he pours, they order their oysters.

"To Chester," Doozy says, picking up her glass.

"To Chester," Ruby says. "So what did you want to tell me? Thought we told each other everything."

"I ain't told nobody about this. Not a soul. Just the money guy," Doozy says.

"What money guy?" Ruby asks.

"Hold your horses. Well, you remember Pat McClement?"

"Sure. Made all that money selling hamburgers. Patty O'Patties."

"Right. Always crazy about my mother," Doozy says. "For years and years. Before he got so rich *and* after. He wanted to marry her, 'cept he was married."

"And your momma was black," Ruby says.

"And she was black. And she run a house," Doozy says. "And she don't want to marry him anyway. Nice guy, she say. But she ain't marrying nobody. Not even Patty O'Patties. They stay friends after the house close down—he still thinking Miss Georgia the limit. Called her sometimes just to talk, brought her gifts. Lot of them fellows did."

"I got no earthly idea where you're going with this."

"I'm getting there. So then, 1965. That's the year Patty O'Patties, they was a big chain by then, had a whatchacallit, on the market. Stock market. One of them things. And he gave Miss Georgia one hundred shares. Told her not to touch it. And she never did. Gave it to me, she told me not to touch it. And I never did."

Ruby's mouth is hanging open, her eyes wide, her eyebrows at the top of her forehead.

"Here are your oysters, ladies. Enjoy." The waiter refills their champagne glasses.

Ruby is waving her hand by her face rapidly. "Oh Lord. Lord Lord Lord. Doozy, I . . . well, you sly old fox. That is something. Mm, mm, mm. One hundred shares, oh my good Lord! How—how—how—"

"How much now?" Doozy asks. Then she whispers. "'Bout twelve million. Over."

"Lunch is on you!"

Doozy laughs and slurps an oyster.

"Doozy! Why didn't you . . . why're you still at the Chicken Shack?"

"'Cause that's my job. And I own it."

"How d'you own it?" Ruby asks. "Thought you never spent any of the money."

"Naw, I didn't. Miss Georgia made plenty of money over the years herself. Peoples that owned the Shack wanted to retire in 1970, so my mama bought it dirt cheap."

"Well, why you're driving that old Chevette?"

"'Cause it still works. Mostly. What would I do with all that money, Ruby? Half the time I don't even believe it's real. I didn't earn it. So I never touched it, never thought about it. Money guy say do this, do that. Don't mean nothin' to me. 'Cept now I gotta think about it. Don't have no kids. That money's gotta go somewhere."

"Don't you have a will?! You're ninety-three, Doozy!"

"'Course I got a will. Spreads it around. But now I'm thinking I might do something a little different. Still want to give it to some people, thems that's not dead. Been thinking lately, maybe something else, too."

Ruby eats an oyster. "Something else like what?"

"I don't know. You good at ideas. Something you can . . . see. Or touch."

"What do you think Chester would have said?"

"What he always say: 'hot diggity dog.' Then he laugh. Then he leave it up to me. Wanna split a pan roast?"

"You know I do." Ruby says. "You want me to come up for a week?"

"You know I do," Doozy says.

Since the election, Rufus has been spending most evenings at the Elks. Tonight he is three beers in when Mange, the Lodge's Exalted Ruler, sits down next to him.

"What are you gonna do next, Rufus, now that you're out of the politics game?"

"Dunno, Mange. Dunno," Rufus says.

"You remember my cousin Alphonse?"

"Yeah, sure. Why?"

Mange says, "He got a steal at auction on a used soft-serve ice cream truck. Those things go for forty thousand for a fully-equipped rig. He was gonna run the operation, but on account of his gout he doesn't think he could handle it now. Selling it at twenty thousand. You won't find that anywhere else! Him and me was talking and your name came up—thought you might want to get in on that."

"Food trucks are cash machines these days. Ice cream? Huh. People love ice cream. Yeah, I might be interested in that."

"He told me," Mange says, "that if you were interested, he'd sell it to you with a friends-and-family discount. Eighteen thousand dollars. Lot of beautiful women with their kids, coming up to your window, you making everybody happy. It's a sweet deal, Rufus. Get it? A sweet deal."

Rufus sits up. "When could I get the truck?"

"How about tomorrow, Rufus?"

"Hooo, Emma Rose!"

No answer.

"Emma Rose?"

Doozy hurries into Emma Rose's bedroom and turns on the light.

"You scared me!" Doozy says.

"Hard to breathe," Emma Rose says.

"Hold on," Doozy says, reaching for the phone.

The paramedics are there in minutes and Emma Rose is rushed to the hospital. After they leave, Doozy looks around at Emma Rose's tidy, cheerful room, which has traces of Norell, her favorite perfume, in the air. She makes the bed and then sits down on it. Doozy picks up the phone, looks at the speed-dial choices, and pushes the one that says "Cathy."

"Cathy, it's Doozy. Your mama's on her way to the hospital . . . I don't know, Cathy. I just got here. Trouble breathing . . . Dagnabbit, them pills ain't for trouble breathing . . . Okay, listen. Your mama's going to the hospital. And I'm hanging up."

She hangs up and shakes her head. She picks up the receiver again and her bony fingers slowly stab the buttons.

"What's the matter?" Ruby asks as soon as she picks up.

"They just took her to the hospital. Trouble breathing. I got a bad feeling."

"I'll get the next train."

***

Doozy and Ruby decide to leave the hospital for lunch since Emma Rose's daughter is with her. They walk to The Shack.

Sal comes over and asks, "How is she?"

"Not so good," Doozy says.

Sal sighs. "Hiya, Ruby. Good to see you. Fried chicken?"

"Thanks, Sal," Ruby says.

Doozy and Ruby sit quietly, grief stealing around the corner.

At the next booth Trevor and Susanne are talking with Jenny and attorney Jewel Guldens about their idea for Van Dalen Park. Jewel is saying, "Guys, I love the idea. Of course. What Ivan did was despicable. But the fact is he owns the land and he'll just find another use for it."

"I hear that his Japanese funding has decided to invest in South Carolina instead," Trevor says. "He's held onto that land for a long time and my bet is he'd take a halfway decent offer and get out. He's *persona non grata* around here now."

"Look, a park in that location would be an incredible thing for AF," Jenny says. "The Council would go for it in a minute. But the town doesn't have that kind of money available. If you could find a buyer, you *might* get him to sell, but, let's face it, Ivan Borger is a miserable bastard and he could hold onto the property out of spite."

Doozy, who has been eavesdropping intently, stands up and walks in front of their table. "You want to make that a park? Where the Dutch House was? How much that land cost?"

Jewel says, "It's prime real estate near the river. Off the top of my head, I'd say he'd sell the two parcels for, maybe, a million three. That sound right, Jenny?"

"I think that's the ballpark," Jenny says. "Why do you ask?"

"I might know someone," Doozy says. "Then you got to make the park. How much that cost?"

Jewel says, "That's a tough one to answer. There are so many variables."

"Try," says Aunt Doozy.

"Maybe half a million to do it right," Jewel says, looking at Jenny. Jenny nods as Sal brings food to Doozy and Ruby's table.

"I gotta eat something. Jenny, you want to take a walk with me after lunch?"

"Love to, Aunt Doozy."

CHAPTER TWENTY-FIVE

Will Loses a Bet

Word started to spread that Campfire had bought the TV rights to "Mischief in Merryvale," Alex Barnsdorf's *New Yorker* series, but rather than rely on Arnold Falls' magpies, I tracked down the brief article in *Variety*. All I learned was that the show would be called *Merryvale*, that they expected to begin production in the summer, and casting was already underway. I check the AF community board to find there are already plenty of comments and complaints.

WhoMe?57: We're gonna lose lots of business when they block off streets for filming. This sucks!

Obviously a High Street antique dealer or restaurant owner.

UsernameMYOB: Citiots have already killed the town's character. We don't need to broadcast it to the world.

An old-timer.

DudeAbides: Town is already losing its edge.

The hipster cri de coeur.

Fleck: Why didn't Jagoda stop this?

Petalia: Save the Loomworks Garage!

Chief Williams: The Police Department is already stretched thin and we are concerned about managing this kind of ongoing disruption.

AFDPW: Public Works got concerns too. About the hit to our infrastructure. Stressed already to the max

Nurse Ratched: We already don't have enough parking near the hospital. Just sayin'

PolatinosRule: Titties

Dubsack, obviously.

Merryvale, it seemed, was less welcome than a tire factory.

The day after the *Variety* announcement, the *Times* ran a short article with some additional details. It was revealed that Giles Morris would be directing the first three episodes, that Christine Baranski would star, and that the series would shoot in Blue Birch Corners. The comments take a turn.

WhoMe?57: Blue Birch Corners' boon will be our loss. This sucks!

UsernameMYOB: Arnold Falls always had much more character than Blue Birch Corners. This must be a sick joke.

DudeAbides: AF losing its edge.

Fleck: Why didn't Jagoda fight for this?

AFDPW: Bye bye lots of overtime pay. Screwed again.

Polyjuice Potion: @Fleck Nothing to do with Jenny. Ask Rufus McDufus if he ever returned the production company's calls. (Spoiler alert: he didn't)

Petalia: Where is Merryvale?

"What happened in here?" I ask.

"What do you mean, what happened?" Bridget says.

"It's so . . . tidy. When I was here for the ACs, it didn't look like this."

"It's important to make room," Bridget says.

"Where are the airline barf bags? I love those."

"In the downstairs bathroom. They look quite festive there."

Gussie comes running down the stairs to greet me and I sit on the floor for a cuddle with him. "Gussie, did you have peanut butter for breakfast?"

"It's his favorite," Bridget says.

"What did you want to talk with me about?"

"It's important to make room," Bridget says, "Open things up."

"It is. You've moved the dinosaur teeth."

"The Cretaceous period isn't one of Trudy's favorites. She's prefers Mid-Century Modern. There's still a jar of them by the front door."

"Good job saving Martha Washington," I say.

"Thank you. You would have been shocked by her sweater. But that's—"

"Maybe you can start a collection of First Lady hats or something like that. Now that you have some room for new things."

"*Exactly!* That's what I wanted to say to you. Time to make room for something new," Bridget says.

"You want me to build you more bookshelves?"

"No, no, that's not it."

"Oh, you want me to go all Marie Kondo on you! I can do that."

"No, Jeebie. What I am trying to say is, my home is full. I only need to make room. It's not about *stuff*. Do you see?"

"I, uh . . . no. Lost the plot."

"When I came over a couple of weeks ago to plan the Chaplin rescue, you said to me something about beefing up security protocols. 'Can't have just anyone turning up here' were your words."

"That's because you didn't knock or ring the doorbell."

"Life doesn't always knock, Jeebie."

"Opportunity knocks," I say.

"Jeebie. Stop that flippancy. Who's 'turning up'? Tell me. And if they do, will you let them in? Anybody home?"

"You didn't ask me over to help with your house, did you?"

"My God you can be a dense thicket," she says.

Bridget actually escorts me off the premises.

I've just stepped out of the shower when I hear my cell ringing. I wrap a towel around my waist and grab the phone from the dresser.

"Hi, Jeebie. This is Will Shaffer."

"Hi," I say.

"I hope it's okay to call you. Nelle gave me your number."

"Oh, she did? Where did you run into her?"

"I didn't run into her. We're friends on Facebook. I had an idea I wanted to run by you. Do you want to have a drink with me? Tonight, maybe?"

There's a phone app that will take any song you have and slow it way down so that you can hear with clarity what's going on from note to note. I need something like that right now—and more time to reflect on the fact that Will is on the phone, that Nelle has given him my number, that she has not told me this, and that they're Facebook friends. And when did all this friending happen, I would like to know? And what could he want to talk with me about? And does Nelle already know what that is? And should I consider that a betrayal or am I being ridiculous and of course she only wants the best for me, but, come on, you have to admit it seems like something sneaky is going on, and how many other sneaky things are going on of the 'Don't Tell Jeebie' variety? I include Bridget Helen Roberts in that! And Nelle and I have only known each other for two months although it does feel like a lifetime, and you never know about people, do you? And do I want to have a drink with him tonight? And am I overthinking things? Okay, obviously yes, but under-thinking things, well, that way lies danger for a control freak, and I might be a bit on that side of the spectrum. Is under-thinking a word? Sounds made up. And it's cold standing here in just my towel. He's seen me in my boxer shorts, when he was here for the fire, and now he's on the phone, thanks to Nelle giving him my number without mentioning it.

"Sure," I say, clearing my throat. "Want to meet at Argos at seven-thirty?"

"Great, see you then," Will says.

"Okay, bye, uh . . ."

"Will."

"I know your name. I know your name."

I sit for a moment and then dial Ms. Clark.

"Hello, *Lanelle Clark*," I say.

"Hello, *Jeffrey Walker*." There's a pause. "What can I do for you?"

"*Oh, I think you know,*" I say witheringly.

"Let me guess. Will called you."

"Correct."

"And you want to know how he got your number."

"*Way* ahead of you. You are *friends* on *Facebook!*" I say with just the right amount of dudgeon. "Are you *laughing?*"

"Yeah," Nelle says.

"Thanks to you, Will has my number."

"Everyone's got your number, Jeebie. Especially Will."

"Witty, very witty. When did he friend you?"

"He didn't. I friended him," Nelle says.

"*You* friended *him?*" I sputter.

"Jeebie, you're behaving like you're in high school. May I remind you how old you are? In reality?"

"No," I say.

"Are you going out for a drink with him?" Nelle asks.

"I'm sure you already know the answer to that."

"Jeebie! Stop it!"

"We're going out tonight," I say.

"Good. Have fun. Gotta get to work," she says and hangs up.

Since it's not too cold this evening, the back terrace at Argos is open and the outdoor fireplace is going. We have it to ourselves. We sit on the couch facing the fire. Manny comes out to take our order. I have a glass of red, Will orders porter.

"What is porter, anyway?" I ask.

Will explains it to me and he seems to know his beer. It turns out he's a home brewer, too.

"Did you finish your application to Cornell?" I ask.

"Just about done," he says. "I'm cutting it close."

"I thought you said December first?"

"That's only two weeks away," Will says.

Manny brings us our drinks.

"Cheers," I say.

"Cheers. So, what I wanted to talk to you about is this," he says with his green eyes and his cowlick. "I got a call yesterday out of the blue from an editor at Burgess Books. She asked me if I'd ever thought of turning my monkeys into some kind of book. I told her no, because I never had, and she said she thought they could make a funny, illustrated book and would I consider it? I said 'Sure' but I've never written a book and she said no one's written a book until they have."

"Will, that's wonderful! Good for you! You should do it. Would it be a book for kids or adults?"

"No idea. I just started doing the illustrations for fun and then I thought I could maybe sell a few and send some money to the Goodall Foundation. The first monkey . . . the first monkey I ever did was of you."

"Really? The one in the tux?"

"Yeah, I put it in a drawer because I didn't know if you would like it. I drew it not because you look like a monkey because you don't at all. But you're mischievous like one. Funny. Sly."

I feel pleasantly warm from the flattery.

"Anyway, this book idea seems pretty far-fetched but she asked me to think about it so I'm thinking about it. She also said I might want to work with a partner. They could match me up or maybe I knew someone. And I thought . . ." Will hesitates for a moment. "I thought that maybe with your humor and intelligence and . . . your way with words . . . that you might want to work on it with me."

No, absolutely not, I think to myself, but my mouth has different ideas and from it come the words "I think I'd like that."

Will smiles. "I thought you'd say no."

"My brain said no. My mouth said yes."

"Then I thank your mouth," Will says.

We watch the fire for a moment.

"How's G. I. Joe?" I ask.

"Who?"

"FBI G. I. Joe," I say.

"He asked me out." Will says. "I wanted to be sitting at your table."

One of the logs in the fireplace splits.

"If you could be anywhere in the world right now," Will asks, "where would you be? And you can't say 'here'—that's corny."

"I would say . . . Mexico City."

"Not what I expected," he says. "Why Mexico City?"

"Because there's a small hotel there that is the warmest and most welcoming I've ever been to. I could have stayed forever."

"Is that why you were interested in *Auberge of the Flowering Hearth*?"

I look at him. "I hadn't thought of that. Maybe so."

"It's really wonderful," Will says.

"What is?"

"The book."

"You've read it?"

"I just finished it."

"I should read it," I say.

"I thought you'd read it," he says.

"I . . . I was babbling."

"I noticed," he says.

I look straight into his green eyes and I am suddenly tumbling.

"I won't, I won't," I whisper.

"You won't what?" Will whispers back.

"Forget my shoes," and then we kiss and kiss some more.

When I open my eyes, I notice Sofia, Madora, and Manny at the window, looking out at us. Sofia's arms are up in the air giving the victory sign.

"I'm really glad you said yes about the book,' Will says. "Except . . ."

"Except what?"

"Except I just lost a ten-dollar bet to Nelle," he says and smiles that beautiful smile.

"Everyone seems to have been way ahead of me," I say.

"*Everyone*," Nelle agrees.

Nelle had wanted to go for a backroads drive, so she left work early and we're tootling around in her car along the far reaches of Queechy.

"I guess that's what Bridget was going on about," I say. "She asked me over a couple of days ago and kept talking about making more room and then she threw me out of her house. I thought she was talking about bookshelves. Everyone seems to know a lot about this."

"That's Arnold Falls," Nelle says. "You'll get used to it."

"Very funny. Heard you won ten dollars."

"Girl's gotta live."

"Will and I didn't sleep together," I say.

"What's your point?" Nelle asks.

"What do you mean, 'What's my point?' My point is we didn't sleep together. We met at Argos and he asked me to work on a book involving his monkeys and I said yes and you are ten dollars richer. He's also a home-brewer. So that's where things are."

"Jeebie."

"Nelle."

"Jeebie, that is not 'where things are.' That is your brain firing random neurons and verbalizing the results."

"Sometimes you speak in riddles," I say.

"You know perfectly well what I'm talking about. I can read you like a book. And yet you still think you can charm and deflect *me*. And don't sit there in a snit for ten minutes while you weigh your various options. If you're going to do that, I'll put on some music."

After I moment, I say, "He's great. I like being with him. I like listening to him. I like his voice. I like looking at him. I like his smile. I like making him laugh. He's smart and sweet and different. And I . . . trust him."

"*That's* what's got you spooked," Nelle says. "You trust him."

"Yeah. How about Nils?"

"I would say many of the same things about him."

"But?" I ask. "Black and white? Let's face it, you can't get much whiter than the Nyqvists."

"That's the truth. But, no, that's not it. It's more . . . with Nils, you don't just get Nils. He comes with a big, tight family."

"I see what you mean. You never had that. Hard to navigate?"

"Right," she says.

"What terrible problems we have!"

"I know," she says.

After a moment, I say, "Nils is *really* hot."

"Hooooooo, lawsy, is he hot!" she says, cracking herself up.

"I could go for a Darlene burger, what about you?"

Nelle slams on the breaks, still laughing, pulls a U-ie and heads toward the bridge. Just then, I get a text.

Emma Rose has died.

CHAPTER TWENTY-SIX

Milestones

E ven though she had lived in Manhattan for decades, Ruby always felt part of Arnold Falls or maybe it was that Arnold Falls always felt a part of her, and never more so than right now with Doozy next to her, utterly still, seated in Our Lady of Lourdes. Ruby looks around to the closed casket up front, she looks across the church and notices there are no empty seats, she turns around to glance at the faces behind her, some still familiar. She puts her hand over Doozy's hand.

Emma Rose had died early Thursday morning, just after five. She and Doozy were sitting at her bedside when she stopped breathing. They had gotten the nurse but Emma Rose was gone.

After a homily, Communion, and prayers, the casket is brought down the aisle and out of the church. They proceed to the cemetery behind Our Lady of Lourdes where Emma Rose is laid to rest next to her husband, Clayton.

"So many people loved her," Ruby says to Doozy.

"Yes, they did," Doozy says.

———

Leaving the church, Doozy and Ruby walk slowly, in silence, each wearing a pink rose pinned to their overcoats.

"Let's go to the Dutch House. Where it was," Doozy says.

As they make their way down the steps toward the waterfront, they meet Luther and Elma Green and their two children.

"How do, Doozy, Ruby," Luther says. "Very sorry to hear about Emma Rose."

"So sorry for your loss," Elma says.

"Thank you. How you doin' young ladies?" Doozy says to the girls.

"Fine, Aunt Doozy!" they say in unison.

Doozy asks, "You get into the new house, where's it? Old Post?"

"We're moving in this weekend."

Ruby asks Elma quietly, "How are the children dealing with it?"

"Oh, you know," Elma says, "they bounce back."

"You coming to the big Thanksgiving dinner?" Doozy asks.

"We'll be there," Luther says. "Lot to be thankful for."

Doozy and Ruby continue down the stairs and around the bend to see all that is left of the Dutch House: a pile of bricks and rubble.

"Mm, mm, mm," Ruby says, shaking her head. "What a damn shame."

\

"It is," Doozy agrees. "Oh, dagnabbit," Doozy says with a long sigh. "So, Van Dalen Park, Ruby."

"I can picture it," Ruby says.

"Me, too," Doozy says.

"Doozy! I have an idea! You're paying for this park, so it's yours in a way."

"Naw, it's a gift. That don't make it mine. Opposite."

"Okay, but maybe you could suggest something for the park," Ruby says.

"Like what?"

"What about a memorial to Chester?"

"That's a good one, Ruby! Chester and the whole 761st. Maybe a rose garden, too."

Jenny is on her way to a meeting with the City Clerk. As she's about to go into the building, Dubsack is walking out.

"Hello, Mayor!

"Mayor-*elect*, Dubsack."

"Congratulations on a hard-fought campaign," Dubsack says, extending his hand, which Jenny shakes.

"The blueberry won—isn't that amazing?" Jenny says. "Especially since hardly anyone knew my real name when I had so few campaign signs."

"I wouldn't know about that," Dubsack says.

"How's your chlamydia?" asks Jenny.

"I didn't have—" Dubsack says, and then he realizes, turning to look at her with some admiration. "You!"

"I wouldn't know about that," Jenny says.

"So, Jenny. We've known each other since we were kids."

Look at those wide-eyes. He's working her, she knows

he's working her, he knows she knows he's working her. "And?" Jenny says.

"You know, if you ever need anything."

"How many dead people voted this time?"

"Not that many," Dubsack says. "Hard to get them to turn out in an off-year election."

Jenny laughs in spite of herself, shaking her head. She says, "You knocked over gravestones in the cemetery two Halloweens ago."

"I did, yeah." Dubsack says.

"You're a gambler," she says, "and a bookie."

"We prefer 'wager concierge.'"

"You once put maple syrup in Phil Fleck's gas tank."

"Come on, the guy's annoying."

"You cut down the rose bushes by City Hall."

"Coulda been."

"You stenciled 'Danger: cooties' all over the elementary school's brand-new jungle gym."

"Ounce of prevention," Dubsack says.

"You ran naked through the Big Y."

"Forgot about that one!"

"People who saw you will never forget it," Jenny says. "How about doing an honest day's work?"

"I am employed by the county of Queechy," he says.

"Really? And what is it you do for them?"

"Whatever they need me to do."

"Do you have a job title? Do you receive a weekly paycheck?" Jenny asks.

"No, no, cash only," Dubsack says. "So let me know if I can be of service."

"With a resume like that, I'd be a fool not to. I'll keep what you said in mind."

"Thanks, Mayor. Elect."

CHAPTER TWENTY-SEVEN

The Bay Leaf Debacle

"How are things going with Will?"

Duncan likes to get right the point. He's called as I'm roasting Brussels sprouts for Thanksgiving tomorrow.

"We've spent a lot of time together this past week."

"And?"

"And things are good. Great, actually."

"Marybeth!" Duncan yells. "Jeebie says things are great with Will."

"You could wait to get off the phone before gossiping about your favorite charming mess," I say, though I'm touched by his enthusiasm. "Wait, I buried the lede!"

"Will's not the lede?"

"Yes, he is, but you'll love this: I spoke with my friend Meg at *Epicurious* and Annie is in big trouble! Did you watch her special?"

"No way."

"I didn't either."

"So Meg told me that, thanks to all the publicity, the show got a bump in the ratings even though Chaplin didn't appear. Anyway, as Annie is making the stuffing, she goes on a rant about bay leaves, claiming they're a scam, did nothing for any recipe ever, and says, 'Bay leaves should be tossed into the dustbin of culinary history.'"

"That's it?"

"No, that's not it! Big trouble!"

"Marybeth! Get on the phone! Annie slagged bay leaves and now she's in big trouble!"

She gets on the phone. "What?!"

"On her special," I say. "Called them a scam. The next day, something called the Bay Leaf Growers Consortium wages a fierce attack on Annie and her comments, quoting 'serious chefs' defending the leaf's uses. Meg said the BLGC turned out to be surprisingly adept at social media and just battered O'Dell relentlessly and anyone else who might doubt the wonders of the bay leaf. Annie was forced to issue a full-throated apology from Chiang Mai, where she and her husband are now."

Duncan and Marybeth are hooting and hollering.

"Wait, there's more. Apparently, the BLGC emailed Annie a contract to give the keynote speech at their annual, five-day convention taking place in Buffalo. In February. They've chosen her to be the worldwide Ambassador for Bay Leaves. She's always mocking her sister for being the Ambassador to Andorra, and now she's the *Ambassador for Bay Leaves*."

CHAPTER TWENTY-EIGHT

To the Next Chapter

Rufus gets all the permits needed for Sweet Deal, as he decides to call the truck, rushed through, thanks to friends in the right places. He's feeling good this gray Monday before Thanksgiving, pulling the truck onto High Street for the lunchtime crowd, just up the block from City Hall.

As he raises the flip-up window, it begins to hail heavily, dispersing the few people on High Street. Rufus quickly lowers the window and ducks back into the truck.

He looks around at his new surroundings, listening to the hail pound the top of the truck, and wonders if he should have done a business plan. Rufus pulls the lever on the vanilla soft-serve and fills a paper cup, putting on several spoonfuls of sprinkles. He sits there rhythmically spooning up the ice cream, staring at his reflection on the back of the flip-up window. By the time he finishes, he is shivering, and drives the truck back home.

"That smells so good, Trudy!" Kenny says. "What are you making?"

"They're my mom's Königsberger *klopse*. Meatballs. I have to say, they're divine."

"Prussian, huh?"

"Exactly," Trudy says. "Bridget, do you have a slotted spoon?

"Yes, in the bottom drawer. A small collection of them. More wine, Kenny?"

"Yes, please. I had another idea."

"Tell!"

"What if we did a monthly event at the carriage house— a talk, with guest speakers? A broad range but having to do with art and design, and how it impacts our lives. Why we preserve. Historical periods in art and furniture. Things like that.

"That's great!" Trudy says, bringing the klopse to the table.

Bridget is putting the salad she made on small plates. "That's a wonderful idea. Almost like a salon," she says, bringing over the salads. They sit down at the table.

"Cheers," says Kenny. "Thanks for having me over."

Gussie and Delphy walk in with their noses twitching.

"My God! These meatballs!" Kenny says. "They are off-the-charts!"

"Glad you like them," Trudy says. "I love the flavors— they really say home to me."

"Klopse 1, Swedish meatballs 0," Kenny says.

"That reminds me!" Bridget says. "I heard today that the Nyqvists are interested in buying a building on High Street."

Trudy looks at Kenny. "They could buy yours!"

Kenny nods. "I ran into the Nyqvists after Emma Rose's funeral and we talked about it. Nils heard I might want to sell. He told me they want to open a storefront for his sister, Stella, to sell her baked goods. They already asked Elma Green if she would bake her apple pies for the shop and she said yes. I think it sounds wonderful. But we'll see."

"That does sound wonderful. Let's drink to the next chapter," Trudy says.

"To the next chapter," they say.

The next day, Bridget and Trudy are walking Gussy and Delphy in the cemetery. Delphy is moving slowly and Gussy has adjusted his pace to hers, sniffing the many piles of brown leaves until she catches up.

"What would you think," Bridget asks, "if I got a Martha Washington for myself?"

Trudy stops and looks at her. "That you're as batty as everyone says."

"Oh, they don't say that," Bridget says. "They say I'm charmingly eccentric, an interesting character, that I'm never-a-dull-moment."

"No, I've never heard anyone say any of those things," Trudy says, then sees that Bridget has taken this more seriously than she intended. She puts her arm around her. "What would you do with Martha?"

"I don't know exactly. I just think she would be a nice friend. Low-maintenance, good listener, never has a cross word for anyone. But I'd like one without sinus problems. The other one had sinus problems."

"Bridget, tell me you're joking."

"No, she had Afrin in her purse."

"I mean about getting her at all."

"Half," Bridget says. "Maybe she could just sit on the porch—you know, put her in charge of neighborhood watch."

Trudy considers this for a moment. There is something . . . what is in the air here? Delphy has stopped to rest, so they pause to look around this beautiful, forlorn cemetery. So peaceful, until she hears a cracking. "What was that noise?"

"Corn Nut," Bridget says. "Want one?"

"Bridget, are your teeth really up for those things? As for neighborhood watch, don't you think there are better first ladies for that? What's wrong with Mary Todd Lincoln?"

"I don't know. I never really considered her. Although, Mary Todd held séances in the White House, so I'd say she's a contender."

"Let's put her in the 'maybe' column," Trudy says. "Florence Harding?"

"Not sure about the vibe. She may have poisoned Warren G." Bridget says.

"I don't think he was any great prize."

"No. I suppose not. What about Bess Truman?"

"Oh, no, Bridget, I think she was a handful. She sent her laundry from the White House back to Kansas City for cleaning."

"She wouldn't!" Bridget says, genuinely shocked.

"Oh, yes, she did."

"What would you do," Bridget asks, "if I sent my laundry back to Ashtabula?"

"I'd send your remains back with it. I'd say Martha Washington is looking better and better." She begins shaking.

"Trudy! What is it?"

"I've . . . I've . . . "

"What, Trudy?"

"Oh, my God! I've caught your crazy!"

"No, Trudy, it's not me! It's Arnold Falls! Highly contagious!"

"You're right!" gasps Trudy. "Prognosis negative!"

Delphy looks up as Trudy shakes with laughter. When she catches her breath, Trudy asks, "Bridget, aren't *I* all the things you say about Martha? I'm a good listener, reasonably low-maintenance. And I don't trash people unless it's deserved."

"Yes," Bridget says. "You are all those things."

"We should get married," Trudy says.

Now it's Bridget's turn to gasp.

"Bridget, will you marry me?"

"Yes, Trudy! Of course I will! When?"

"Soon. Whenever you want," Trudy says.

Jenny is staring at Ivan Borger, who is clinging to his office chair, his comb-over a fizzle of keratin and delusion.

He's the only person sitting. Jenny has wrapped her arm around Doozy's shoulder and they're standing side-by-side next to Judge Harschly, Jewel Guldens, and Chief Williams. They've come to confront Ivan like a tribunal delivering a verdict.

"I can do what I want with land I own," Ivan says.

Jenny says, "Ivan, you know perfectly well that that is not the whole story. There are all kind of restrictions on land use. Not to mention your obligations to the community.

"Community!" Ivan scoffs. "I've gotten two death threats!"

"Three," says Judge Harschly. "I'd like to kill you myself, Ivan."

"Chief, do you hear that?" Ivan pleads.

"Four," says Chief Williams.

"Five," says Jewel.

"Six," says Doozy. "And another thing. You're banned from the Shack."

"You can't ban me!" Ivan says.

"I can. Just did. I ban you," Doozy says.

"I'll talk to Sal," Ivan says.

"Go right ahead. Sal don't own it. *I* do."

"*You* own it? You know how I love that fried chicken!"

"Enough of this bippety-bop. Shoulda thought about that before. The peoples in this town don't want you here no more. Arnold Falls is changing and you part of that change. You know what a snowbird is? That's you. You flyin' out this winter. But you ain't flyin' back."

"Ivan," Jenny says. "You ripped down the Dutch House but you didn't have the say-so from the town to do that. The town wanted that house *saved*. You wanted to put a goddamn tire factory in the middle of our community, next to the Hudson River. How did you expect people to act?"

"The injunction was still in effect," Judge Harschly says. "I could make you rebuild it, brick by brick. And if I had my way, you'd do all the work yourself."

"Your Japanese money has dried up, Ivan," Jewel says. "No one wants to do business with you."

"Here's your best offer and your only offer," Doozy says. "I'm ninety-three, so it won't last long. Go 'head, Jewel, tell him and let's get outta here."

CHAPTER TWENTY-NINE

Thanksgiving

We luck out with the weather: It's in the mid-thirties on Thanksgiving morning and the sun is bright and warming.

High Street is hopping when I arrive outside Argos. A group of us has volunteered to try and pull off whatever this parade is supposed to be. Arnold Falls is always up for a parade, but we've never had one, that I know of, on Thanksgiving. The national reports on Chaplin must account, in part, for the size of today's crowds. Our sidewalks are as close to clogged as I've ever seen them.

Queechy Caliente is rehearsing, Jenny arrives and goes to test the sound system she'll use to give a short kickoff speech, and shopkeepers are opening up their stores to lend support as needed. Walkie-talkies are distributed, two golf carts arrive to ferry anyone who needs ferrying, and Fair Trade has been nice enough to set up a table of complimentary coffee and doughnuts. The vintage fire truck arrives followed by a line of private vintage cars and several floats deftly rustled up by Chesty Biddle. Ginger Abrams of the *Observer* has her notepad out.

Maybe it's the sunshine, maybe it's Chaplin, or maybe it's the first woman mayor and the end of the tire factory, but Arnold Falls seems in the mood to celebrate. Just after eleven, Jenny stands on a crate and gives them one more reason. She announces the financing of a new park on the former site of the Dutch House to be called Van Dalen Park, funded by a private citizen who wishes to remain anonymous. "We have preliminary agreement from the seller and with any luck, we'll have a groundbreaking in early spring. We have so much to be thankful for."

And we're off! The mariachi band plays "Cielito Lindo" as they begin marching. Grand Marshal Chaplin leads the way, followed closely by Serena and Venus, along with the Pluggy's gang to keep the Naggs on track. Theo Nyqvist makes his entrance from Ledyard Street on stilts, dressed as Charlie Chaplin's Little Tramp. He's impossibly cute.

I'm walking with the Friends of Chaplin group—the sun feels good on my face, the crowds are cheering, and the mariachi music matches everyone's high spirits. The whole thing is an unlikely bliss-out. Chaplin seems blissed out, too, having been born, as he was, to lead a parade. Head held high, feathers fanned, strutting and gobbling, turning his head left and right to acknowledge the crowds. He is eating it up. People shout, "We love you, Chaplin!" and Chaplin gobbles back.

We're about halfway along the parade route when Chaplin spots Bridget. He stops and yelps. Venus and Serena stop. Everybody behind them stops. Chaplin yelps again and then runs over to Bridget. "Hellooooo, Chaplin," she says.

Chaplin begins rubbing his head against her.

"No, no, Chaplin! We can't go on like this!" Bridget cries.

When Chaplin doesn't stop, Bridget runs across the street to the opposite sidewalk but Chaplin is right behind her. She turns around and sees him, makes a cartoonish "Aah!" sound, and hightails it down the sidewalk, ahead of the parade, Chaplin in hot pursuit.

Since no one can think of a quick fix to this (and no one really wants to), the parade continues on. Queechy Caliente is playing "Las Alazanas," which is the very mariachi tune you want when you're being chased by a turkey.

Trudy comes up to me and says, "Jeebie, should I help her?"

"Are you kidding? They're both having the time of their lives."

Bridget is now backed into a doorway. "Officer Velez!" she cries. "I need your assistance!"

Officer Velez says, "Isn't it nice to be pursued for love?"

"But he's a turkey!" Bridget says.

"Judge not."

And now Chaplin is rubbing his head on Bridget's backside. "AH!" Bridget cries, bolting upright.

"Best parade ever," I say to Trudy.

As soon as the Raffertys, owners of Dragon Hill, heard about the town-wide Thanksgiving dinner idea, they offered their very large barn, which had been turned into an event space several years ago.

The sky has clouded over since the parade, giving Arnold Falls a wintry cast, but the lights are on in the barn and at least three dozen people are inside, cooking in the kitchen, setting up the tables, dance floor, and turkey pen, testing the sound system, and putting up little white lights. Noly Spinoly, having pulled off the parade, is troubleshooting and keeping things on track. Everyone's chatting as they work to the sound of Smokey Robinson and the Miracles playing over the sound system, thanks to yours truly.

The large kitchen is crowded. Some have brought over finished dishes but others are working away over hot stoves and sharp knives. Given that this is Chaplin Day in addition to Thanksgiving, the dinner organizers had decided to keep the meal meatless. I walk into the kitchen and smell the butter and onions being sautéed by Madora, and that particular aroma always makes me happy. In the corner near the pantry, Elma Green looks to be making at least a dozen cinnamon crumble apple pies, assisted by her two daughters, who are taking the work very seriously. Marybeth and Duncan have dropped off baskets and baskets of fall veggies and big wheels of Riverwind cheese. There is a line of choppers, including Judge Harschly and his wife, Elena, working through the leeks, carrots, onions, and string beans.

Doozy is saying to Elena, "I guess the judge is useless in the kitchen."

"Outside of his courtroom," Elena says, "there's no known use for him."

"Thank you, dear," Judge Harschly says, kissing her cheek.

Mrs. Patel, who is standing with a furrowed brow at the

kitchen island, calls to me, "Jeebie, please come and taste this."

I've only eaten Mrs. Patel's Gujarati home-cooking once, but I dream of it sometimes. I smell basmati rice and see *dal*, *pakoras*, and what I think is a vegetable curry.

"Please taste this *kadhi*."

"Is that a curry?"

"It is a yogurt curry and it should be a little sour. Is it too spicy?"

"No! It's delicious. Oh, that's delicious!"

"Okay, good. Thank you."

I walk out into the big room and Nelle is in the bar area, unpacking the cases of wine donated by the wine store. Sofia and Manny are at her side, dealing with ice, glasses, and soft drinks. Lust for Crust fired up their ovens this morning just to bake dozens of baguettes and olive loaves for dinner. They're piled up in baskets by the wait station and I stand for a moment inhaling the yeasty smell.

Will is on duty at the fire house until two and he'll be here after that. My phone rings and I hope it's him calling but I see it's Bridget.

"Hello, Bridget Helen Roberts," I say.

"Hellooooo, Jeebie," she says in her low voice.

"Are you and Chaplin having a cigarette at some hot-sheets motel?"

"Jeebie, you're always so amusing," she says. "I'd pat your cheek if I could."

"I hate that, you know."

"I know," Bridget says. "Listen, do you know if Judge Harschly is going to be at the dinner?"

"What have you done now?"

"Nothing. Do you know?"

"I do. As a matter of fact, he and his wife are already here, working in the kitchen."

"Would you ask him something for me?"

"Sure," I say, walking back into the kitchen.

"Would you ask him if he'd be willing to marry Trudy and me this afternoon during the meal? We'd like to have a pop-up wedding."

"Bridget! Congratulations!"

"Thank you, dear."

"Hold on a second. Judge Harschly, Bridget Roberts is on the phone and she wants to know if you would marry her and Trudy Bettenauer this afternoon?"

The judge continues chopping carrots. "She on or off the Clagger?"

"Tell him I'm off at the moment," Bridget says.

"She says 'off.'"

Judge Harschly scoops his carrot slices into a bowl. "In that case, it would be my pleasure. I assume Chaplin is heartbroken."

"Bridget, he says yes, but he's worried that Chaplin will be heartbroken."

"We'll always have Paris," Bridget says.

When I relay that, it gets a solid, barking laugh out of Judge Harschly. I find Noly and tell her to add a wedding to her to-do list. People will start arriving at three, which means we've got about ninety minutes to finish everything. I let people know in my best *Great British Bake-Off* voice to pick up the pace.

The table setup crew seems to be the most behind, so I lend them a hand. When I look up next, we've got the tables finished and Will is walking toward me.

"Hi," he says, and kisses me.

"Hi."

"Did any apples arrive?" Will asks.

"Three bushels," I say. "Wait, did *you*—"

Will smiles.

"Are those Cox Orange Pippins?"

"Affirmative. I asked Ed and Louisa and they were happy to do it. Now, what can I do to help?"

"Walk with me to the coat room."

"Okay," he says.

We emerge a few minutes later well-kissed.

Nelle looks up from the bar and smiles. "Hi, Will," she says.

"Hey, Nelle. Happy Thanksgiving."

"You, too."

"Are you singing later?" Will asks.

"Three songs."

"She won't tell you what they are, though," I say. "She's got to have her little secrets."

"I'm singing Esperanza Spalding's 'I Know You Know,' 'Ain't No Mountain High Enough,' and 'Better Things.'"

"Ray Davies. Nice," Will says.

"I'm having trouble remembering why I ever had fond feelings for you, Lanelle."

"Beats me," she says. "Maybe it's because I'm singing 'Ain't No Mountain High Enough' for you?"

I try to look unmollified. "Whose version?"

"*My* version," Nelle says.

"Based on whose version?" I ask.

"Your skinny little Miss Ross' version. Okay? Except in my version, the backup singers don't do all the heavy lifting."

Jenny interrupts this abomination. "I'm going to offer Deputy Mayor to Noly. Don't you think? She can pull anything off."

I nod. "Good choice, Jenny. Perfect choice."

Proving the point, Noly walks over to us and says, "So, the order is Nelle's set, then the wedding, then the band from Traitor's. Is that okay with you, Nelle?"

"Absolutely," Nelle says.

"Nelle!"

Nelle looks to the front of the barn. "Auntie! Uncle Damon! What are you *doing* here?!" She runs to hug them. "I thought you were going to be in Cape May."

"We were. A little birdie changed our minds," Myra says, looking at me.

"How did you do that?!" Nelle asks me.

"Myra and I are friends on Facebook," I say "Two can play that game."

She whispers in my ear, "I adore you."

"As you should," I say.

The rest of the Traitor's house band has assembled and is doing a quick run-through. They start playing "I've Got You Under My Skin" and it gives me a rush of pleasure even before Will points to the band, to me, and back to himself.

Dubsack walks in with a shopping cart he's stolen from the Big Y and shouts, "Clagger Jell-O shots! Get yer Clagger Jell-O shots!" which he begins unloading onto the bar.

"Jeebie?"

"Yes, Mayor-Elect?"

"Would you grab two of Dubsack's Clagger shots and join me for a moment in the hayloft?"

"Uh, sure, okay," I say.

Once we're sitting at the top of the stairs, I wait for her to explain, but she's just looking at me.

"You're freaking me out a little," I say.

"I'm freaked out a little," she says. "Jeebie. Do you

remember when you first brought up me running for mayor?"

"Of course."

"I said I was intrigued by the idea and I might have an ulterior motive. And you said—"

"I said, 'Everybody has an ulterior motive.'"

"Right. Wilky is a six-year-old orphaned boy from Haiti," she says. "And it just became official yesterday. He's going to be my son."

Well, I just lose it. We sob into each other's shoulders.

"You are going to be the best mother." Holding up my Jello-shot, I say, "To Wilky," and we clink and laugh and cry all over again.

"I have a thousand questions," I say.

"Tomorrow," she says.

We walk unsteadily back down the stairs and into the maelstrom. Before I can truly process what Jenny has told me, Tishy Mustelle arrives wearing a sweater festooned with plastic cranberries, proudly bearing a tray of Pickle Stretcher Salad, which she describes to Dubsack as "dill pickles, olives and lime gelatin." It is a hideous, neon-green clump, but maybe it will go well with the Jell-O shots. Besides, Tishy seems pleased with it, so I go over and say, "Tishy, that looks delicious! And I bet yours is the only one! Let's take that right into the kitchen."

"It's a family favorite," she says.

"I'm sure it is."

Tishy grabs a Jell-O shot from Dubsack and we head to the kitchen, as Sal carries in two large baking trays.

"And, Jeebie . . . " Tishy says.

"Yeah?"

"Rufus is parked outside in his ice cream truck."

I look for Jenny, who's talking with Noly near the kitchen, and relay the info about Rufus.

"Tell me he's not selling ice cream today?" she asks.

"My guess is he wants to come in but he doesn't know if he's welcome."

"Is his family here?"

"No. It's only been a few days since the funeral."

"For God's sake, Rufus," Jenny says.

Madora calls from the doorway, "Jeebie, can you help me?" I follow her back into the kitchen, delighted to note she's made her penne alla vodka, which I eat at least once a month at Argos and never tire of. "Can you help me get the pasta into serving dishes?"

Davis walks into the kitchen and walks over to give me a hug.

"Hey, Jeebie! Happy Thanksgiving!"

"Happy Thanksgiving. Pumphrey's is closed and you're here to work anyway?" I taste the penne sauce with my finger and Madora hits my arm with a dishtowel. "Delicious."

"I didn't bring anything so I thought I'd lend a hand," says Davis.

"Perfect timing," I say. "We could definitely use help getting the stuff out onto the buffet."

"Your parents here?" he asks.

"No, they're in Santa Fe with what's-her-name, my sisternal unit. Where's your girlfriend?"

"She's in Ithaca with her family," Davis says.

Will walks up to me and wipes off a bit of penne sauce next to my lips.

"Davis, do you know Will?"

"Uh, yeah. You came into Pumphrey's last month."

"Yeah, I was with G. I. Joe," Will says, smiling. "Happy Thanksgiving."

"Happy Thanksgiving. Lots to be grateful for," Davis says.

"Nelle is looking for you, Jeebie," Will says.

I walk out to Nelle, who's standing at her microphone by the band. "What does her ladyship require?"

"I want to know if I should talk between songs."

"No. Quite enough from you," I say.

"Really?"

"Just say, 'Happy Thanksgiving, everyone,' and keep it moving."

"Okay, that sounds right," she says. "And Bridget just called me. I'm singing 'Dedicated to You' from the piano for the first dance. Noly knows."

People in Arnold Falls make it a point to come late for meetings and early for parties, so there's a steady trickle of guests and it's only quarter to three.

Ginger Abrams brings in matzo brei, Mimi Unter der Treppe has made poutine ("Vegetarian," Mimi says. "Mushrooms for the gravy"), Wanda Velez carries in a giant bowl of pisto, and the Hubbles baked pot brownies with the word "weed" thoughtfully iced on each square. Jenny walks Rufus inside, hands him a Jell-O shot, and points him in Dubsack's direction.

"Look, the Animatronics are here," I say to Nelle.

"Stop calling them that," she says. "You're too young to be so bitter."

"At least I'm too young for *something*."

Greetings all around from the murmuration of Nyqvists. Nils gives a kiss to Nelle and a hug to me. They've brought pumpkin-shaped piñatas that they have *made*. Filled with Swedish candies, I guarantee you.

Someone taps me on the shoulder and I turn around to see Juliet, everyone's favorite librarian, arm in arm with Alec Barnsdorf.

"Oh. *Oh!*" I say.

"Hi, Jeebie, Happy Thanksgiving."

"Hi, Juliet. Same to you."

"Do you know Alec Barnsdorf?" she asks.

"Yes, we've . . . traveled together."

He gives me a hug. It's not a good hug—he's clearly not a hugger—but I am pleasantly surprised at the effort.

Will comes up to me and hands me a glass of wine. Juliet looks at him standing next to me and says, "*Oh!* Hi, Will."

"Oh, hi, Juliet."

Juliet says, "Will, this Alec Barnsdorf. Alec, Will Schaffer."

Will says, "*Oh!*"

"Oh, you're Will Shaffer? I love your monkeys!" Alec says.

"Oh, thanks! I'm a big fan of your writing. But I'm not sure I agree with you on Rational Choice Theory."

"Oh?" says Alec.

"It's not a good explanation for love," Will says, smiling at me.

Alec looks at Juliet. "You may be right."

The Minuet of Ohs comes to end.

Then, as if someone flipped a light-switch, it's a party. There's a processional of the Pluggies, Chaplin, Venus, and Serena, who arrive to a sustained ovation, played in by Queechy Caliente. I shout to Duncan, "You know how to make an entrance! And you call *me* the drama queen!" He gives me two thumbs up.

I realize that Bridget and Trudy haven't appeared yet,

and it occurs to me that they're somewhere outside, timing their entrance for maximum impact. And sure enough, a minute later, in they come.

Bridget is wearing a black-and-white Chanel wool suit and Trudy is wearing what I'm guessing is a Jil Sander cocktail dress. They both look radiant. And beautiful. They get their own rousing welcome.

That's how it goes for the next few hours: people stop in for a drink on their way to other festivities, extended families settle in for dinner next to other extended families. "Hey, it's been too long" greetings are followed by bear hugs, confidences are shared, accomplishments noted, memories jogged, old jokes retold, the departed remembered, photos taken, photos forwarded. I see Sofia sitting with the Nyqvists, Dr. Jantzen with a tongue depressor at the ready, and a table of our new friends, the Wiccans. The swing of the music and the whirl of people dancing send a warm thrum throughout the old barn. And Chaplin. Every time I check on the Naggs, someone is stroking Chaplin's feathers or slipping the turkeys treats from the dinner spread. You've never seen happier birds.

I go up to the buffet table for more kadhi and pakoras and notice no one has touched the Pickle Stretcher Salad. I do a stealth recon of the area—peripheral vision and all that —no Tishy. Grabbing a bunch of napkins, I cut off about two-thirds of the glob, wrap it, and go into the kitchen to dispose of the hazmat.

There's applause in the dining room so I hurry back out to see Nelle has walked up to the band and is ready to start her mini-set. People are streaming back from the dance floor to their tables.

Nelle starts right into "I Know You Know" and she glides through the samba so effortlessly that the room seems to levitate. I'm a table away from Aunt Doozy and her face is lit up like a young girl's. Nelle scats the last bit to a high-note finish.

"Good evening, friends. Happy Thanksgiving and happy Chaplin Day," she says. "And thanks to my Auntie Myra and Uncle Damon for being here." Nelle begins "Ain't No Mountain High Enough" much like the Diana Ross version, which is a slow build to the flashpoint chorus. Watching Will's face as Nelle pulls this off is half the fun. And true to her word, Nelle does the heavy lifting.

Then she sings "Better Things" within an inch of its life, turning a sweet breakup song into one of those anthems of hope. Nils, who is seated just a few feet away from Nelle, is as close to kvelling as Swedes are allowed to get.

After much cheering, Nelle thanks the crowd and then says, "Now I'll turn it over to Judge Harschly."

"Thank you, Nelle. You are a tough act to follow. For my first song, I'd like to kick things off with 'Born to Run.'"

For a moment, there is a horrified silence and then a stunned realization that Judge Harschly has made a joke. The room bursts out laughing.

"I guess we'll save that for another time. It is my great honor and pleasure to marry two very special ladies, Bridget Roberts and Trudy Bettenauer."

Everyone applauds as Bridget and Trudy walk over to stand before Judge Harschly. Bridget takes the mic and says, "Trudy and I were meant to be together and I knew it from the moment I met her. It did take her longer, bit of a rocky start there. Anyway, we had decided to get married but hadn't set a date. The spirit moved us to have the ceremony today and so thank you for sharing it. In case you're worried, Chaplin knows that I still love him even if it wasn't meant to be.

"Trudy and I haven't written vows, but we decided to surround ourselves by something old, something new, something borrowed, and something blue. Trudy has the first two, I have the borrowed and blue, and we've kept them secret from each other. Trudy?"

Bridget hands the mic to Trudy.

"Mine was easy. It's something old and something new all together, and it was something Bridget wanted."

Noly wheels in Martha Washington. The crowd gets it immediately.

Bridget laughs. "I love her. And I love you."

Noly pushes Martha next to the turkey pen, where Chaplin gobbles a greeting. Then Trudy hands the mic back to Bridget.

"For something borrowed," Bridget says, "I have here the keys to a silver Rascal parked outside. Will the gentleman whose pocket they came from allow us to borrow them for the ceremony?

Dubsack jumps up. "Hey, those are mine!"

The room erupts in laughter again.

"Okay to hold on to them?" Bridget asks.

"Yeah, sure, but you have to teach me how to do that!"

"Talk to me later," Bridget says. "And for something blue, Trudy, look in the inside pocket of your jacket."

Trudy, surprised, pulls out an Hermès scarf, with roses on its aqua background. "How did you know?!"

"I know things. Gussie?"

Trudy nods and Bridget ties it around her neck.

"Now we're ready, Judge," Bridget says.

Judge Harschly performs the ceremony. After Susanne Nyqvist brings forward two rings she designed, and Trudy and Bridget place a ring on each other's fingers, he pronounces them "partners for life." Nelle sits down at the piano and plays the opening notes of "Dedicated to You," and Trudy and Bridget have their first dance as Nelle serenades them.

Then the Traitor's Band fires up again and people hit the dance floor.

After dancing for a few minutes, Will and I step off to watch, our arms around each other's backs.

"I don't think I've ever seen the town happier than right this minute," he says into my ear.

"Want to head out?" I ask.

"Yeah, let's *boogie*," Will says, smiling.

"That's not funny," I say.

"Ah, but it is," he says.

I'm about to respond when he trains those green eyes on me and says, "Why don't you go get our coats?"

I go get our coats.

As we slip out into the night, Will says, "Snow! The first snow!"

We stare up at the flakes as our ears adjust to the stillness.

"That was a Thanksgiving for the books," I say.

"So much love. And music. And food," he says.

"And wine," I say.

"And wine."

The noise from the barn grows faint as we walk past the birch grove. We kiss.

"Where are your gloves?" I ask.

"Forgot 'em," Will says, pushing his hands into his coat pockets. "Before you say anything, who walked out of his smoky house—"

"Raging inferno," I interject.

" . . . out of your no-alarm fire barefoot and in boxer shorts? Hmmm? Cat got your tongue?"

I take a glove off and slip my hand into his coat pocket. We hold hands.

"Someone needs to keep an eye on you," Will says.

"Pffffft."

"Home?" he asks.

"Home."

ACKNOWLEDGMENTS

Boundless gratitude to my editor, Andrea Robinson, for her wise counsel, to supportive early readers Bill Foley, Bill Melamed, Nina Skriloff, Nealla Spano, and Debora Weston. Special thanks to Gary Gunas, Bill Rosenfield, and John Gibson, whose enthusiasm for AF kept me going. And to Rainer Facklam, thanks for your help in a thousand ways.

ABOUT THE AUTHOR

Charlie Suisman is the founder and publisher of Manhattan User's Guide, the longest running city newsletter. *Arnold Falls* is his first novel. Join him at charliesuisman.com

Made in the USA
Middletown, DE
12 May 2020